THE CHOSEN

Hecate's Rebellion Book 2

Jade Hayes

TCA Publishing LLC

PROLOGUE

Thick, choking smoke rose from the fire on the cavern floor. The gray swirl obscured much of the light from the flickering flames. Hecate stood to the side, surveying her work. Her laughter, gleefully evil, rang through the chamber and echoed off the walls. She watched as the smoke ascended to the ceiling and flowed through the cracks in the roof, on its way to wreak havoc in her great-granddaughter's life. The meddlesome young woman was in for a surprise she would never see coming. Keira's amateurish witchcraft would never detect the potent spells she just sent her way.

Hecate twirled her fingers through the wisps as they rose. She was done playing nice and biding her time. Victor was supposed to defeat that little twit, Penny, so Hecate could take possession of the belt, but he failed miserably. It was unfortunate Hades got involved, but Hecate wouldn't let that stop her plans. She had waited far too long to get what she wanted. The god of the underworld would not stop her, and neither would a troublesome band of gifted humans.

No. Hecate would get her revenge and show the world that she alone controlled her fate.

CHAPTER 1

A light breeze blew through the trees, making the leaves whisper a soft song. The hot September sun tried to penetrate the lush canopy, but only dappled sunlight fell over Leo Devereaux's face. Straddling a tree limb some twenty-feet off the ground, his thighs gripped the sturdy branch as he worked on the security camera, peering out from the tree's thick foliage. He was thankful for both the breeze and the thick leaf cover. He would roast without them. Changing camera batteries was hot, sweaty work. Today was no different, but at least up here, he got a bit of a break from the relentless Carolina sun.

He wouldn't be out of the heat at all if it weren't for the fact this tree offered an amazing view of the road running along the backside of the estate owned by his friends Ty and Penny Farris. Leo had been staying with them for the last couple months after the shit storm that went down at his home in Louisiana eighty days ago.

He was determined no one would sneak up on them here. Since he got his hands on the security, he'd locked the estate down like a gator's jaw on a chicken. A squirrel didn't eat a nut on the property without him knowing about it.

Despite all the security measures he put in place, he still felt vulnerable. He could ward the grounds against human invaders all day long. But it didn't do shit against the supernatural. For that, he had to rely on the still fledgling knowledge of all things magic held by their resident witch-slash-demigoddess, Keira Artherton. It irked him to no end he couldn't protect them all better. Protection was what he did. He had joined the Navy to protect his country. Had done unspeakable things in the name of protecting the world. Now, he couldn't even fully protect fifty acres of land in South Carolina. Some SEAL he was.

Jesus. Leo swiped a hand down his face. Could he be more of a Debbie Downer? Maudlin seemed to be his go to emotion nowadays.

He scoffed at himself. Having the Greek god of the dead steal your soul and threaten to keep it for all eternity tended to mess with one's emotional stability.

But he was still better than this. He had been trying so hard to go on as if nothing was wrong. But now, with only ten days remaining of their ninety-day limit, he was beginning to wonder if they would succeed. As far as he knew, Keira had made little headway in finding Hecate, even though she holed up with her books and herbs all day, every day. She hadn't told him anything about her progress.

He hadn't asked, though. Leo didn't figure she needed the added pressure of him nagging her about it.

So, here he was perched in a frickin' tree high off the ground, protecting the estate from an enemy they would never see coming, no matter how many cameras he put up.

Shaking his head to rid it of his depressing thoughts, Leo pried the cover off the back of the camera and popped out the batteries, quickly swapping them for the spares in his pocket.

He stretched his arms out to replace the cover, when the air around him took on an electric feel just before a fine gray linen covered his previously bare arms.

"What in the hell?" He stared down at himself in disbelief.

His eyes traveled the length of his arm before landing on the rest of his god-awful outfit. The gray linen was attached to the rest of a Victorian-era tailcoat. His t-shirt was gone, replaced by a soft, white silk shirt, its ruffled collar strangling him. The jeans he donned that morning were gone, too. Thin, fawn-colored, moleskin breeches, tucked into tall black boots, covered his legs now. Without the protection of the heavy denim, tree bark bit into his inner thighs.

Leo shifted his weight and blew out a harsh breath. He was going to kill Keira. The little witch had left him alone lately. He couldn't help but wonder what he did to piss her off now.

It couldn't have been anything too terrible. He usually remembered stoking her fire. It was fun to watch the annoyance flash in her eyes and her spine go ramrod straight. She reminded him of a pissed off kitten. Teasing her was a pleasant distraction from his own problems.

Doing his best to stretch in the restrictive coat, Leo put the cover back on the camera. The tree bit into his legs once again as he shifted his weight to climb down.

As gracefully as his clothing allowed, he swung down off the branch into a fork made by two lower branches. He straddled the sturdier of the two and swung down, dangling six feet from the ground, and let go. His brand new, tall riding boots did little to absorb the shock of his landing.

His dog, Clyde, stood up from his resting spot at the base of the tree. He looked up at his master and whined.

"I know, Clyde. I look ridiculous. Let's go find Keira and get my normal clothes back." Straightening the coat, Leo strode determinedly toward the house and the demigoddess responsible for his wardrobe.

CHAPTER 2

"**D**ammit, Keira!"

Out for a stroll to clear her head, Keira Artherton whirled around at the sound of the angry male voice coming down the path from the garden to the house.

"Would you please stop altering my clothes?" Leo growled as he stormed down the path. His dog, a giant chocolate lab, trotted along beside him. "Do you have any idea how hard it is to climb out of a tree and to work in tight places in breeches and a tailcoat? Not to mention this—this thing!" He flicked the ruffled collar of his shirt, glaring at her.

Keira could only stand there, mouth agape at the sight of Leo striding toward her in leg-hugging, fawn-colored breeches and a dove gray tailcoat, the ruffled collar of the flowy, white shirt beneath spilling out the opening at the top. The cut of the coat made his already broad shoulders even wider and emphasized the strength of his upper body while accentuating the narrowness of his waist. Sunlight glinted off his sun-bleached, tousled blond hair, giving him a rakish look. His dark eyes pinned her in place as he walked with purpose toward her.

Throat suddenly tight, Keira gulped and edged back a step. Leo Devereaux was a devastatingly handsome man. He had been a threat to her sanity from the moment they met. Most days he looked like some beach bum surfer boy, but she knew he was anything but. His bearing—whether he wore his usual jeans and a t-shirt, or the eighteenth-century outfit he wore now—screamed a man with confidence, and dangerous, deadly abilities.

Yes, the ex-SEAL was a dangerous man on many, many levels.

Keira looked up—way up—as Leo stopped directly in front of her, crowding her. At five-foot-two, she had to crane her neck way back to look at Leo's face. He topped her by at least a foot, which made her feel simultaneously pissed and protected.

Annoyed at her wandering hormones, Keira shoved those thoughts away and concentrated on the ticked off man in front of her.

"Seriously, Keira. Why am I in this getup?" He gestured to the ridiculous, yet sexy as hell outfit. "I've barely seen you all day and then suddenly, poof!" One hand flew up above his head and back down quickly. "I look like some Victorian dandy. Why?"

Eyeing him up and down once more, Keira could see why he was upset. While to her he looked drool-worthy, the outfit was rather impractical for doing more than looking pretty.

"I would have said you look more like a rake, but that's just me," she quipped. She couldn't resist poking the bear. Just a little. He was, after all, her distraction from the matters clogging up her brain.

He didn't disappoint.

Leo's brows slammed down over his milk chocolate eyes. "Keira." His voice was like thunder rolling over the hills.

Okay, maybe that backfired a bit, Keira thought with a delicious shiver. The low growl of his voice rumbled tantalizingly along her nerve endings. She rolled her shoulders, shrugging off the tingles he evoked, and took a step around him in an attempt to disguise how he made her feel.

It would be a terrible idea to let on to Leo what he did to her. It would only give him more ammunition to use against her. He found enough material on a daily basis to mercilessly tease her with. He didn't need anymore.

She stopped a couple feet away and turned to look up at him, deciding to explain herself before he used that tone on her again and she couldn't hide what he did to her. "I'm sorry. I was frustrated and needed an outlet. Changing you into a Jane Austen hero seemed like a harmless way to blow off some steam. I didn't mean to interrupt your work." Honestly, she hadn't given it any thought when she did it. She knew he was out changing batteries in the surveillance cameras, but she hadn't realized what all that entailed. She could see how it would be difficult to climb and reach in the restrictive coat.

Leo's posture and expression relaxed with her explanation.

"Why are you frustrated?"

Keira frowned fiercely at the question. He really had to ask that?

"Maybe because I can't make any headway on finding Hecate." She tapped her chin thoughtfully, anger and frustration brewing in her voice. "Or maybe it's because I feel like I should have at least been close by now and I'm not. Or, just possibly, it's because I keep failing and I hate failing, and that's all I seem to do lately." She advanced until she was toe-to-toe with him again as she growled out all her frustrations.

Clyde whined and nudged her hand. Keira reached down absently and stroked the dog's head. He had grown on her in the time they'd been living together. She took a deep breath and tried to get herself under control again.

The last eleven weeks had been the longest of her life. Ever since she awakened to the thick, noxious smoke filling the living room of her best friend, Penny Dimas's house, Keira felt like life was one frustrating challenge after another. She went from an up-and-coming, badass, prosecuting attorney for the city of Austin, Texas, to a real-life witch with no job and no family except for her now estranged parents and uncle.

But that's what happened when one had a charming, yet psycho grandfather who was a minion for a deranged Greek goddess bent on avenging a centuries-old affront. All her relatives sided with him and left her to figure things out on her own.

Keira couldn't help but roll her eyes at her self-pitying thoughts. She wasn't normally like this, but she was just so damn *frustrated*. She had tried and tried to find Hecate, and it didn't matter what she did, she came up blank every single time.

It didn't help, either, that things had been... weird around the estate. The electricity kept blinking in and out. Leo's cameras would stop working, only for him to go out and check them and find nothing wrong. Clyde would work himself into a frenzy, barking at shadows and lead them on frantic chases around the grounds, only to suddenly quit mid-search and turn back to the house.

And the strangest thing was they kept finding animals inside the house. All manner of raccoons, snakes—even birds—had ended up inside. Ty and Leo had captured or chased out at least a dozen animals in the last couple months. Keira had replaced her herb stores four times, because the animals would unerringly make their way into the room where she kept them and dump everything. She knew it was all Hecate's doing, but she couldn't figure out the spell to counteract it. It was beyond frustrating and it pissed her off. She hated being second best, even to a goddess, but most especially to Hecate. The bitch was going to go down. She just had to find her first.

Keira looked out over the expanse of yard to avoid looking at Leo. He just reminded her of her failures every time she saw him. If she didn't find Hecate soon so they could turn her over to Hades, Leo would lose his soul forever. She always thought Hades got a bad rap in the Greek mythology texts. Not anymore. He was an asshole, and she couldn't wait to turn Hecate over to him and wash her hands of the jerk. She wished she'd thrown him farther when he pissed her off.

Why she had to be a descendant of a Greek goddess, she didn't know. It was even more puzzling why she had to be co-guardian of a magical belt with Penny and Penny's new husband, Ty Farris. It was Penny's birthright as a descendant of Thetis. For Ty, it was a matter of using his ancestry as a descendant of Hercules to protect his wife.

But for Keira, it was a situation she was thrust into thanks to her greedy, conniving, ruthless family. She wished she didn't have a conscience like the rest of them. Then she could just walk away and it wouldn't bother her in the least. Instead, she was floundering, out of her element, and she only had ten days left to find Hecate and deliver her to Hades before the rat-bastard kept Leo's soul forever. She just wished she could think of, or find a way to do that.

Leo grasped her shoulders, bringing her out of her thoughts. "You are not a failure, Keira. You just haven't found the solution yet, but you will."

She scoffed in disbelief. She didn't have any more solutions to try.

"You are the most stubborn, determined woman I've ever met in my life. If anyone can figure this out, it's you."

His earnest expression had her slumping as the fight drained out of her. She wished she had the faith in herself Leo had in her. "I don't know where to go from here, Leo. I've gone through every locating spell I could find, even the one that used my blood to try to link my lineage. I found my parents and my uncle, even a couple of cousins in Russia I didn't know existed, but nothing on Hecate. It blipped over Greece, then disappeared. I don't know what else to try." Keira's voice broke on the last word. Leo pulled her in for a hug.

"You're trying too hard. You need to think more simply."

A snort escaped her. "There's nothing simple about magic."

Leo shrugged, continuing to run his hands up and down her spine. Keira felt like purring.

"Who says it has to be about magic?"

His words took a moment to register over the heat building in her belly from his touch. She pulled back to look up at him, puzzled.

"What do you mean?"

"You're trying to use magic to find her. What about good old-fashioned police work? There's a detective living under the same roof." Leo gestured at the house behind them. "Why don't you ask Ty?"

"Treat her like a missing person, you mean?"

Leo nodded.

Her eyes widened at his suggestion. She whacked him on the shoulder. "Why the hell didn't you suggest this before now?" Tempered excitement zinged through Keira. She hadn't really thought to look for Hecate through conventional means. It seemed a little implausible to be able to find her through normal methods, but Keira was shit out of options at this point and willing to try anything.

Leo shrugged. "It never occurred to me until you told me all you tried. You haven't exactly been forthcoming with me about what you're doing to locate Hecate. You hole up in your magic room and I hardly ever see you. I think the only person you really talk to is Penny. Even then, I think you keep things from her. Like just how frustrated you really are."

Keira frowned as guilt flooded her. He was right. She had kept him out of the loop, and she didn't talk to anyone the way she should. It wasn't intentional. She was just so used to solving problems on her own, and she was the only one who could perform the spells to locate the goddess. Keeping to herself had just been her absorbed in her work.

But that was changing as of now, she vowed. She needed to find Ty so she could pursue this new avenue of inquiry. And she needed to be upfront with both him and Penny about everything.

Keira stood on her tiptoes and placed a quick kiss on Leo's cheek. "I knew you were more than just something pretty to look at." She beamed up at him.

He just rolled his eyes at her. "Can I have my normal clothes back now, please?"

With a laugh, Keira nodded. She had forgotten all about his outfit. Messing with Leo had become second nature; she didn't even need to concentrate to hold an illusion on him.

"It's a shame you don't like those clothes," she teased as she walked backward toward the house. "Those pants do something amazing for your legs." She eyed the aforementioned appendages like she wanted to take a bite out of them, tilting her head over-dramatically. She did, but she didn't need him to realize that.

Leo grinned devilishly, adding to his rakish air. "We've had this discussion. If you want to see my manly bits, all you need to do is ask."

Keira fought the blush that wanted to break free and backed away several more paces. She released the illusion keeping him in Victorian clothing and tried not to stare at his now denim-clad legs and the pecs highlighted by the snug t-shirt that read, "The name Pavlov rings a bell," with a salivating dog beneath the words.

"Keep dreaming, Devereaux. Keep dreaming." She whirled away and ran up the porch steps to the front door. It would not do for Leo to see the thoughts she was sure were plastered across her face right now. One of these days, he was going to make that offer and she was going to take him up on it.

Winding her way through the enormous house, Keira found Ty ensconced in his office, papers spread around him on the desk. He had taken to working from home as much as possible, and today was no exception. He and his partner, Colin Jacobs, worked a lot through video chat. Ty only left the estate grounds when they had to track down leads for a case. His boss had been surprisingly okay with it once Ty explained someone had a vendetta against his wife. Ty left out all the details, of course, telling his captain it had to do with her Uncle Theo's salvage business.

Energy vibrating from every pore, Keira perched in the guest chair in front of the desk.

Ty arched a brow and tossed his pen down. "Hi, Keira. You look like you have something on your mind."

Keira nodded at the big man. She had been intimidated by him at one time—he was the size of a mountain, and she had seen him do some pretty scary stuff with just his bare hands—but now she counted him as a friend. A very knowledgeable friend.

"I need some advice, and Leo suggested you'd be the person to help."

Ty frowned. "What kind of advice?"

She leaned forward. "On how to find Hecate."

Ty shook his head. "I'm not a witch, Keira. I don't have the first clue how to help you."

Keira waved at his concern. "I'm not talking about anything like that. Leo said maybe I should try conventional methods to find her. I don't know if it'll work, but I'm out of ideas. I don't know where to start, though. How do you go about finding a missing person when a case comes to you?"

Ty sat back and stared at her a moment in thought before answering. "Well, I'd start with the person's family and friends. Talk to them and see where he or she was last seen."

Keira bit her lip thoughtfully. "So, I need to talk to someone who knows Hecate?"

Ty nodded. "I'd say so."

Keira slumped in her chair. "I don't know who she knows."

"You might not," Ty said, holding up a finger while a lopsided smile lightened his face. "But I know someone who does. Or can at least find out."

Curiosity now aroused, Keira leaned forward. "Who?"

"My dad."

Of course, Keira mused. If anyone would know who Hecate's associates were, it would be Jack Farris. She should have thought of him to begin with. The scholar was the one to not only help Ty and Penny get to the bottom of who was after Penny and the belt, but also the one to suggest uniting Penny and Ty's abilities so they would have a better chance of capturing Hecate once they found her.

"We can call him this evening and you can ask him."

She really hoped Jack could help. Short of just using the coins Hades gave them and going to the underworld to search for Hecate, she didn't know what else to do.

CHAPTER 3

Keira rubbed her tired eyes as she walked down the dim hallway to the kitchen in search of a warm drink to help her sleep. She talked to Jack earlier. He promised to do some research and get back to her. As a result, she was still wide awake at two o'clock in the morning, impatient, and wondering how long it would be before she heard from him.

Waiting had never been her strong suit. Her mind kept whirling with possibilities of who Hecate's buddies might be, as well as plans for what she was going to do to track them down once Jack got back to her.

Entering the kitchen, Keira nearly did an about-face and went back to her room. Leo leaned against the counter, staring out the window. His arms were crossed over his naked chest, a coffee mug clasped in his fingers. A pair of navy blue cotton pajama pants rode low on his hips.

A shiver ripped through Keira at the sight of Leo's muscles on such blatant display. Tattoos dotted his biceps, enhancing their definition. The man was seriously hot.

And he knew it.

Before she could retreat, Clyde spotted her from under the table and let out a soft woof in greeting. Leo snapped out of his thoughts and turned his head toward her.

Cursing the dog for ruining her moment to escape without being seen, Keira squared her shoulders and sauntered into the room, trying to appear as unaffected by his low-slung pants and lack of shirt as she possibly could. She quickly disappeared into the pantry in search of tea, hoping he hadn't seen the blush she was sure stained her cheeks.

She lingered as long as she could, but it only took so long to take a tea bag from the box on the shelf. She inhaled deeply and tossed her hair back, silently kicking herself. She was a grown-ass woman. She had seen plenty of men without their shirts in her twenty-six years. She'd even seen a few completely naked. Leo was no different.

Yeah, right. And she could be a supermodel.

Keira rolled her eyes at herself and took another deep breath, squaring her shoulders once more. A mantra on repeat in her head that he was just a man, she left the pantry, tea bag clutched so tightly in her fingers the thin paper threatened to tear. She walked out to see he'd grabbed the teapot and was filling it with water.

"I could have done that," she told him. "Thank you."

He nodded in acknowledgement and set the pot on the stove to heat.

"You couldn't sleep either, huh?" she asked. Her eyes darted to the cabinet with the coffee mugs and she bit her lip. It was right next to where he rested against the counter again. She wasn't sure standing that close to him was a good idea.

Oh, stop being such a ninny! He was a man, for crap's sake. This was getting ridiculous.

Feeling determined, Keira crossed the kitchen and opened the cabinet to get a mug. She pretended not to notice the heat coming from his naked torso or the clean scent of soap clinging to his skin.

Leo shook his head in response to her question. "No. I keep having nightmares," he said, his voice quiet.

Keira's heart broke right then. This brave, honorable man did not deserve to have this happen to him. If she hadn't already vowed to do everything she could to get his soul back, she would have done so then. It killed her she hadn't been more successful. She really hoped Jack came through with names and that she could get some answers from whoever he found.

Without thinking it through, Keira reached over and wrapped her arms around Leo's torso in a hug. The instant she felt the silky warmth of his bare skin beneath her cheek and hands, she knew the hug had been a huge mistake. Warmth flooded her veins and her belly clenched.

She pulled away even as he stiffened at her touch.

"I'm sorry," she said. She kept her face averted and busied herself unwrapping the string from the tea bag.

Leo's finger under her chin made her lift her gaze to his. "You don't have anything to be sorry for, *chère*. Thank you for trying to comfort me. This isn't easy on any of us, and I know you're taking it hard. Probably harder than you should. You just surprised me. You don't normally touch me unless it's to pummel my bicep." A half smile tilted his mouth.

Her own mouth quirked up in response. "Well, if you didn't make me so crazy…"

One perfect eyebrow arched over his dark eyes. "Where would be the fun in that?"

Keira rolled her eyes at him and stepped away to grab the whistling teakettle from the stove, flipping off the burner as she went. "Do you want some tea? It might relax you some."

He shook his head. "No, I'm good. I can't stand that stuff. I'll stick with coffee." He raised his mug and took a sip.

"Well, I want to sleep." She poured the hot water over the tea bag and set the kettle back on the stove.

"What's keeping you awake?" Leo asked, taking another sip of his coffee.

Keira fiddled with the tag on the tea bag and shrugged. "Waiting."

"Waiting?"

She nodded. "I hate waiting." She looked at him then. "I took your advice and talked to Ty. He suggested I talk to his dad to get an idea of who might be Hecate's confidantes. I called him earlier, and he said he would do some research and get back to me. Now, I have to wait, and I hate to wait. I'd rather do."

Leo nodded in agreement.

An awkward silence fell then. Keira stirred her tea, willing it to steep faster so she could retreat to her room and away from Leo's muscles and surfer boy good looks.

She chanced a glance at him and found him staring at her.

"What?"

He shook his head and looked down at his coffee mug with a frown. "Nothing."

Keira frowned back and was about to shrug the whole thing off when he reached around her with one long arm to deposit his now empty coffee mug in the sink. A zing of pure lust shot through her as the masculine scent clinging to his bare skin filled her senses. She held her breath, trying to regain her equilibrium only to have it blown to bits when she looked up at him through her lashes to find him staring down at her with an intensity she felt all the way to her bones.

He straightened to tower over her, one hand on either side of her hips, bracketing her against the counter. Rather than feel intimidated by his size, she felt protected. Like he would stand between her and the big, bad world.

Leo brushed a curl away from her face. Keira felt the contact of his fingers skimming over her cheek all the way to her toes. She didn't want to be attracted to this man. He was a distraction when she didn't need one. Not to mention, he was usually on her last nerve.

She brought her hand up to wrap around his wrist as he threaded his long fingers through her curls.

"Leo." Her voice came out a breathy whisper and not the forceful admonition she had been hoping for.

He pressed a gentle, tender kiss to her forehead and gathered her close. "I know, *chère*."

Heat flowing between them, Keira closed her eyes and rested her forehead against his naked chest, trying desperately to fight the urge to lean back in his embrace and kiss him square on the lips. At least she wasn't the only one fighting their attraction. She could feel the tension in his body as he held her. His fingers alternately dug into the back of her head, then caressed, as if they couldn't quite decide whether to give in to the feelings or not.

Unable to stop herself, she touched his waist and ran her hand up his side. His skin was silk over steel beneath her touch. He sucked in a breath, his fingers clenching in her hair.

Abruptly, he released her and stepped back.

Keira reached back for the counter to hold herself up. Her knees threatened to buckle from the desire thrumming through her veins. How a simple embrace could light her on fire like that, she didn't know. Her hand bumped her teacup as she grappled with the countertop, causing some of the liquid to splash onto the granite surface. Keira seized the distraction and whirled around to clean up the mess. She grabbed a dish towel and dabbed at the spill.

The honey bottle landed next to her cup, making her jump. Her eyes followed the long, tanned fingers wrapped around it, up a sinewy forearm and over a sleek, carved, tattooed bicep to Leo's handsome face. She swallowed hard and willed her libido back under control. He needed to step back before she completely unraveled and jumped on him.

"I'm going to head to bed. I hope you get some sleep, *chère*." His eyes burned into her as he stared down at her for a brief moment, like he could tell exactly what she was thinking, before he turned and strode from the kitchen. Keira stood stock still, watching the muscles ripple in his back as he walked away from her.

She snapped out of her trance when Clyde stood from his position under the table and followed his master out of the room.

Keira sagged against the counter, her head in her hands. So much for hiding her feelings from Leo. She took a smidgen of comfort in the fact that at least he felt something, too.

She sucked in a shaky breath and picked up the honey bottle to squeeze some into her tea.

If she made it through the next nine days without giving in to her attraction to that man, it would be a miracle. She really didn't know how she hadn't already.

CHAPTER 4

The door to the bedroom closed with a soft snick. Leo's bare feet sank into the plush carpet as he crossed the room to the bed. He perched on the edge, cradling his head, trying to get a rein on his rioting emotions.

He nearly kissed Keira in the kitchen. Even now, he couldn't say what stopped him. Maybe the sheer force of the desire that smacked into him when she stroked his side.

All he knew was she had kicked off a firestorm inside of him. It still flared bright, ratcheting up all of his emotions and making it harder for him to ignore the gaping chasm left behind by his missing soul. Its loss still reverberated through him every second of every day. A yawning, aching blackness that, if he let it, would swallow him whole. Tonight, with the emotions Keira stirred up, he was having a very hard time keeping a lid on things.

Only his years of military training had allowed him to compartmentalize it at all, so he could function as well as he did. To pretend he was okay when he really wasn't. He refused to think about what would happen if Keira failed to locate Hecate in the next nine days. He was already clinging to his sanity by a thread.

Leo drew in a deep breath, counted to ten, and attempted to put a firm lid on his emotions. He needed a clear head so he could focus. Emotions would only cloud his thinking. That meant he needed to keep his distance from a certain witchy demigoddess.

Another deep breath had the fire banked to embers, and the darkness pushed back to a manageable level.

Leo rubbed at the ache deep in his chest. The next nine days couldn't go fast enough.

CHAPTER 5

Keira scribbled furiously on the notebook in front of her as Jack rattled off all he found out about Hecate's associates. She was amazed to see Hades's wife, Persephone, among them and wondered if the god had thought to ask his wife if she knew Hecate's whereabouts.

A smirk spread across her face. He probably had, and she told to stuff it. Persephone wasn't exactly known for being nice to her husband. Keira wouldn't be, either, if she was forced to marry against her will.

"Persephone will likely be the easiest for you to find. It's summer, so she should be up here with us mere mortals. That scrying ability of yours is going to come in handy."

Keira let out a little grunt of agreement. No kidding. How else was she going to track down the goddess of fertility? Not to mention Hermes and the Furies.

"Do be careful when you talk to them. Don't agree to any deals or stipulations. You don't want to get trapped into owing a god anything. I'm still not entirely convinced Hades will keep his word once you bring him Hecate."

Keira's head snapped up, her eyes hard. "Oh, he will, or I will find a way to make his eternal life a living hell."

Jack chuckled. "I have a feeling you, of all people, could do that."

Oh, he had no idea, Keira thought, determination surging. This was going to end with Hecate at Hades's feet and Leo's soul back in his body where it belonged, one way or another.

"Be careful contacting these gods. I doubt they'll take kindly to being found by a human."

"I'll be careful, I promise." She thanked Jack for his help and severed the connection.

At least she had a place to start now.

Notebook in hand, Keira left her bedroom and headed down the hall to the room she had affectionately dubbed "The Magic Room." When she moved in, they decided Keira needed a space for all of her shiny new magic potion ingredients and books. Since the house had six bedrooms and only three were in use, she took over one of the larger ones to work in.

She walked to the desk and set the notebook down before pulling out a world map and the small obsidian arrowhead she used for scrying spells. It wasn't the most conventional form of scrying—many people she had read about used mirrors or crystals—but it worked rather well for her.

She set the arrowhead on the map and rested a finger on it. With a deep breath, she closed her eyes and muttered her locating spell. Keira pictured Persephone—at least what she thought the woman represented, since she didn't actually know what she looked like—and waited for the arrowhead to move.

When it stayed put, Keira frowned and opened her eyes to look down at the stone. It was resisting her and almost seemed stuck to the map. Like a bolt of lightning, Keira realized it was fighting the danger inherent in trying to locate such a strong deity.

She closed her eyes again, adjusting the force behind her spell. After a moment, the arrowhead drifted across the map. When it came to an abrupt halt, she opened her eyes and looked at where it stopped.

A deep frown furrowed her brows as she stared at the map.

Great Britain.

She hadn't been expecting that. And she didn't have a detailed map of Britain, either. Only of Greece and the United States. Apparently, a trip to the bookstore was in order if she wanted to get a more precise location on Persephone.

Quickly, Keira gathered up all her materials and put them back in the desk before heading downstairs to the study in search of Penny. Her friend told her earlier she would be working most of the day in there.

She walked into the room and stopped short at the sight in front of her.

"Oh, geez. Can't you guys at least close the door first so people knock before coming in?" She stared at her friend perched atop Ty's lap, arms wrapped around his neck, one of his hands buried beneath her shirt. They had been fused at the mouth, but Keira's interruption made them break apart.

Penny turned her head to smile sheepishly at Keira.

"Keeping the door open keeps us from, um, not working," Ty said, withdrawing his hand from beneath his wife's shirt. He tugged the fabric back into place, but made no move to push her from his lap.

Keira grinned. "Yes, because you look like you're hard at work now."

He laughed. "But we would be working much less if the door was closed."

Penny snickered. "He's not wrong. So, what's up?"

Keira leaned against the doorjamb. "I came to see if I could borrow you," she said, addressing Penny. "I need to go to the bookstore to get a map of Great Britain."

Penny frowned. "Great Britain? Why do you need that? And why not just pull one up on the computer?"

Before she could answer, Ty jumped in, eyes wide, immediately understanding why she needed the map. "You talked to Dad, didn't you? He gave you a lead?"

Keira nodded, a satisfied smile spreading over her face. "Yes, and yes. He gave me some names." She quickly explained all that Jack told her and what she did upstairs.

"Keira, that's awesome news!" Penny exclaimed. "I know how hard you've been trying, and this could be just what we need."

"I know, which is why I want to go get that map. So, can you come?" Keira was more than willing to go alone, but they had all agreed Keira went nowhere by herself. They wouldn't put it past Hecate to attack her. Keira had argued she was fully capable of defending herself, especially with her abilities, but it made Penny feel better, so she relented.

Penny frowned and sat up, swinging her legs around so her feet touched the floor. "I wish I could, but one of my salvage crew captains is calling in about twenty minutes. He's been having a lot of problems on his dive and wanted to discuss it with me." Penny had really taken to running Theo's salvage operation. Even though she only had three-quarters of an accounting degree, she discovered she had quite the knack for business.

"I'd go with you, but I'm leaving soon to meet Colin. We got a lead on one of our cases we need to follow up on."

Penny looked back at Ty. "What about Leo? Is he free?"

Ty shrugged and grabbed his phone off the desk. "I don't know. Let me check."

Keira bit back a groan. She really didn't want to be trapped in a vehicle with Leo after their encounter last night. Her nerves still hadn't settled from it, and she just wanted to avoid him until the awkward phase passed.

Her shoulders drooped slightly in dismay when Ty hung up and told her Leo would be up to the house in a couple minutes to go with her into the city.

Not wanting Penny and Ty to think anything was amiss between her and Leo, Keira pasted a bright smile on her face. "Okay, thanks. If you see him first, tell him I'm getting my purse and I'll meet him in the garage."

"Will do," Ty said, his tone distracted as he had already turned his attention back to his wife.

"Bye, Keira," Penny called with a wave of her hand, eyes on Ty.

Keira rolled her eyes good-naturedly and smiled as she left the study. It was nice to see Penny so happy. She had been alone since her parents died and just kind of going through the motions of life. Ty brought the light back to her eyes.

Keira rounded the corner of the hallway, headed for the kitchen and the area by the interior garage door where they all dropped their bags and shoes. Her thoughts on what she might find out once she got a more detailed map, Keira didn't hear Leo approach and ran headlong into him.

"Whoa, there." Leo's arms whipped out to grasp her biceps, so she wouldn't hit the floor as she bounced off his chest. Today's t-shirt, Keira noted absently, featured a T-Rex trying to do push-ups.

"Sorry, *chère*. You all right?"

Stepping back out of his hands, Keira nodded. She resisted the urge to rub her arms where his touch seared her flesh. So much for avoiding him and letting things die down. If he kept touching her—even inadvertently—she was going to melt into a puddle at his feet.

He stuffed his now empty hands into his pockets. "So, Ty said you need to go to the bookstore?"

Again, she nodded. "I got a lead from Jack, but I need to get a map before I can go any further with the information." She quickly explained what she discovered upstairs.

"Let's go, then." He pulled his truck keys from his pocket and turned around, heading for the garage.

Keira followed, pausing long enough to slip on some flats and grab her purse. In the garage, she let him help her into his truck—there was no way she was getting up into the beast without help or jumping, and she wasn't about to jump—and they were soon on their way.

"Where am I going?" Leo asked once they were on the road headed into Charleston.

Keira named the large chain bookstore in the shopping district on this side of the city she knew carried maps.

Strained silence fell as their proximity and memories from last night hit them. Keira hugged the door and stared out the window at the passing scenery, trying hard not to let her mind dwell on the fact Leo was only feet away. She could hear him shift in his seat every so often and drum his fingers on the steering wheel as he drove.

When he finally broke the silence, Keira fought hard not to jump out of her skin.

"So, what's the plan once you locate Persephone?"

She looked at him then. He stared straight ahead, watching the road, but there was a tension to the way he sat. Ready to spring into action, his body looked almost coiled in the seat, even though he was trying to appear relaxed.

"We go after her, I guess."

"In Britain?"

Keira nodded. "I don't think she'll speak to me over the phone. I'm not even sure how I'm going to get her to speak to me in person, but it'll likely be easier than trying to cold call her. I'm also hoping once she hears me out that, if she doesn't know where Hecate is, she'll at least convince Hermes and the Furies to talk to me and save me the trouble of having to track them down."

Leo tipped his head. "That's actually a really good plan."

Keira arched an eyebrow. "I'm not an idiot, you know."

"I never said you were. You're just thinking strategically, and I didn't really expect that from you. You always seemed a bit of a 'fly by the seat of your pants' kind of person. You think things through, but you have to admit, you are somewhat impulsive."

Keira flushed. He wasn't wrong. He'd been on the end of her impulsiveness more than once, she thought. Her mind jumped to yesterday's Victorian gentleman's outfit as a prime example.

Still, she wasn't always that impulsive. "Well, I'm treating this like I would a case I had to bring to court. I throw impulsiveness out the window when it comes to the law. To build an effective case, you have to explore all avenues and make plans for your plans, so you make sure you cover every potential line of questioning. I'm trying to apply the same ideas here."

He nodded. "You let me know if you need help." He looked at her then for a long moment. "You're not in this alone, *chère*."

Her impulse showing, she reached over and patted his thigh. "I know."

He covered her hand with his, giving it a squeeze before releasing her.

Keira pulled her hand back to her lap, fingers tingling.

CHAPTER 6

Leo stared down at the little woman in front of him, her back to him as she perused the maps on the display, wondering what the hell he was doing here. He totally should have told Ty that Keira could wait until Penny could go with her.

But here he was, in close proximity to the one woman in the world who drove him to distraction. Even after his pep talk to himself last night, he still remembered the feel of her fingers trailing up his side. He craved for her to do it again. He wanted to reciprocate.

Leo stuffed his hands in his pockets so he didn't thrust his fingers into her curly hair. This was friggin' torture.

He willed her to hurry up so he could take her back to the house and go build something or fix something to take his mind off of her. How long did it take to pick out a map, anyway? There were like three different maps of Great Britain right in front of her. She just needed to pick one. Or all of them. He didn't particularly care. He just wanted to leave so he could get away from her and regain his equilibrium.

She picked up each one in turn and examined them all before finally deciding on one.

"Okay. I think this will do."

Thank the Lord. If he had to stand here any longer, staring down at her biting her lip while she looked over the maps, he was going to take over the biting.

Leo whirled and marched toward the checkout counters, eyes sweeping from side to side, automatically looking for danger. It was something the military ingrained in him and a habit he still carried to this day. When he reached the counter, he plucked the map from her fingers and handed it to the girl behind the register.

"Leo, what are you doing?"

He looked down at her, eyebrows bent in a frown, and dared her to argue with him as the girl rang up the map. "You're trying to save my eternal soul," he said quietly. "The least I can do to help is buy a map."

Keira frowned up at him, but didn't argue. He had a feeling that was more in deference to the fact they were in public than anything else. A smile quirked one side of his mouth as he wondered what magical thing she would do to him to express her displeasure. He had actually started to look forward to her antics. She had a creative mind and never ceased to amaze him with the things she came up with.

That outfit yesterday was brilliant, even if it had been uncomfortable. He really had looked like he just stepped off the cover of a historical romance novel. The detail was amazing.

Taking the bag from the clerk, they left the store. Back in the truck, Leo turned to Keira. "Say it," he demanded.

She crossed her arms over her chest and glared. "Say what?"

"Whatever it was you wanted to say in the store."

She shook her head and looked out the window, sinking into the truck seat, the fight leaving her. "It doesn't matter, Leo. Let's just go home."

"It does matter, Keira. I don't want you to hide your emotions from me. This isn't a game, and we all need to be a hundred percent honest with each other to succeed."

"I know it's not a game!" she shot back, her tone harsh and her eyes flashing.

"Then tell me what's bothering you." He wanted to shout the words at her, but held back. Barely. Instead, he stared her down, trying to use his combat face to make her talk.

Her jaw worked while she thought about what he said. Finally, a hard glint in her eyes, she relented.

"I'm pissed, okay?"

He opened his mouth to protest that it was just a map, but she held up a hand and spoke before he could get the words out.

"Not about the map. I'm pissed this has happened to you. You had nothing to do with any of this until we came to you for refuge. It wasn't really your fight. And you wish you could help? Well, I wish I could snap my fingers and fix it all. I've got all this power inside me, all these special abilities, and I haven't been able to do a damn thing. Some witch I am." She crossed her arms over her chest and glared out the windshield.

Leo's eyebrows slammed down in another frown. "Hey. You're not giving yourself enough credit. You're brand new to this and have been busting your ass trying to find the witch-bitch. So, it took you a while. We'd still be chasing our tails if we tried to find Persephone without your abilities. There's no way the three of us could find Hecate without you before time ran out.

"And for as far as it not being my fight, that doesn't matter. Ty is my friend—my brother-in-arms. I will *always* fight for him and with him no matter what or who the foe may be." Leo sat back, elbow on the windowsill, and propped his head against his fingers. He stared out the windshield, lost in thought. It bugged him she was so stuck on his predicament. Yes, he wanted his soul back. There was a gaping void inside him, gnawing at him every second. He was pissed at Hades for sure, but this was bigger than Leo. If Hades was right, failing meant the end of the world as they knew it.

"I want you to promise me something, *chère*."

She looked at him warily. "What?"

"You need to stop making this about me. This is about saving our way of life. If we don't find Hecate and deliver her to Hades, it won't just be me who suffers. We all will. She has to be stopped. That's what I want you to focus on. Stopping her." He leaned forward and took her hands in his. "Can you do that for me?"

Her shoulders fell, and a confused frown marred her pretty face. "Leo. I—"

"Promise me, Keira. I don't want this on your shoulders if we fail to find her by Hades's deadline. You have tried so hard, and I have no doubt you will keep trying until you find her, but please stop making this about me. It's so much bigger than that."

Tears welled in her eyes, and Leo felt his heart clench. He hated to see women cry, especially this one.

"I promise I will try. But that's about as good as you're going to get," she admonished.

Leo squeezed her hands. "We'll work on it." He grinned at her.

She smiled back and swiped at her cheeks before pointing out the window. "Just drive, bayou boy."

Leo laughed and started the truck. "Yes, ma'am."

This time, the silence on the ride home was companionable. Leo sensed they had broken through a wall with that conversation. He felt like they were, if not actually friends, then on their way to that now instead of merely tolerating each other.

They were passing through the miles of farmland separating Theo's estate from the city and were nearly home when something caught his attention. In one of the fields was a dog, running toward the road at full tilt.

Realizing he was going to hit it if he didn't stop, Leo slammed on the brakes. The car coming from the opposite direction wasn't paying as close attention and didn't see the dog until it was in the road. He heard Keira shriek as she realized at the same time he did that the oncoming car was going to hit them.

CHAPTER 7

L eo swung the truck sideways and braced himself, praying the car hit the back of the truck cab and not his door or the truck bed. *Oh, this was going to hurt.*

The car bounced off the back of the truck cab, tipping them onto two wheels. Leo fought to right the truck, but it kept going and crashed onto the roadway on its side. They skidded several yards before finally coming to a halt.

Leo groaned, slightly dazed from the abrupt stop, but not hurt. He looked over at Keira. What he saw had his heart jumping into his throat. Blood flowed down the right side of her face and from her nose. Her eyes, glassy with pain, struggled to stay open.

"Keira. *Chère*, talk to me." Leo struggled with his seat belt, but his weight kept it snug in the buckle. Cursing, he stuffed his hand into his jeans pocket and pulled out his knife. Within moments he freed himself from the tight belt and gingerly lowered himself to Keira's side of the truck.

He cupped Keira's face in one palm and turned her to face him. "Baby, wake up. You need to talk to me."

"Leo?"

Relief flowed through him. Her voice was rough and barely above a whisper, but her eyes cleared the longer she looked at him.

"We need to get you out of here, but you're going to have to climb. Can you do that?"

She blinked slowly a couple times before taking a deep breath and shaking off some of the fog from the blow to the head. Finally, she nodded. "I think so."

Leo wrapped an arm around her waist and stood, pulling her up with him in the tight space. He helped her lean against the seats.

"I'm going to climb out, then I'll help you up."

She nodded. "Okay."

Window already broken from the impact, Leo cleared the glass from the edges of the window frame and pulled himself up and through.

He glanced around for the other car and found it spun out on the other side of the road on the berm. The front was smashed, and the driver still sat in the car, looking dazed.

Another car pulled up just then. The driver stuck his head out of the window. Leo didn't give the man a chance to ask if he needed help. "Check on the other car and call 911," he yelled at the man.

Turning his attention back to Keira, he kneeled the best he could on the door frame and reached a hand through the window. "Grab my hand, *chère*."

She did as told, and he pulled her up, lifting her through the window. Bracing her free hand on the door, Keira helped hoist herself from the wrecked truck. Leo jumped down to the ground and lifted her off the truck. When her knees buckled as soon as he put her down, he scooped her up and carried her to the grass.

Gently, he set her down. "Let me see your head, baby." He pushed the curls away from her face. She had a nasty gash on her temple and her nose was bloody.

Suspicion crept in at the sight of her nose. Incredulous, he looked back at his truck. While it was on its side, the dent where the car hit was minimal. There should have been much more damage for as fast as both vehicles had been traveling.

He turned back to the still dazed woman sitting on the ground in front of him. "Did you deflect the other car?"

She looked up at him and winced. "I tried. I put a bubble around us, but the car was coming too fast and had too much mass. It bounced and kind of squished the bubble into us. I couldn't keep it from pushing us over."

Leo just shook his head. Keira's mojo was freaky, but he couldn't say he wasn't glad she had it. It had at least saved them from some very serious injuries.

"What happened to the dog?" Keira asked, peering around him.

That was a good question. Leo looked around as well, but didn't see any sign of it. "I'm not sure. It probably ran off."

"Where?" Keira gestured around them. It was nothing but open fields in all directions.

Leo looked around once more. It was weird that the dog had just disappeared. Even running at top speed, they should still be able to see it in the distance.

Before he could think on that oddity anymore, the passerby ambled up.

"I called for an ambulance. Are you two okay?"

Leo stood. "We're all right. Just some cuts. Thanks for stopping."

"No problem. I'm glad it looks worse than it is."

Leo nodded, noncommittally. "How's the woman in the other car?"

"Some cuts and she's dazed, but seems okay. What happened, anyway? She muttered something about a dog."

Leo nodded, looking around once more for the elusive animal. "There was. Some big mutt. Came barreling across the field right in front of us."

The hairs on the back of his neck rose. Something about this was hinky. That animal should have still been visible after the crash. He had watched it continue across the road unharmed.

So what did happen to the dog? Leo had a feeling that answer wouldn't come anytime soon.

CHAPTER 8

Feeling like someone beat the stuffing out of her, Keira let her head rest against the crinkly pillow on the hard bed in the emergency room cubicle. She closed her eyes against the harsh lights, which were exacerbating the headache pounding through her brain. After a battery of tests, the doctor had declared she had a mild concussion, and stitched her up. He left her with instructions to rest for a few days.

Keira had nodded to appease the man—and Leo, who hovered silently in the corner—but she had no intention of spending the next several days lounging on the sofa. They didn't have time for that.

Speaking of, that nurse needed to hurry with her discharge instructions so they could leave.

Keira's hand edged toward the call button, intent on finding out what was taking so long, when footsteps in the hallway drew her attention.

She opened her eyes in time to see the curtain covering the cubicle entrance whip to the side, revealing Penny's tall frame. Her jade eyes, wide with concern, quickly searched the room, landing on Keira's prone form. "Oh my God, Keira. Are you okay?"

Keira winced at the volume of Penny's voice as she walked into the tiny space, Ty on her heels.

Pressing her hand to the side of her head over the bandage there, Keira nodded. "I'm fine, Penny. Just a bump."

"She has a mild concussion," Leo stated from his chair against the wall. He looked relaxed with his legs extended and his arms crossed over his chest, but Keira could feel the tension vibrating off of him.

Keira glared at him. "You didn't need to tell her that. I'm fine. You heard the doctor. I just need some rest and I'll be right as rain in a few days."

He arched an eyebrow at her. "Like you'll take it easy? I saw that look in your eyes when you told the doctor you would rest. It's going to take all of us to make sure you do."

Keira frowned fiercely. She didn't have time to take it easy. She had a goddess to find.

Ignoring his comment, she changed the subject. "Did you get the map out of the truck?"

With a sigh, Leo nodded. He sat up and rested his forearms on his knees. "You can use it tomorrow if you're feeling well enough."

Keira shook her head before he ever finished, bristling at his dictatorial words. "I'll use it tonight. I'm fine."

Leo's frown and steely glare surpassed hers. "You're not fine. You have a concussion."

"*Mild* concussion."

"And you pushed your ability too far, trying to keep us safe," he continued, as if she hadn't spoken. "You need to rest."

Keira wanted to scream. She could feel the press of time closing in on her. She did not want to put this off. "You really think I'll be able to rest without finding Persephone?" She willed him to remember what happened last night when she couldn't sleep, hoping to compel him to back down.

His eyes lit with the memory, but he stayed silent and continued to glower at her.

She arched an eyebrow at him, daring him to deny her.

He stared at her hard for a moment before responding. "I'll agree to it, so long as you rest for a bit when we get home, and I'm in the room with you when you use the map. Knowing you, you'll push it till you pass out and then *really* hurt yourself when you fall."

Keira rolled her eyes. He was probably right, but it didn't mean she had to like it.

"Fine. But you stay out of my way."

Leo held up his hands in surrender. "I'll be wallpaper. I just want you to be safe."

Tears welled in Keira's eyes suddenly, and she rubbed her face, feigning a headache to disguise her reaction. She wanted to scream again. Only Leo could make her emotions bounce from righteous anger to overwhelming gratitude in the span of a couple seconds.

"Um, what was that all about?" Penny asked. She looked at Ty. "Did we miss something?"

His mouth quirked. "Apparently."

Keira bit her lip and averted her eyes from everyone. She knew if she looked at Leo or Penny, Penny would know instantly something was happening between them. She probably already suspected, but Keira wasn't about to confirm it for her.

Thankfully, she was saved from having to say or do anything when the nurse pushed aside the curtain and stepped in with Keira's discharge paperwork.

"Whoa," the nurse said, stopping short when she nearly ran into Ty as she stepped in. She looked the tall man up and down, her eyes pausing on the gun and badge strapped to his waist, before turning to Keira with a smile. "I see you have some visitors."

"We're here to take them home, ma'am," Ty told the woman.

The nurse smiled and turned to Keira. "Well then, as soon as I get your Jane Hancock on these papers, you are free to go." She waved a sheaf of paperwork in the air.

Keira reached for the papers and pen, eager to leave. The sooner she got out of here, the sooner she could "rest" and get on with finding Persephone.

She scrawled her name where the nurse pointed and took the home care instruction sheet for her *mild* concussion.

"All right. You're all set. Make sure you stay hydrated and if your symptoms get worse, come straight back here."

Keira resisted the urge to jump off the bed to put her shoes on. She was eager to leave, but she knew if she tried that she would end up on her butt on the floor, and Leo would go into super-protector mode and hide the map from her until morning. She didn't want to have to fight with him anymore tonight.

She swung her legs over the side of the bed as normally as she could and stood slowly. Things tilted, but quickly righted themselves. A quick glance around the tiny room revealed her shoes tucked beneath the other chair. Keira bent to pull them out so she could put them on, only to have to make a quick grab for the chair as the room spun wildly around her.

Strong arms wrapped around her and lifted her off her feet. Keira tucked her face against Leo's neck and closed her eyes, trying to make the room stop spinning. "I'm okay," she told him softly. "I just bent down too fast."

He didn't respond, instead sitting her back on the edge of the bed. He retrieved her shoes and slid them onto her feet. Once done, he stood before her, bent at the waist with his fists propped on the mattress on either side of her hips. "You are going to *rest* when we get home, *chère*. I won't stop you from doing your thing later, but I swear to all that's holy that even if I have to lie down in bed with you to make sure you stay there, you are going to at least attempt to take a nap."

Keira's eyes widened as his words registered. Sleep would be the last thing on her mind if he climbed into bed with her. But she believed he would do what he said if she didn't try to rest.

She bit her lip and nodded. It was the only answer she could give if she wanted to hang on to her sanity today.

Leo gave a quick nod in response and stepped back. He held out a hand to help her up.

"You okay to walk, or do you want a wheelchair?"

"I can walk."

He cupped her elbow to steady her as they left. Keira was grateful for the support. She was a tad shaky on her feet. Most of that was from the painkiller the nurse gave her earlier. She hoped a few hours of sleep would help it wear off so she would feel more like herself.

The ride home from the hospital was thankfully uneventful. Penny helped Keira up the stairs and into a pair of leggings and a t-shirt so she could nap. Keira still wasn't sure she would be able to fall asleep, but she was willing to try. She knew herself well enough to know if she tried to find Persephone in the state she was in right now, she wouldn't be able to unstick the arrowhead from the map, let alone get an accurate reading.

Penny pulled the drapes on the windows, plunging the room into semi-darkness as Keira pulled the covers up over herself.

After one last twitch of the curtains to fully block out the light, Penny walked back over to the bed and laid her hand over Keira's. "Do you need anything before I leave you alone?"

Keira rolled her head side to side on her pillow, growing drowsy, much to her surprise. "No. I'm okay."

Penny grinned. "What about Leo? Do you need him?"

Keira's lips pursed. "No," she replied, even as her heart and body screamed yes.

A chuckle slipped past Penny's lips. "You keep telling yourself that." She patted Keira's hand again. "Rest. I'll see you in a few hours."

Keira nodded and smiled softly. "Thanks, Pen."

"Anytime."

Keira turned onto her side and closed her eyes, already half asleep as Penny closed the door. She sank into oblivion with visions of warm brown eyes and sunlit, golden hair floating through her head.

CHAPTER 9

When Keira woke hours later, the sun was down and her room was completely dark. Only the red glow from her alarm clock offered any light. Her eyes bugged when she saw how late it was. She had slept the rest of the day and well past dinner.

Shrugging off the blankets, Keira flipped on the bedside lamp and stood up slowly. Once on steady legs, she shuffled toward her bathroom. Quickly taking care of business, Keira moved to the medicine cabinet and downed a couple of ibuprofen to ease the throb in her head.

Stepping in front of the mirror, she unwound the bandage from around her head. The bleeding had stopped, and she was ready to ditch the head wrap for a smaller bandage.

The last of the gauze fell away, and Keira let out a squawk as she got her first good look at the injury. A gash marred her forehead just above her temple. Blood still dotted her face over the purple bruise. Steri-strips and stitches held it together, giving her a bit of a Frankenstein look.

Leaning closer, she noticed blood still on her scalp under her hair. She brushed at the curls, grimacing when she felt the stiffness of dried blood in the strands. A shower would be lovely, but the discharge instruction said to wait twenty-four to forty-eight hours before she got the wound wet.

She let out a sigh. Maybe if she asked Penny to help, they could wash her hair and keep the wound dry.

It was going to have to wait until morning, though. Right now, she wanted to eat something and then use that map.

Feeling bolstered by the long nap, Keira left the bathroom and went downstairs to the kitchen. She dug through the fridge and found some leftover chicken salad. After quickly eating and downing a cup of coffee—she wanted to stay awake tonight—she headed off in search of Leo.

It briefly crossed her mind to leave him out of her search, but not only did he have the map still, she didn't want to alienate him. It really didn't matter if he was in the room, and leaving him out would only create unnecessary tension in the house.

Figuring he would be out in the garage, puttering around on his electronic gadgets at the workstation he and Ty set up for that express purpose, Keira went out there first. Softly playing rock music greeted her when she opened the door. Leo sat at the long table, the pieces of some gadget laid out in front of him as he worked on it.

She called his name as she crossed the room. He turned, standing when he saw her. He had changed into fresh clothes and his t-shirt this time made her smile. It had a picture of an alligator and read, "Common Name: Murder Log."

"You're awake. How are you feeling?"

Keira gingerly touched the new bandage on her head as she stopped a few feet from him. "Better. The nap was a good idea."

"Good. I suppose you want to use that map now."

Keira nodded. "Yes, I do."

"Did you eat?"

Again, she nodded. "Yes, Dad."

He rolled his eyes. "Watch it or I'll change my mind." He put down the parts to what he was working on and started for the house. "Let's go."

Keira frowned, then blinked in disbelief. "You're not going to try to put me off until tomorrow?"

He turned back and shook his head. "No. You honored your part of our agreement and you look better than when we left the hospital. Let's go find us a goddess." He headed for the house again. Not about to argue, Keira hurried after him.

After a quick stop in his room for the map, they soon stood over her desk, staring down at it.

Keira took the arrowhead from her desk and placed it on the map. She looked at Leo, who was hovering only a couple feet away at the edge of the desk, leaning over on his fists. "Don't touch the map. It might throw off the spell."

He straightened and thrust his hands in his pockets. "I'm a statue. Pretend I'm not here."

Keira's mouth quirked. That was much easier said than done.

Pushing thoughts of Leo and what he did to her equilibrium from her head, Keira took a deep breath and touched the arrowhead. She muttered her locating spell and once again pictured what she thought Persephone represented. This time the arrowhead moved easily as Keira put the necessary force behind the spell. Within moments, the arrowhead stopped. Keira opened her eyes and looked down. It rested over Norwich on the east coast of England, just north of London.

CHAPTER 10

Leo watched Keira weave her magic. It never ceased to amaze him to see what she could do. All of this divine power stuff still astounded him. He had grown up believing in the weird—he was Cajun, after all—but he'd never experienced anything quite like this.

"Well, that's random," Keira said, staring down at the map, snapping Leo out of his thoughts. "I figured she'd be in London or in the absolute middle of nowhere. Norwich seems kind of normal."

Leo stepped closer and looked over her shoulder. Huh. That was interesting. He should have thought of that. "It's not really that surprising if you think about it," he said.

She looked back at him, her breath catching. She cleared her throat before replying. "What do you mean?"

Leo felt his pulse kick up at her proximity. He took a step back to keep a clear head and pointed at the map. "That part of England is the most heavily farmed part of the country. It makes sense that's where she's holed up."

"How on earth do you know that?" Incredulity tinged her voice.

"I was stationed there one summer when I did some training with the British SAS. One of them was bemoaning the stench from the fertilizer they used, saying how he didn't miss it when they were in other parts of the world during the growing season." He shrugged. "It made me curious about their farming practices, so I looked it up. It really was some smelly fertilizer. Turned out to be manure."

Keira wrinkled her nose. "Yuck. No thanks."

Leo smiled. "Well, you can't avoid it, *chère*." He pointed at the map again. "We have to go there."

Her shoulders slumped, and she sighed. "You have gas masks in your bag of tricks, right?"

He barked out a laugh and wrapped an arm around her in a half hug. "It's not that bad. You'll survive."

She rolled her eyes. Her hand landed on his chest and she looked up at him with a genuine smile on her pretty face.

Desire lanced through him, fast and hot. This woman lit him up like no other. Nothing phased her for long. She just rolled with the punches and somehow kept coming out on top. She was incredible.

Leo lowered his head. He could no more stop himself from bending down to kiss her right now than he could the Earth turning. All of his earlier promises to himself to keep his distance flew out the window.

The first tentative touch of her mouth to his left him reeling. Intense need roared to life. He brought a hand up and cupped the side of her face. He pulled back slightly and opened his eyes, looking down at her, wanting to know if she wanted this as much as he did.

Desire as deep as his own shone from the dark brown depths of her eyes, ratcheting up the fire lighting his blood. Pulling her closer, Leo caressed her face and ran his thumb over her plump lips. Heat from her breath washed over his thumb and his control snapped. He lowered his mouth to hers once again, but this time there was no gentle touch or soft melding of mouths. Flames erupted and fused them together. She clutched his shirt and parted her lips for him. He swept inside, tangling his tongue with hers.

One of them groaned. Leo couldn't be sure it wasn't him. In the end, it didn't matter. It still served to make them both burn. She released his shirt and let her hands roam. Up over his shoulders and into his hair, her nails raked his scalp. Leo locked his knees as they threatened to turn to liquid. He let his own hands wander. The fingers of one hand gripped her hair at the back of her neck while his other hand traveled around her hip and up her back before heading down to cup the curve of her bottom. He gave her a gentle squeeze, and she arched into him, moaning her pleasure.

His fingers grazed the bandage at her temple. It was like an instant bucket of cold water over the head, reminding him she was injured and wasn't up to the kind of activity his body had in mind. Gentling the kiss, Leo placed one last, lingering caress on her lips before pulling back. He settled his hands at her waist and leaned his forehead against hers.

"That map isn't the only thing you've put a spell on, *chère*," he told her, breathing hard.

"Yeah, well, you've weaved your own magic." Inhaling deeply, she stepped out of his arms. Leo felt the loss down to his bones.

She began gathering up her scrying materials and Leo felt a distance spreading between them.

"Keira."

She looked at him as she closed the desk drawer, her face shuttered. "I don't want to talk about it, Leo. It happened and we need to make sure it doesn't happen again. It's a distraction we don't need."

Leo felt anger surge. She was fooling herself if she thought they would be better off ignoring the attraction. It hadn't worked well for them so far. "You need to think on that again, *chère*. I don't know about you, but I'm going to spend a lot of time wanting more, and it sure as hell will be a distraction."

He stepped around her and headed for the door before he did something they'd regret—like grab her and kiss her again until neither of them could think straight. "I'm going to go book us tickets to London. You should get some more rest."

With that, he left the room, still fuming she could dismiss his feelings and her own so easily. That kiss had rocked his world. Now that he knew what he had been missing—how it felt to hold her and to touch her—not being able to have her would be a bigger distraction than the emotions she evoked ever would. He wasn't going to give up without a fight.

CHAPTER II

Keira woke to a scream. Eyes darting to the clock, she was amazed to see only an hour had passed since she finally drifted off around three a.m. Sleep had been elusive after her encounter with Leo in the magic room. She kept replaying what he said through her head.

An angry male shout echoed down the hallway, bringing her thoughts back to what awakened her. Keira threw off the covers and rushed from her room. She screeched to a halt in her doorway as Leo nearly ran her over as he barreled down the hall toward Ty and Penny's bedroom. It was Ty's voice she heard bellowing.

Alarmed and feeling the fear rising, Keira followed behind him. She didn't know what they would find. She couldn't imagine what would make a man like Ty sound like he wanted to commit murder.

Leo flung open the bedroom door. They both stopped dead in their tracks at the sight before them. Whatever Keira had expected, it hadn't been this. Ty, clad only in a pair of black boxer briefs, chased Penny around the room. His eyes glowed an icy blue, a menacing snarl on his normally handsome face. Penny kept dodging away from him by shifting from one animal to the next so fast Keira could hardly keep pace with the changes. Over the bed as a cat, under the bed as a mouse, above them all as a bird, Penny shifted, trying desperately to elude her husband. Ty kept shifting with her, turning predator to whatever animal Penny chose.

Penny saw them and darted away from Ty quickly. She shifted human. "Stop him! He started yelling, then tried to choke me. I don't know what's going on!"

"He's locked in a nightmare," Leo said. "Can you get your arms around him from behind? Use the strength you got from him against him?"

Penny shifted into a cat again and streaked across the room as Ty, human again, barreled at her once more.

She shifted back. "I can try, but I think he's still stronger than me. And he could shift into something small and get out of my hold."

"Not if I keep him from shifting," Keira said, a plan forming.

"Can you do that?" Leo asked.

Keira nodded. Running an enchantment through her head. "I think so. Leo, I need you to go down the hall and get some things from my magic room while Penny and I get him under control." She quickly rattled off the list of supplies she needed.

He took off.

Keira turned her attention to Penny. "Okay, Pen. Get behind him and wrap him up like a bear. Use your arms and your legs and hang on tight."

Penny waited until Ty was almost on her before she shifted into a bird and flew around him. Before he could turn around, she shifted back and wrapped him up.

Keira immediately wrapped magical chains around him, muttering an enchantment that kept him from shifting. She could feel his power pushing against hers. He seemed to blink as he tried to shift and couldn't. Bellowing in rage, Ty struggled against their hold. He was angry and determined to get what he wanted. She was glad for Penny's help. Neither one of them could have held him alone.

Leo rushed back into the room with the items Keira requested. She quickly grabbed several of them to mix together in a glass she found sitting on the dresser.

"What are you going to do?" he asked, pouring things as she handed them to him. She was grateful for his help. It allowed her to keep most of her concentration on keeping Ty immobile for the moment. She kept having to mumble the enchantment to strengthen the bonds holding him. His abilities were strong.

"This should sedate him long enough for us to figure out what the hell is going on. I hope." This needed to work. The potion felt right, but it had just come to her, like the enchantment holding him. She was trying to get used to that and to trusting her gut. But not having recognized she had this ability until the last few weeks made her leery. And Ty had some serious mojo. She had to make the potion strong enough to dampen his abilities, but not kill him.

She shoved the glass at Leo. "Put some water in that—about half full—and stir it with his toothbrush or something."

Leo raced off to the bathroom and returned within moments.

"We need to get it in him."

Leo looked at her like she had lost her mind. It felt like she had when she eyed the snarling, glowing, deranged grandson of a god, held immobile by his wife and some magical chains.

He handed her the glass. "I'll get his mouth open. You pour."

Leo dragged the only chair in the room in front of Ty and stood on it. He held out a hand to Keira and helped her up next to him.

Ty continued to bellow and strain against his bonds.

"Ready?"

With a deep breath, she nodded. "Tip his head back so it goes down and doesn't dribble down his chest. He's going to need it all."

Using the leverage he created by standing on the chair, Leo put Ty in a headlock as best he could and pried his mouth open by pushing on the pressure points on his jaw.

Keira didn't waste any time. She poured the potion into his mouth, forcing him to swallow or choke. She hated having to do this, but something was going on and they needed to find out what. The only way to do that was to get him calm first.

In seconds, all the potion was in. "You can let him go, Leo." Keira stepped down from the chair.

"What about me?" Penny asked.

"Soon." Keira took a few steps back and watched for signs the potion was working. "It should take effect rather quickly."

Almost as soon as the words left her mouth, the blue glow started to fade from Ty's eyes. Some of the tension leached from his muscles and he relaxed.

"You can get down, Penny."

"Are you sure?" A slight tinge of panic laced Penny's words. Keira could tell she was close to losing it over this. She couldn't blame her. Keira would too if her husband went into a nightmare-induced rage and tried to kill her.

"I'm sure," she told Penny. "Let him go and step over here."

Penny did as Keira said. Once Penny was clear of the big man, Keira used her abilities to lift him off his feet and put him on the bed, prone. By the time he hit the mattress, he was sound asleep again.

Keira released the chains as well as her breath. That was intense.

She turned to Penny. "Are you okay?"

Penny nodded, shakily. "He didn't really hurt me."

Keira grasped Penny's arm. "I didn't mean physically."

Staring down at her sleeping husband, Penny ran a hand through her hair and collected herself before nodding. "I will be. Once I know why he did that. He's never done anything like that before, Keira. He's had nightmares since we've been together, but never like that." The tears threatened to make a reappearance and Penny sucked in a breath to hold them back. She turned to Leo. "Were there any missions you guys went on that would provoke a response like that?"

Leo immediately shook his head. "No. We had a couple that went sideways and then some, but I've never seen him react like that to a dream, and I've seen him have some doozies in the field."

Keira walked back to the dresser where she had mixed up the sleeping potion. She picked up the other items she had Leo grab and turned back to them. "I need a clean glass or bowl and a drop of his blood."

"Why do you need his blood?" Penny asked.

"Something weird is going on. His blood can likely tell me what."

"Like an illness?"

Keira shrugged. "Kind of. But he's not sick. At least not with a normal, human illness."

Leo looked back and forth between her and Ty, confusion written all over his handsome face. "He has a magical illness? Is there such a thing?"

Again, she shrugged. "It's possible, and I won't know until I test his blood."

Leo pulled a knife from his pocket, flipping open the blade. "Let's find out, then, because I don't like this. Having a deranged man with the strength of Hercules is a bad idea."

Keira agreed. They needed to figure out what was happening pronto. She couldn't keep Ty sedated indefinitely.

Working quickly, they gathered all they needed for the test. Penny found another glass in the bathroom and washed it while Keira measured ingredients. They dumped the herbs into the glass, added some water and a drop of Ty's blood.

Keira swirled the liquid to combine things. In a matter of moments, it turned black and congealed.

"I knew it." Victory surged through her that she got the potion right, swiftly followed by a healthy dose of dread. The implications of what the test revealed were frightening.

"Why is it black and gooey?" Penny asked.

Keira took a deep, steadying breath. "Hecate got to him. I don't know how, but this," she held up the cup, "means he's had a dark magic spell used on him." It was just one more in the long line of weird things that had happened lately. Keira couldn't wait to get her hands on Hecate. The goddess was going to regret messing with Keira's family.

Penny's eyes widened. "Can you fix it?"

Keira stared down at the congealed mass, combining ingredients in her head. "I think so. But we're going to have to keep him sedated until I make an antidote. That sleeping potion I gave him is the only thing keeping the dark spell at bay."

"How long and what do you need?" Leo asked, cutting to the chase.

Keira thought about what she had in her magic room. "I need to get a couple things, but I can't do that until morning. Once I have them, though, it shouldn't take much time to put it together."

"Do you have enough of the ingredients to keep him asleep until you can reverse the other spell?"

She nodded. "Definitely. But we'll have to dose him probably every hour. With his size and heritage, it will wear off quickly."

"Then that's what we'll do. *Chère*, show me how to make this magic elixir of yours. You need to go back to sleep for a couple hours."

Keira frowned fiercely. "I'm fine, Leo."

He was shaking his head before she even finished speaking, deepening her frown. "You've taxed yourself quite a bit already tonight. You're going to rest again. Penny and I can handle dosing Ty with his sleepy juice."

It didn't matter to her that he was right or that her head throbbed. It was the principle of the thing. She was the witch. It was her potion and her responsibility. And she didn't like taking orders.

Keira opened her mouth to launch another protest when he walked over to her and gently took her face in his hands. "Please, *chère*? You need to rest. We really can handle this. You don't need to save the world single-handedly."

His soft, sensitive tactic accomplished what his demanding, dictatorial tone had not. The fight left her, and she nodded at him, laying her hands over his. "Okay. But the herbal place I go to opens at nine. I want to be there *at nine*."

Leo grinned. "I'll get you there. Now show me how to make this stuff so you can get some rest."

With one last mock glare, Keira did as he requested.

CHAPTER 12

P enny hovered over Ty, watching for signs he was coming out of his nightmare. "I think it's working."

Keira stood to the side, watching nervously. They had given him the potion to reverse the effects of Hecate's spell. True to his word, Leo had her at the herbalist at nine sharp. She had been waiting on the sidewalk when the proprietor opened the door. In no time at all, Keira got what she needed and mixed up the elixir to counteract Hecate's spell.

Ty stirred on the bed and blinked several times, stretching like a cat. He saw Penny hovering over him and smiled, reaching for her. She fell into his arms, sobbing.

"What the hell, Pen? Why are you crying?" He looked up after a moment and noticed Keira and Leo standing at the foot of the bed, watching him. A frown creased his brow. "Why are you two in here?"

"You really don't remember what happened last night?" Leo asked.

Ty frowned and stroked Penny's hair as she wrapped herself around him. She hiccupped as her sobs slowed. Tears still trickled down her cheeks.

"I remember having a wicked nightmare, but that's it. Why?"

"What was your nightmare about?" Keira asked, wondering if any of it would mirror what had happened in real life.

Ty sighed and thought about it. "I was chasing someone. Or some*thing*. Yeah, it was a thing. It wasn't human. It was a demon or some other creature like that."

Keira shared a look with Leo. That would explain why he was trying to kill Penny. In his mind, she was the thing from his nightmare.

Leo moved around the side of the bed and stood next to Ty, who had pulled himself up into a sitting position. Penny still sat in his lap, arms wrapped tight around him. Keira didn't see her moving from that spot anytime soon.

"Ty, you went berserk last night. You tried to kill Penny," Leo told him.

Ty's eyes went wide. He looked down at his wife in horror. "Oh my God. Did I really?"

Penny nodded, more tears welling. "You started shouting in your sleep, and when I tried to wake you, you attacked me." Her voice broke on the last words and she bit back another sob.

Ty pulled Penny close and blinked back his own tears. "I'm so sorry, baby. I don't know why I did that. I would never intentionally hurt you. I love you so much." He kissed her hard. "I'm so sorry," he murmured again into her hair. Tears leaked out of his eyes as he rocked his wife.

"You weren't aware of what you did. In fact, it wasn't even you who did it. Or at least, it wasn't really you in your mind telling you too," Keira said.

Ty frowned at Keira. "What the hell do you mean, it wasn't me? You just said it was me."

She was botching this explanation badly. She took a breath and tried again. "It was Hecate. She put a spell on you that tricked you into thinking Penny was a creature from your nightmare. That's why you attacked her. The spell made you do it."

"A spell? How did she put a spell on me?"

Keira wished she knew the answer to that. "I don't know. It's possible she's strong enough to do it from the underworld. Or she could have gotten it up here somehow and slipped it into something you ate or drank. Of all of us, you're the most vulnerable because you're away from the estate the most."

Penny sat back and turned Ty's face to look at her. "Maybe you should take some time off. I don't like the idea of her being able to get to you."

Ty covered her hand where it rested on his cheek. "We can't live in fear of Hecate. We'll never catch her if we do that."

"Ty's right," Leo said. "We can't let her get to us. She's trying to distract us and keep us from finding her." He turned to Keira. "I bet our accident wasn't purely an accident. I bet she sent that dog and that's why we couldn't see it afterward."

Keira nodded. She agreed. It was just too odd for the animal to vanish the way it did. "We need to be careful. This probably won't be the last thing she tries on us."

"I booked the tickets to Britain for just the two of us," Leo said to Keira thoughtfully. "Maybe I should book seats for Ty and Penny as well."

"No," Ty said before Keira could answer. "You'll draw less attention if it's just you two. People tend to notice me." He smiled wryly. "Besides, it leaves Penny and the belt less vulnerable if we stay here. This house is the safest place she can be. It's fortified like Fort Knox now that you two have gotten your hands on it."

He wasn't wrong, Keira thought. Leo had taken the already good security on the estate and turned it into something that rivaled the best in the world. He was a whiz with electronics and at finding vulnerable entry points. Keira had warded the outer perimeter the best she could against the supernatural. It had kept the worst out so far.

"We don't know what Hecate's endgame is with these attacks," Ty continued. "Yeah, she might be trying to distract us from finding her, but she could also be trying to get Penny alone somewhere we can't protect her, so she can get to the belt. That's been her goal all along. I doubt she's abandoned it just because Hades took out her unwitting henchmen."

Keira felt the same pain lance her heart that always did anytime someone reminded of her brother, cousins, and grandfather who died at Hades's hand. She couldn't exactly blame Hades for doing what he did; her family had done some awful, awful things in their quest to get the belt Penny guarded. But it didn't change the fact she wished they weren't dead. It still hurt every time she thought of them.

Ty was right, though. Penny *was* still in danger and needed to keep a low profile. Jetting across the pond to England was the antithesis to that.

"All right, then." Leo ran a hand through his hair. "I guess it's just you and me, *chère.*"

"Good. Glad that's decided," Ty stated. "Now can you two leave, so I can apologize to my wife the right way?"

Keira couldn't help but chuckle at the sight of the couple on the bed. Discussion over and done about who was going to England, Ty and Penny had turned their focus on each other. He was looking at her with such longing and love, it almost hurt to see. Penny looked right back, oblivious to anyone and everything else.

Beating a hasty retreat, Keira grabbed all her potion supplies and went to pack.

CHAPTER 13

A soft knock on his door made Leo look up from packing later that afternoon. Ty's massive frame filled the doorway.

"Hey. What's up?" Leo tossed a rolled t-shirt into the open duffel on his bed.

"I wanted to thank you for helping me earlier," Ty said, striding into the room.

Leo shrugged and rolled another t-shirt. "There's nothing to thank me for. Keira and Penny did all the work." He had actually felt rather helpless. With no special abilities, he had been forced to stand back and watch. It wasn't a feeling he particularly cared for.

Ty leaned against the dresser, propping one arm on the top. "You shoved that elixir down my throat all night. That counts for something."

Leo just slanted a look Ty's way before turning back to his packing.

"Look, I know this has been hard on you."

"I'm fine."

"You're not. You pretend you are, but I've known you a long time, Leo. We've been through a lot of shit together. You can't hide how you're feeling from me."

Leo threw the ball of socks he just folded into his duffel, his temper flaring as the emotions he had been fighting to keep in check pushed out of their box. "What do you want me to say, Ty? You're right. I'm eight days away from being fucked for all eternity, and there isn't a damn thing I can do about it. So, yeah. I'm not all right. But it doesn't help me—or anyone else—if I sit around and wallow in my misery."

"I'm not saying you need to do that. I just—" Ty broke off to stare briefly at a point on the wall, gathering his thoughts. "I just want you to know you're not alone. That we all carry this burden."

Leo barked out a harsh laugh. "I'm pretty sure I'm the only one with the gaping hole in my psyche."

Ty rolled his eyes and straightened away from the dresser. "You know what I mean. We're all in this together. We all have a part to play. I just want to make sure your head is in the right place."

Leo blew out a long breath and sank onto the bed, a bit ashamed of his outburst. Ty was only worried about him, and Leo practically bit his head off.

"I'm sorry, Ty. I'm not fine, but I am okay. Thank you for worrying about me, but my focus is exactly where it needs to be."

"I hope so, because that woman who saved my sanity this morning is going to need you at the top of your game. She might be able to defend herself with her magic and her potions, but she's counting on you to see the bad stuff coming."

A fierce protectiveness stole over Leo at Ty's words. Leo might not have Keira's magic, but he was still determined no harm would come to her.

He looked his best friend in the eye. "I know, and I've got her six."

A knowing gleam entered Ty's eyes. His mouth quirked. "Among other parts, I'm guessing."

Leo glared, his hackles rising. "Watch it."

Ty laughed and threw up his hands. "No disrespect. Penny and I noticed the fire between the two of you. I think it's a good thing."

He couldn't argue with Ty there. He was beginning to think so, too.

"Yeah, well, we'll see. She's not exactly jumping on the relationship bandwagon."

Ty's brow quirked, incredulous. "And you are?"

Leo heaved a sigh and scrubbed a hand down his face. "Hell, I don't know. She's amazing, but right now isn't exactly the time to start something. Our focus needs to be on finding Hecate and stopping her, so I can get my soul back, not on each other."

Ty leaned against the dresser again. "If you two are anything like Penny and me, it won't matter. Things will just naturally evolve. It'll be like it was always there, and it will blend seamlessly into your lives. I'm not saying it won't have an effect on your life, just that it will strengthen you instead of weakening you like you seem to think it might."

A frown marred Leo's face as he contemplated what Ty said. He hoped his friend was right. He didn't think he could just walk away from Keira. Not anymore.

He stood and resumed his packing. "Well, your theory's going to be put to the test, because I'm about to be alone and in close quarters with her for the foreseeable future."

Ty pushed off the dresser to come and stand next to Leo. All traces of amusement had disappeared from his face. "You two be careful. There's no safety net past the estate walls. You'll be entirely on your own."

Leo looked his old friend in the eye. "I know. And the same goes for you. The closer Keira and I get to Hecate, the more desperate she's going to be. She may try to get to Penny here."

Ty's face hardened. "I hope she does. She won't know what hit her when I'm done with her."

While Leo echoed the sentiment, he wasn't too sure Ty and Penny could defeat the goddess on their own. Leo's gut was telling him there was more to this story than any of them knew. He couldn't help but think the next week and a half was going to be interesting.

CHAPTER 14

Trans-Atlantic flights were a bitch. Leo scrubbed his hands over his face and yawned. They left Charleston nearly twelve hours ago and were on the train north to Norwich from Heathrow in London. He couldn't wait until they reached their hotel. He was going to collapse on the bed and sleep as long as Keira would let him. He'd like eight hours straight, but he doubted he'd be able to put her off all day. Plus, he wanted to sleep tonight so he could get used to being on British time. Even two hours of shut eye would be welcome right now, though.

He glanced over at Keira beside him, who had her head tipped back against her seat, resting. She had done a good job hiding her head wound with makeup, her hairstyle, and a hat. The stitches were hidden beneath the fall of her curly hair, which the hat held in place. Her makeup still looked subtle, but he knew she had caked it on to hide the giant purple bruise still coloring her temple. At least the swelling went down, so her face didn't look lopsided. She'd held up remarkably well for having a recent head injury. Leo had been a little worried about her flying so soon after a concussion, but she just popped a couple of ibuprofen and took a nap.

Leo yawned again. He wished he had been able to nap. Unfortunately, sleep and travel never really mixed for him. Too many years of having to be on alert for any and all potential dangers kept him from taking more than a quick cat nap any time he traveled. While the dangers from his military career weren't there anymore, the threat to his life and Keira's was still very real.

Keira shifted in her seat until she was slanted his way and opened her eyes. Leo felt his breath catch, just like it did every time she turned those dark chocolate eyes on him. Their rich, warm depths drew him in and held tight.

"Are we almost there?"

"Just about."

She sat up and stretched, sending Leo's libido into overdrive.

"So, where are we staying? You never said."

Leo bit back a smile. That was a surprise. He booked them into a bed-and-breakfast he heard about from a friend years ago. It was in the heart of Norwich's historic district. After the last few weeks, they both deserved something better than a cramped, crappy, standard hotel room on the outskirts of the city.

"You'll see when we get there."

She glared at him, eyes narrowed. Leo couldn't stop the smile this time. He did enjoy toying with her. The fire that sparked in her eyes always got his blood pumping.

"You better not be taking me to some dive."

Leo shook his head and drew an X over his heart. "No dive. I promise."

She continued to look at him through narrowed eyes. "You're not going to tell me, are you?"

Leo shook his head.

She heaved a sigh and curled up in her seat again, closing her eyes. "Fine. Wake me when we get there."

He chuckled and settled deeper into his own seat, watching the countryside fly past. At least the trip here wouldn't be dull with her along.

CHAPTER 15

"Holy crap." Keira spun in a circle as she took in their room. "Leo, this is amazing!" And it truly was. The room was large—probably twice the size of a standard hotel room. But that wasn't its most impressive feature. That went to the hardwood floors that gleamed golden in the sunlight, the crystal chandelier sending rainbows onto the light blue walls, and the frosted glass French doors leading to a bathroom that was close to half the size of the rest of the suite. She could see an enormous, freestanding, white claw-foot bathtub sitting in the middle of the bathroom floor on beautiful blue and white tiles that complemented the blue walls. She couldn't wait to climb into that thing and soak. Oh, how she hoped the B&B supplied some bubble bath.

"I told you I wasn't taking you to a dive." Leo closed the door and set their luggage off to the side. "This is better than I hoped, though. It's bigger than I thought it would be."

"It's wonderful. Thank you!" She walked over to the bed and flopped onto it on her back with a laugh. "I've never been in such an opulent hotel room before. And this bed is awesome. It feels like a cloud." She wiggled and settled deeper into it before she looked over at Leo. He was still standing by the luggage, just staring at her. There was a strange look on his face, almost like he was in pain.

Keira propped up on her elbows and frowned. "Leo, are you okay?"

Her words seemed to snap him out of his thoughts and he turned away to rummage in his suitcase as he answered her.

"I'm fine. Just tired." He straightened with some clean clothes in his hands. "I'm going to take a shower and then pass out."

Keira started to nod when she realized they had a problem. "Um, Leo?"

He halted on his way into the spacious bathroom and arched an eyebrow at her in question.

"There's only one bed."

He grinned devilishly, the fatigue vanishing from his handsome face.

Keira felt her eyes widen. He wouldn't seriously get them a room with only one bed, so they had to sleep together. If she had learned one thing about Leo over the last couple of months, it was that he was a gentleman first.

She frowned at him fiercely and sat up. "Leo."

His smile turned playful. "Relax. The couch pulls out. I'll sleep on that."

She grabbed a pillow off the bed and chucked it at him. "You're terrible."

With a laugh, he ducked into the bathroom to dodge the flying cushion, and shut the doors. Keira flopped back on the bed again and stared at the ceiling with its embossed tiles. It really was the most amazing room. She was touched Leo had been so thoughtful. He was helping to make the most of a stressful situation.

He was also making it difficult to ignore how he made her feel. When he was being snarky and argumentative, it was easy to forget he made her blood burn in a delicious way. But when he was all sweet like this and booked her into the biggest, flashiest, most spectacular room she had ever seen, it was all she could do not to open those beautiful bathroom doors and join him in the shower.

With a groan, Keira rolled onto her side and tucked her hands up under her pillow. It was going to be a long few days of nothing but pent-up sexual frustration if he kept this up.

CHAPTER 16

"Are you enjoying that?" Leo asked with a chuckle.

Keira wiped a crumb from the corner of her lips and smiled sheepishly. "Sorry. It's really good." They had napped for a couple hours before venturing out for an early dinner. Keira ate all of her food and was rather stuffed, but she still could not resist the smell of the pastries from the bakery they walked past on their way to the bookstore.

"Try some." She held the pastry up to his lips.

Leo bent and took a bite, his eyes meeting hers as he bit down.

Keira gulped and looked away, face flaming. There was that damn fire again.

"You're right, that is good." He grabbed her wrist and took another bite, leaving her with only a small piece.

"Hey! Don't you know better than to steal a woman's dessert?" She quickly downed the last bite before he could take that, too.

Suddenly, she found herself wrapped in his arms. "Leo?"

"I'm sorry, *chère*. Here, you can have the last taste."

Keira let out a squawk as she found her mouth pressed to his. He took advantage of her open mouth and slid his tongue along hers. Absentmindedly, Keira noted that he did indeed taste like her pastry.

Her mind screamed at her to push him away, but her body failed to listen. Her arms rose of their own volition to circle his neck. She toyed with the hair at his nape, letting herself relax into his kiss. She couldn't remember why she was fighting their attraction at the moment. He had her senses on overload.

All too soon, Leo pulled back. He pressed one last soft kiss on her lips before releasing her.

"Come on." He took her hand. "Let's go find that city map so you can do your thing."

Too flummoxed to remind him that kiss shouldn't have happened, Keira followed him down the street to the bookstore.

It didn't take them long to find a map of Norwich. Keira bought one of the county too, just to be safe.

"Do you need anything else while we're out?" Leo asked as they left.

"It probably wouldn't hurt for us to explore a bit and see if there's an herbalist nearby. I couldn't bring any of my stash with me because of the customs laws on plants." She actually felt rather vulnerable without all her supplies. It was amazing how fast she had come to rely on magic. A little disturbing, too. It hadn't taken long for her new skills to become second nature.

She still wanted her herbs, though. Her natural illusion and telekinetic abilities would only get her so far. Her illusion ability—other than what she did to Leo—was relatively weak still, and the telekinesis took a lot of concentration. Most of her focus had been on potions because they were what she needed to find Hecate. Her other abilities were good for quick self-defense, but not for long-term.

A group of youths stumbled out of a shop, laughing and not paying attention. Keira sidestepped, but one of them still bumped her, sending her toppling into Leo. He wrapped his arms around her and pulled her in to his body to keep her on her feet.

"Oh, sorry, ma'am," the group apologized.

"Be a little more careful," Leo admonished the group.

They all nodded and walked on, still talking and enjoying their evening, but more subdued.

Leo let her go, but held onto her hand. "Are you okay?"

Keira nodded. "I'm fine. They just knocked me off balance." She tugged on her hand, but he held fast, pulling on it to bring her closer.

"Nope. You're staying close now. There won't be any more injuries for you on my watch."

Keira rolled her eyes, but didn't pull away. Instead, she turned her attention to their surroundings. Downtown Norwich was beautiful. The area they were in was pedestrian only. It boasted stone buildings and brick streets and sidewalks, helping it to retain an old-world charm. Parts of it even seemed medieval in feel. The shops had kept up the theme by using old-fashioned script on their signs. The one herbal store they found looked like it should have people in period costumes manning the desk. Everything was stored in glass jars with corks and stocked on rough wooden shelves. The floor even creaked when they walked on it.

"It's like stepping into another world, isn't it?" Leo remarked, reading her thoughts.

Keira nodded. "Being here makes you realize how young the United States is in comparison. I bet some of these buildings are as old as the U.S., if not older."

"The Middle East is like that too. I went to Egypt on leave once. Seeing the pyramids and some of the other ancient sites—" He broke off and shook his head in wonder. "It's amazing what people are capable of with the most rudimentary of tools."

"Do you miss the military? Being able to travel?"

Leo shook his head. "Not really. I mean, part of me misses getting to experience new cultures and see things I've only ever read about, but I don't miss the work. Some guys can do the special forces thing until their bodies give out. They live for the adrenaline and the thrill. I just found it tiresome. I know what I did was important and made a difference, but it just got to the point where I felt like it was eating away at my soul. The killing and the sight of what other people did to each other in the name of power."

He scoffed. "It's a bit ironic that I left the military to save my soul and ended up losing it anyway."

Keira stopped and faced him. She brought her hand up to cup his face. "I'm going to get it back. Hades picked the wrong person to challenge," she said, her voice hard and earnest.

One side of Leo's quirked up. "I know. If there is one thing you are, it's fierce. I wouldn't want to be on your bad side."

She looked at him quizzically. "What are you talking about? You've been on my bad side practically since we met."

Leo shook his head. "No, *chère*. I annoy you. You don't hate me or want to do me harm."

Keira smiled softly. "I guess I can't argue with that. I definitely don't want to hurt you. Annoy you back sometimes, yes, but never hurt you."

He kissed her softly. Keira felt the touch bone deep. He was getting to her, breaking through her defenses and demanding she acknowledge her feelings for him. She was starting to think he was right; denying how she felt was more of a distraction than letting what they had the chance to flourish.

"Let's head back. You find Persephone, and we can come up with a plan on how to approach her."

They turned back toward their B&B, a companionable silence between them. It felt like their relationship had changed—at least to Keira. Maybe it was because she was loosening up and not fighting her attraction to him as much. She also felt she knew him better now. He was a protector first and foremost, and it was killing him he couldn't do more to fix their situation, so when he could protect her, he did.

It didn't take them long to reach their B&B, and within minutes they were inside the old stone building, climbing the tight staircase to their room on the second floor. Keira's mind was on her revelations about Leo and their relationship and not paying attention to her surroundings. When Leo stopped abruptly and thrust her behind him, she had to throw her hands out to grasp his back so she didn't fall.

"What? What's going on?"

He motioned her to be quiet and pointed at the door to their suite. It was slightly ajar.

Keira's eyes widened. She scanned the hallway, looking for someone lurking.

Leo moved her so her back was to the wall next to the door. "You stay right here until I give you the all clear," he whispered.

Keira nodded and rooted her feet to the floor.

CHAPTER 17

Body tense, Leo pushed the door open and stepped into the room. Their suitcases were open and their clothes were strewn all over the floor. Keira's toiletry kit had been dumped on the top of the dresser. The sheets had been pulled from the bed and cushions removed from the sofa, their innards pulled from the covers.

Leo picked up a heavy statue from the table by the sofa and crept into the bathroom. He checked both the shower stall and the small room with the toilet and sink, but found no one. Whoever did this was long gone.

He went back to the hallway, where Keira waited. "You can come in, *chère*. It's a mess, but I don't think they took anything."

Keira walked in and immediately covered her mouth as she saw the damage. "Wow."

Leo reached for the phone and called the front desk to report the break-in.

"Don't touch anything," he told her when he hung up. "The police will want to take photographs."

Keira nodded absently, looking at the items strewn across the dresser.

Leo didn't like this. It couldn't be random. Their room seemed to be the only one disturbed, and this was a posh place. Vandals didn't come in and ransack rooms for no reason. Keira had brought some expensive jewelry with her in case they needed to dress up to get close to Persephone, and it was all still here. He had seen it on the dresser with all of her makeup and hair products.

"Leo."

He turned at the slightly panicked tone of her voice.

"Leo, I can't find my arrowhead. The one I use for scrying. It's gone!"

Alarmed, he went to her. "Where was it?"

She pointed at a small leather pouch. "I keep it in there. I put it in my toiletry case so I could keep it in my carry-on and not risk it getting lost if my suitcase didn't make it." She poked the pouch. "It was open like that and it's empty."

Leo crouched down. "Maybe it fell on the floor." He pulled his phone out and turned on the flashlight to shine it under the dresser. He found a tube of lipstick, but nothing else. A quick search around the area revealed nothing more than a receipt and a Band-Aid.

This was not good. The break-in definitely wasn't random if the only thing missing was Keira's scrying stone.

"This is terrible. I knew I should have kept it on me." She sagged against the dresser and scrubbed her face with her hands.

Leo set his hand on her shoulder and gently squeezed. "This is not your fault. We had no reason to think we were followed here, and we weren't gone long. Whoever did this is much more prepared than we thought. Now we know to be on the lookout. They won't catch us off guard like this again." He wished he had his surveillance equipment. It might not be a bad idea for him to seek out a small electronics shop while they were here.

"Can you still find Persephone without that stone?"

"Yes, but I need another stone and some supplies so I can put an enchantment on it. I hope I can get the new one as sensitive as the arrowhead. Part of my success with it was because it meant something to me. I had a connection with it."

Leo frowned, curious. "What kind of connection? I thought you found that thing in Theo's collection of rocks and other stuff he had on display." In addition to the things Theo found on dives, he had an astonishing array of artifacts from around the world on display in his home. Penny hadn't moved any of it, liking the connection to the past. Leo, who also had a thing for archaeology, had spent hours going through the house looking at everything.

Keira shook her head. "No. It was part of my things I had shipped from Austin. I found it as a girl on vacation one year out west. It was my most prized possession for a long time."

Leo pondered that thoughtfully when inspiration struck him. "What about this?" he asked, pulling the ring off his right hand. It was his signet ring from the Naval War College. "It may not mean anything to you, but it does to me. Would it work?"

She took the ring and looked at the stone. "What's the stone?"

"A garnet. It's my birthstone."

"And it's a real one? Not synthetic?"

He nodded.

She smiled up at him. "It will work, then."

"Even though it means nothing to you? Will it still work as well?" He wanted this to have the best chance of succeeding. They didn't have time to repeat the process.

She took his hand and slid the ring back on his finger. "You're wrong, Leo. It does mean something to me, because you offered it to me. That alone gives it meaning. Thank you."

He smiled back at her, but before he could reply, there was a knock on the door. Leo opened it to reveal the B&B manager, Caitlyn Sheffield, and a pair of police constables.

"Mr. Devereaux, this is PCs Abernathy and Hall. They're here to take a report on the break-in," the manager said, introducing the officers.

Leo stood back so the officers and manager could enter.

"They really did a number on this place," PC Abernathy remarked, perusing the room. He was a tall, lanky man in his late thirties. With his light complexion and glasses, he looked a bit nerdy for a cop, but he was built like a runner. Leo bet many criminals underestimated this man and paid the price for it.

His partner, a very fit young woman close to Keira's age, with dark hair wound into a severe bun, snapped pictures of the disarray. "Was anything taken?"

Leo gave Keira a look, silently telling her not to mention the arrowhead. "No," he said. "It was just ransacked."

PC Hall looked up, a frown marring her brow. "Nothing? No money? Jewelry? Your electronics?"

Leo shook his head. Keira echoed his reply.

"That's very odd," Abernathy said. He removed his hat and scratched his head, making the wild strawberry blond hair stand on end further. He turned to the B&B manager. "Mrs. Sheffield, has anyone else complained of a disturbance?"

"No, sir."

PC Abernathy scratched his head again. "Very odd, indeed. I shall need to see your CCTV footage."

Mrs. Sheffield nodded. "I tasked the concierge with making a copy after I summoned the police. It should be ready when we go back downstairs."

"Right. We'll finish up here and then come down."

"I'd like to take a look at the tapes as well, if you don't mind," Leo said. He'd like to get a look at the faces of the people who broke in so they could keep a lookout for them. If he could get a still image, he could send it to Ty and have facial recognition run. They might get lucky and get a hit on who it was and where they were staying.

PC Abernathy frowned. PC Hall ignored them and broke out the fingerprint powder so she could dust for prints. Leo almost told her not to bother, but figured that would earn him more questions than he wanted to answer.

"That is very unorthodox, sir. We don't normally share things like that with victims unless we need to make an identification."

"I figured, but it's bothering me that nothing was taken," Leo lied smoothly. "I'd like to know who I'm up against." And where they've gone, he added silently.

Abernathy frowned. "Do you think you and your wife are in danger?"

Leo didn't bother to correct the man. They had registered as a married couple to avoid undue attention. Like Ty and Penny, if asked, they just told everyone it was their honeymoon.

He shrugged. "I can protect us if we are, but I'd like to see the danger coming."

"Sir, it's best to let the police handle these things," Abernathy bristled.

"I understand that, but I'm a former spec ops officer. I won't let someone hurt my wife if we're attacked." That much was true. If anyone dared lay a hand on Keira, he would break it as well as a few other bones in the process.

Abernathy's bearing changed, and he looked at Leo in a new light. "Spec ops? What branch?"

"SEALs."

Abernathy waffled in his resolve. Leo could tell the constable was not a stupid man; he knew enough about spec ops soldiers to know they would not back down if attacked. Leo was certainly no exception to that rule. He figured, for the constable, it was just a question of whether giving Leo—a man trained to kill—the identity of the person or persons responsible for the damage and threat to Leo's "wife" would be a wise decision.

"I'll show you the footage on one condition," Abernathy finally relented. "You only fight if provoked. If they don't take a swing at you, you detain them and call the police. Any other scenario will land your spec ops arse in jail. Understand?"

"Completely," Leo responded immediately. He had no desire to get into a fight. He'd rather follow and take out the bastards on his own terms, if necessary. Abernathy didn't need to know that, though.

"PC Hall?"

The young woman looked up at her partner from where she currently dusted for prints.

"I'm going to take Mr. and Mrs. Devereaux and view the CCTV footage. Meet me downstairs when you're done."

She nodded and went back to work.

Leo arched an eyebrow at Keira at the woman's response. She was an odd duck. Keira just shook her head, not understanding her either.

He held out his hand to her. "Come on, wife. Let's go see who vandalized our room." Leo grinned at her when she stuck her tongue out at him playfully when Abernathy turned his back on them. She had balked a little at playing husband and wife, but once he explained his reasoning for it, she acquiesced. Since then, she had taken to making private jokes about the whole thing. He was enjoying the game as well although, he enjoyed the ring of "wife" attached to Keira even more.

Leo was in deep, he realized. But he was surprisingly all right with that. Keira was an amazing woman. Any man would be lucky to be her husband.

They followed Abernathy downstairs to Mrs. Sheffield's office, where she had the footage queued on a laptop and a copy of it on a thumb drive, which she handed to the constable.

"What time did you two step out?" Abernathy asked, settling into the desk chair. Leo and Keira took up residence behind him, Leo's arm wrapped around Keira's waist so they could fit in the tiny space. Leo told him what time they had left for dinner, and Abernathy quickly pulled up the recording. He tabbed through the tape, looking for anyone in the hall outside their room.

About fifteen minutes after they left, two men came down the hallway. Both were well-dressed and wouldn't have set off any alarms amongst the staff. They stopped in front of Keira and Leo's suite, where one passed a device over the electronic lock. The door popped open and they entered. Leo resisted the urge to slam his fist down. Both men kept their faces averted from the camera.

Abernathy quickly tabbed through the tape until the men emerged from the room ten minutes later. This time they got lucky and one of them turned toward the camera. It looked like he was answering a question the other one asked. There was no audio, so they couldn't hear what was said, but the picture was plain as day.

Leo felt more than heard Keira's quick intake of breath. He looked down at her. Her eyes were wide in shock. He frowned, but she just pursed her lips and tipped her head at the constable, still sorting through the footage. Leo nodded in understanding.

The rest of the footage went by quickly. The men left the building and disappeared from view.

"I'll have a check of the city's CCTV footage once I get back to the station. There's a good chance I can track them down."

"You'll let us know if you find them?"

Abernathy nodded. "Of course. I have to say, though, they won't get more than a slap on the wrist if we do find them. Nothing was taken or destroyed."

He shared a look with Keira. She looked calm on the surface, but he could feel the tension in her body.

"We understand," Leo said, turning back to the constable.

They walked out of the office to find PC Hall standing in the lobby, evidence kit in hand. "I found some prints," she said as the three of them approached her. "But with this being a B&B, that's not unusual. I tried to wipe up as much of the powder as I could. I hope I didn't leave you too big of a mess."

"Thank you for being so considerate. We appreciate it," Keira told her.

The woman nodded. "I just need to take your prints for comparison and we'll leave you be."

Leo and Keira quickly allowed the constable to use her portable scanner and take their prints. It only took a few minutes and both constables were bidding them a good evening.

Leo didn't waste any time ushering Keira back upstairs as soon as the constables were out the door. They practically flew up the steps to their room.

"Okay, spill," he said as soon as the door closed. "What did you see in that footage?"

Keira took a steadying breath. "The man, the one who looked at the camera?"

Leo nodded.

"That was my Uncle Max."

"Christ," Leo muttered, swiping a hand down his face. This was nuts. This trip was last minute. How the hell did Hecate's cronies find them so fast?

Keira stuffed a sofa cushion back into its cover and sat. "I wondered what happened to him after Hades took everyone out. Max wasn't there that night. I guess Hecate got to him and has him following us."

Leo fixed the other cushion and sat next to her. "But how? I used our real names on the flights and on this hotel, but I booked them with a credit card tied to an alias. You would have to have government clearance to access the flight manifests. And it would only do any good if you knew what flight or cities to look at."

"You have an alias?"

His mouth quirked in a smile at her surprised look. He had several, actually. His SEAL days had been interesting. His ability to not only hack and build surveillance equipment, but his knack for getting people to talk to him, didn't go unnoticed. He had been tapped for some very black, black ops involving the CIA more than once.

She waved a hand at him. "You know what? Never mind. I don't want to know. I'm sure it's some clandestine thing you can't tell me about anyway, and it's irrelevant. If Max is involved, then so is Hecate. She probably put a tracker spell on me and has been feeding that information to her lackeys here."

"A tracker spell? Can you shake it? If we're ever going to get one up on her, we need to be invisible."

Keira sighed and dropped her head into her hands. "This is such a cluster." Her head snapped up, eyes flashing fire. "She's doing this deliberately to slow us down." She jumped up with a growl and started pacing.

Leo sat back and just watched, letting her work through her anger. He was pissed off as well. Had been since Hades took his soul, but he was much less boisterous about it.

"As much as I can't stand Hades and hate the idea of making him happy, I can't wait to turn the bitch over to him. I hope he tortures her for a good long while before snuffing out her existence."

Leo stood and intercepted her, holding her loosely with his hands at her waist.

She rested her hands on his biceps and looked up at him. "Ugh. I'm sorry. I'm not normally so bloodthirsty, but she's just pushed me to the edge."

"Don't be sorry. I kind of like this side of you. It's fiery." Leo pushed her hair back off her face and tucked it behind her ear. His thumb whisked over the stitches at her temple. "I'm just as frustrated as you, *chère*, but I have faith in you. In us. We will win, because we're more determined than she is, I think. And I think she underestimates you. I think you underestimate yourself. You are one powerful woman and you don't quit. There isn't anyone I would want fighting for my soul more than you, Keira."

Keira kissed him. Not a little peck, but a full-on melt his boots kiss. Leo wasn't about to complain. He wrapped his arms around her and pulled her close. He was hot and hard in an instant. She revved him up faster than anyone ever had. It was all he could do not to throw her on the disheveled bed and strip her of her clothes. He held on to his restraint, but just barely. The last thing he wanted to do was scare her. This thing between them was so new. Leo didn't want to kill it before it even had a chance to grow.

CHAPTER 18

Keira slid her hands beneath Leo's t-shirt and caressed the muscles she found there. This was absolute madness, but she couldn't stop herself if her life depended on it. That compliment, coming from a man like him who had fought alongside some of the most courageous men the world had ever known, snapped her resolve like a toothpick. Kissing him seemed like such a natural response to his comment, she hadn't given it a second thought.

She ran her hands over his hair-roughened chest once more. He groaned as she raked her nails over his taut nipples. Shivers skated over his skin and gooseflesh erupted beneath her touch. Their tongues tangled and danced for several more moments. When she suddenly realized how close she was to pushing him down on the bed and following this to its natural conclusion, she pulled back. Her body might be ready for more, but her brain still needed to catch up.

"Wow," she breathed, resting her forehead on his chest.

"Wow is right." He ran his hands over her back and down to caress her butt before moving back up again. Keira stood on her tiptoes and nipped at the tendons in his neck in response.

He moaned again. "God, woman. You muddle my brain."

"Ditto." She took a deep breath, trying to clear her head, and nearly went crossed-eyed as his scent filled her nose. Keira closed her eyes and took a step back. She needed some distance if she wanted out of this room without making love to him right this minute.

They had another item on their agenda tonight they needed to get to. "As nice as this is, we need to go see if that herbal shop is still open."

He groaned again and nodded, letting his hands fall away from her body. "You're right." He reached out to caress her cheekbone with his thumb. "You realize I'm not going to give up on us now, right? Not after that."

Keira blew out a breath, understanding what he was saying. Finally, she nodded.

"Good." He took her hand and led her toward the door. "Let's go see someone about some plants."

Keira followed, wondering if she just made a huge mistake in giving in to her feelings for the sexy Cajun.

CHAPTER 19

"Wow." Keira couldn't help but stare as Leo came out of the bathroom clad in a gray suit. It fit him to perfection, outlining his tall, muscular physique. This was almost as good as the breeches and tailcoat. Nothing could match his legs in those breeches, though.

He fiddled with his tie, but stopped with her exclamation. "What?"

"You look... I'm not sure what to say, honestly." It was the truth, too. He left her speechless.

Leo went back to messing with his tie. "It's just a suit, *chère*. Men wear them all the time."

Keira stepped forward and batted his hands out of the way so she could fix his tie. "Yes, but I've never seen *you* in one before. It is certainly a sight to behold."

The devilish smile that made him look like a young boy reappeared seconds before he grasped her face in his hands and kissed her again.

It was brief, but potent.

Keira blinked several times to clear her head. Damn him. "You need to stop doing that."

He gathered her close, one arm around her waist, the other cradling her head. "On the contrary, *chère*. I think I need to do it more."

She stared up at him, her body at war with her mind. She shouldn't be thinking about this right now. Her total focus should be on locating Persephone and getting her to give up Hecate's whereabouts. Not on how delectable Leo looked in a suit and how much she wanted to get him out of it.

Before she could decide one way or the other, he dropped a quick kiss on the end of her nose and released her. "But it'll have to wait until later. We have a goddess to talk to."

He was right. They did. They made it to the herbal store just before it closed last night and got everything Keira needed to put the enchantment on Leo's ring as well as to identify—and hopefully reverse—the tracking spell Hecate placed on them.

Once they returned to the suite—with new key cards and a promise security would watch their room closely—Keira got to work enchanting the ring and nailing down a location for Persephone. The stone led them to two places: what seemed likely to be Persephone's home, and a building in the business district. Leo and Keira decided to wait until morning to approach Persephone at the business address, hoping she would be more receptive to unexpected visitors at the office than at her home.

Keira hadn't been able to do much with the tracking spell other than identify it. She tried to remove it, but didn't have any success. It was frustrating, to say the least. Leo finally made her call it a night after her third failed attempt had her ready to undo all the cleaning they did to put their room back to rights after the break-in. Around two a.m., they fell into a restless sleep—in separate beds. There had been a rather steamy kiss before lights out, but they broke apart and retreated to their separate spaces, both knowing their relationship wasn't ready for that step just yet.

Once in bed and her brain functioning again after the drugging effects of his kiss, Keira realized Leo had been right to call a halt to her attempts to reverse the tracking spell. Her mind was just running in circles, frustrated and sleep deprived.

Now, in the light of day, while not well rested, she was at least more refreshed than she was last night. It had allowed her to see that if she couldn't remove the spell, she might just be able to block it or confuse it.

But that was going to have to wait until after they visited Persephone.

Clothing all in place and looking like two professionals heading to work, they left the B&B and hailed a taxi to take them to the business district. It was a short ride, only a few blocks, but in the morning traffic, it took twice as long as it should have.

When the cab finally pulled up to the address Leo's ring showed them on the map, Keira was feeling a bit like a hot mess. Finding Persephone and coming up with a plan to talk to her was entirely different from executing said plan. Maybe her scrying stones were right to resist locating the goddess. Persephone was married to Hades, after all. She couldn't spend millennia with the bastard and not pick up a few character flaws.

Keira looped her hand through Leo's elbow when he offered it to her and let him lead the way into the building. It was an impressive metal and glass structure, befitting the business tycoons it housed. It was not something she could see a nature goddess in, but perhaps that was the point. No one would suspect who she really was if she hid out in a place like this.

Inside, they made their way over to the directory and began looking over the company names in the book. Keira's scrying only revealed an address, not a name or suite number.

"This would be so much easier if we had a business name," Keira remarked, staring at the list. There had to be fifty different companies in this building. Some of them were large and employed hundreds of people. It was like trying to find a needle in a haystack.

"Let's just see if there's something nature related and go from there," Leo replied. He ran his finger down the list and paused about a third of the way down on a name for an agricultural conglomerate known internationally. "This one." Quickly, he flipped to the correct directory page, and they scanned the list of names. And there were a lot of names. It was one of the largest agricultural companies in the United Kingdom.

They hardly began when a name near the top for the company president jumped out at her. Kore Sito.

"This is her." Keira could hardly believe it was this easy. She supposed they were due for some luck after yesterday.

Leo bent down to look at the name. "You're sure?"

Keira nodded vigorously. "I did my research on all the players involved in this whole situation. 'Kore' is a known alias for Persephone and 'Sito' is an alias for her mother, Demeter."

He scanned the list again before pointing at the page. "So, does that mean this is Demeter, then?"

Keira frowned down at the directory. Sure enough, under "CEO," was the name Demi Sito.

So much for this being easy. Adding another deity to the mix increased the danger. Keira could only hope the goddesses were easygoing and willing to listen to what she and Leo had to say.

"Well, it doesn't change the fact we need to talk to Persephone." Keira closed the directory and placed it back on the shelf. "Let's go."

Determination had an air of confidence radiating from Keira as she strode across the lobby to the bank of elevators. She jabbed the up button and stood there, tapping the toe of her chic peep-toe heels while they waited.

Leo's hand pressed into the small of her back. He tucked her into his side and leaned down, sending Keira's pulse skyrocketing.

"You know, I know you told me you were an attorney, but until now, I couldn't see it. This take charge, I have confidence the size of Texas thing you have going on right now is extraordinarily sexy."

Pleasure at his words raced along Keira's spine. She felt sexy today. It was nice to be back in her business suits and sky-high heels. It gave her back some of the confidence all her failed attempts to locate Hecate took away. It was very nice to feel some of it return.

Before she could do more than murmur a thank you, the elevator doors slid open. They stepped on, and Leo pushed the button that would take them to Persephone's floor. Nerves flooded her belly. She did her best to shove them down deep and keep her air of confidence about her. She refused to show any sign of weakness to the goddess. If they were going to pull this off, they needed to come across confident in their plan.

Still, when the doors slid open to let them off, Keira was very glad to feel Leo's hand on the small of her back, offering her his silent strength.

"Hello. Welcome to East Anglia Agriculture. How may I help you today?" The perky receptionist greeted them as soon as they approached her desk.

Keira smiled brightly at the woman, projecting confidence. "Hi. We're here to see Kore Sito."

"Your names, please?"

Leo spoke up, giving the woman their names. She quickly placed a call to Persephone's assistant. Keira reached for Leo's hand as she concentrated, drawing on his energy to keep her grounded while she tried to put an illusion on Persephone's calendar so they could get in to see her. She had no problem putting an illusion on Leo sight unseen. But he was different. She was tuned into him like no other. A calendar she had never seen before in a place she had never been? That was entirely different.

He squeezed her hand in silent support while they waited. Thankfully, it was a short wait. Within moments, the young receptionist hung up and smiled at them again.

"You just need these," she said, handing them each a visitor's badge. They clipped them to their jackets, and within moments, she and Leo were being escorted down the long hallway to Persephone's office.

"Again, you never cease to amaze me," Leo murmured in her ear as they followed the receptionist.

Keira amazed herself sometimes. She could scarcely believe that worked. There was a lot to be said for determination, though. They absolutely could not fail, and Keira had used that knowledge—that determination to succeed—to create the illusion that they were supposed to be here.

The receptionist pushed open a set of double doors at the end of the long hall and waved them inside. Another young woman sitting behind a desk smiled at them brightly. She rose to greet them.

"Hi, I'm Emma Forsythe, Ms. Sito's assistant." She held out her hand for them to shake.

Keira and Leo introduced themselves.

"I'm sorry, but you're going to have to remind me why you're here. I don't remember adding you to the schedule," Ms. Forsythe said.

"We're here about a research initiative that would benefit East Anglia Ag and its subsidiaries," Keira lied smoothly. She and Leo talked a bit last night about what story they would spin if asked. Not knowing what kind of company they were going to find, they agreed to go with the idea they were executives of some kind and fill in the blanks on the fly. Thankfully, they only needed to be convincing enough to get past the assistant. Once in with Persephone, there would be no need for pretense.

Ms. Forsythe smiled. "That sounds exciting." She picked up her phone. "Please have a seat and I'll just let Ms. Sito know you're here."

Keira tried hard not to fidget while they waited. She crossed her legs and kept her hands clasped in her lap. Leo lounged next to her, appearing much calmer than she knew he was. The tension in his shoulders was back and his eyes had that watchful wariness to them again. He was coiled like a spring, ready for anything.

She, on the other hand, felt like she was a brand-spanking new lawyer again, trying her first big case. Nerves fluttered in her belly. This had to work.

The door to the inner office opened, and a woman stepped into the doorway. Keira fought to keep her composure as she got her first good look at Persephone. The goddess was absolutely stunning. Tall and slender, but nicely curved, she had her long, dark hair pulled into a sleek ponytail. Ivory linen slacks and a soft pink blouse draped her body flatteringly. Sleek, mahogany leather heels—that Keira herself would love to own—added to Persephone's height, making her nearly as tall as Leo, and finished her polished look. Keira could understand why Hades took one look at the goddess and wanted her for his wife.

"Mr. Devereaux and Ms. Artherton?"

They rose.

Persephone smiled. "Please, come in."

Here went nothing.

Keira followed the goddess into her richly appointed office, Leo right behind her. The room was bright. Floor to ceiling windows lined one wall. The other walls were painted a light sage. Natural wood furniture, vases of fresh-cut flowers, and landscape paintings spoke of Persephone's affinity for nature. Altogether, the décor created a relaxing atmosphere that helped soothe Keira's nerves slightly.

The goddess settled behind her desk and motioned for them to sit in the guest chairs. "So, Emma said you're here about a research initiative? I'm afraid I'm not familiar with what it is, so you'll need to bring me up to speed."

Keira glanced at Leo. His brief nod gave her the encouragement she needed to dive in.

"First, let me state we're sorry we lied to you."

Persephone frowned.

"We're not really here about a research initiative for your company. We *are* here for research, but it's for our gain—and maybe yours if you look at the grander picture."

The goddess's frown deepened. "What on earth are you talking about?"

Keira seized the opening the goddess gave her. "That's exactly the problem. It's not on Earth."

Persephone's face shuttered. All traces of confusion left her and an emotionless mask seemed to fall in its place. It was quite scary to see the soft countenance the goddess projected only a few seconds ago turn into the hard, merciless face of an immortal deity. Keira felt her humanity in that moment.

"What Keira's saying," Leo jumped in, saving Keira from responding around the sudden lump in her throat, "is that we need your help."

"I still don't know what you're talking about. If it's not on Earth, then where is it? Space? I run an agricultural company, not an aeronautics business." Her words were firm, her tone stating she was done with the conversation.

Leo leaned forward. "We know who you are. Who you *really* are."

Only a slight widening of Persephone's dark eyes gave any indication that she understood. She'd clearly had enough, though, and stood. "I don't know what you're talking about, and I think it's time you both left."

Keira stood. She was no match for the goddess in size or stature, but at least standing, she didn't feel like a bug about to be squashed.

She squared her shoulders and faced the goddess. The time for easing into this was over. "Please hear us out, Persephone. My name is Keira Artherton. My original family name is Artemenko. I'm a direct descendant of your handmaiden, Hecate, also known as Iphigenia, daughter of Agamemnon, granddaughter of Atreus."

This time, the goddess couldn't keep the shock off her face. She fumbled for her chair and sank into it. Keira remained standing. Leo rose next to her.

"Look, we're not here to expose you or extort you or anything like that," Leo said. "We need information. Hecate is trying to take over the underworld and subsequently the human world by stealing Hippolyta's golden belt, which is currently in the hands of Hippolyta's descendant and our friend, Penny Farris. We have to find Hecate in the next six days or your lovely husband gets to keep my soul for all eternity. If we never find her and she gets her hands on the belt, everything we all know—including the world you inhabit—will change. And not for the better."

Persephone regained some of her equilibrium. "So, what does any of this have to do with me?"

"We hope you know how to find Hecate. She's shielded herself. Hades can't find her and neither can I. We need a physical location so we can go get her," Keira explained.

Persephone laughed. "She's in the underworld. How do you expect to get to her in the realm of the dead? You're alive."

Leo pulled a coin Hades gave them from his pocket. "With this. Your husband gave each of us one of these so we could travel to the underworld and find her."

Persephone's smile this time was smug. "That will get you there, but how do you propose to get home? Hades isn't exactly known for releasing souls from his domain. In fact, he hates doing it."

Keira frowned fiercely. "I blasted his ass across a clearing already. He'll let us leave—*with Leo's soul*—or he will regret it. I might just let Hecate do her thing. I think he underestimates me and my friends and what we're capable of."

A delighted laugh burst from Persephone. "Oh, I quite like you. I always appreciate anyone who wants to cause trouble for my asshole husband. What is it exactly that you are capable of?"

Keira caught the look Leo shot her, warning her to tread carefully. They didn't need to let Persephone know all their secrets.

She smiled coyly at the taller woman. "I'm a mortal descendant of Hecate. You do the math."

Persephone straightened and arched one perfect eyebrow. "You still need to prove it to me."

Figuring as much, she and Leo talked about it last night and came up with a plan. They decided to go with her tried-and-true skill of illusion. It was the one she had the most practice with thanks to Leo.

Keira tuned in to the energy in the room and ran with Persephone's nature theme. Vines began climbing the walls, continuing onto the ceiling. Blooms erupted throughout the room, the flowers opening to reveal a plethora of colors. The sweet scents of roses, jasmine, wisteria, and honeysuckle filled their noses.

Persephone walked over to the wall and stared at the roses growing there. She poked a flower and gasped when she felt the texture.

"Is that all you can do?" Persephone asked, a touch of wonder in her voice.

Keira shrugged. "I can do the basic witchy stuff. I found you, didn't I?"

Persephone's eyebrow twitched again, but she didn't comment on the lack of information. Keira was glad, because she wasn't getting anymore.

"And what about your friends?" Persephone wandered about the room, stopping to smell the different varieties of flowers Keira created.

"Penny's a descendant of Thetis. Her husband, Ty, is a descendant of Hercules," Leo replied.

Keira resisted the urge to roll her eyes as Persephone pondered that information. Her patience was wearing thin. She released the illusion and brought Persephone's attention back to them. "So, are you going to help us or not?"

Persephone returned to her desk and propped her elbows on the blotter. She steepled her fingers, resting her chin atop them. "What happens if I refuse? Hecate is a dear friend. Why should I betray her for my bastard of a husband?"

"Because your 'dear friend' would just as soon see you die as Hades," Keira argued. "She wants to destroy everything to get her revenge. This is all about her, and I don't think she particularly cares who she hurts in her wake."

"On whom does she want her revenge?" Persephone inquired.

"The gods," Keira quickly retorted. "She sees them as the source of her problems. Her father sacrificed her to appease a goddess. While Artemis took pity on her and made her into Hecate, she's been relegated to the fiery realm of the underworld, banished from the light. You, more than most, should be able to understand how much that sucks."

Persephone bristled and sat back, a thoughtful look on her face now. "All the more reason for me to keep silent."

"But do you want to destroy everyone and everything?"

The goddess frowned and Keira held her breath.

Finally, Persephone sighed. "All I can tell you is she is indeed still in the underworld in her domain there. Where she is in that domain, I don't know. Hermes was the one who escorted me to Earth this spring."

"You're sure she's still in *her* domain and not hiding somewhere else in the underworld?" Leo asked.

Persephone nodded. "I'm sure. I demanded to see her when she failed to show up to bring me back here. Hermes took me to her domain. She was there. Unless she's gone somewhere else since I've been here, she's there."

"How do we get in?" Keira asked. "And where is it?" This was her big problem with going to the underworld to find Hecate. They were at a serious disadvantage in a realm where they didn't know where anything was and where magic reigned supreme.

The goddess sighed. "I can't believe I'm helping the jackass," she muttered before grabbing a pen and a legal pad. She paused, hand poised above the paper, and looked up at them. "Fate of the world is at stake? Fire and brimstone and all that?"

Keira nodded, trying to keep the smile off her face at Persephone's obvious distaste for having to help Hades. It wasn't at the top of Keira's favorite things to do, either, but he *was* trying to stop the destruction of the world.

Before Persephone could do more than place the pen on the paper, there was a knock on the door. It opened, and a slightly older version of Persephone poked her head in. Keira felt her eyes widen.

Demeter.

She could ruin everything. Her dislike of Hades was legendary. Keira had a feeling if given half the chance, and if she had the power, Demeter would blast Hades into oblivion and damn the consequences.

Demeter smiled. "Emma called me and said I might be interested in this meeting." She stepped into the room, hand outstretched. "Hi. I'm Demi Sito, CEO."

Leo took her hand and introduced them. Keira held her own hand out for Demeter to shake. She did so, but a frown crossed Demeter's brow at the contact. She stared hard at Keira before releasing her and turning to her daughter.

Keira wondered what Demeter felt at the contact.

"Hi, Mom," Persephone said. "You might as well have a seat. You'll hear about all this soon enough, I'm sure, when Hades calls you to gloat."

Demeter's eyes widened almost comically at the use of her son-in-law's name dropped so casually into the conversation with a pair of strangers.

"Kore!" Demeter admonished.

"They know who we are." Persephone gave her mother a quick rundown of what Keira and Leo explained to her. Demeter's frown deepened with each passing second.

"That sweet girl who accompanies you here every spring wants to destroy us all?" Demeter shook her head. "No. I don't believe it. Persephone, you cannot help these people. It could be a trick. Hades is very, very adept at pulling the wool over people's eyes." She looked at her daughter knowingly, and Persephone blushed.

"I know that, mother, but I don't think they're bluffing. I felt Hades' presence on Earth a couple months ago. He never comes here unless it's extremely important. I asked Hermes if he knew what was going on. He just said Hades came up to take care of a problem and that he was still working on it."

Demeter turned her frown on Keira and Leo. Keira was amazed she didn't wither in her chair from the force of the glare. She could understand why Hades had folded to the woman when it came to Persephone. She was quite scary.

"What do you know about this?"

"She's right," Keira replied immediately. Demeter demanded total honesty if she were to be convinced. Keira was going to give her as much as she could. "He was here. He killed most of my family and took Leo's soul."

Demeter stared at them, shocked. "And you want to *help* him? Why?"

"Believe me, we don't, but he didn't give us much choice," Leo retorted. "I want my soul back. But that's small peanuts compared to what will happen if Hecate gets what she wants. Millions will die and the realm of the gods may end up under her complete control."

Demeter waved a hand. "Zeus will stop her."

Keira resisted the urge to scream. They were so close to getting what they needed. Why couldn't Demeter have stayed away until Persephone gave them whatever she had been about to put on that paper?

"No offense, Demeter, but you're wrong," Leo fired back. Keira looked at him, a bit shocked at the vehemence in his voice. Frustration oozed from every line of his body. She had underestimated how much this was wearing on him. He bore the burden well and hid it from her even better. He must be nearing his breaking point if it was coming out now.

"Really?" Demeter snorted. "Why don't you enlighten me, human?"

Leo grinned that disarming grin. Keira bit back a smile. He was about to lay into the older goddess.

"Hecate wants Hippolyta's golden belt. You know what that is, yes?"

Demeter nodded hesitantly, suddenly wary, as Leo launched a verbal offensive.

"Then you know it renders the wearer invincible. Do you really think Hecate will *ever* take it off once she gets her hands on it? Or that it will matter? Once she has it, the first thing she's going to do is take out Hades and then she's going to go after Zeus. He won't stand a chance so long as she has that belt on."

"But she doesn't have it."

"Not yet, but like you said. We're human. We need to eat. Sleep. *Bathe.* Our friend who has possession of the belt takes it off periodically, which makes her and the belt vulnerable. It's only a matter of time until Hecate secures it for herself if we don't stop her now. Do you really want to be known as the goddess who could have stopped the apocalypse and didn't?"

Keira held her breath. Demeter was not pleased at his impertinence.

Thankfully, Persephone intervened. "Mother, they're right. Hecate needs to be stopped. I don't like it either, but I can't see that we have much choice."

Demeter continued to frown and addressed her daughter. "How do you know they are who they say they are? I sense a power about them, but that doesn't mean they're not trying to pull one over on you."

Keira had had enough. She stood and let her ability loose. In moments, Demeter was bound to her chair, vines aggressively growing out of the floor and wrapping around the goddess. Demeter tried to make them vanish, but Keira just kept bringing them back as fast as Demeter made them wither away.

"I'm not playing, Demeter. I'm angry. Do you know what I've been through in the last three months? I have lost my *entire* family to this. Only my parents and my uncle are still alive. My father and uncle are both on Hecate's side, and my mother has disowned me because I chose not to support my father. My own flesh and blood wants me *dead* because I chose to fight against them. To not be part of their indiscriminate killing spree in their quest for power. My family now is Penny and her husband, and this man—" she pointed at Leo. "He has sacrificed more than any of us. This was never supposed to be his fight, but now he's in a fight for his soul. All because Hecate wants revenge and Hades is an ass-hat."

Demeter fought against her bonds again, but Keira just threw on more vines. She was beyond pissed at this point, and it was fueling her abilities to a new level. Energy crackled in the room as Keira called on it to keep Demeter bound.

Persephone rose from her chair. Keira threw her a look, warning her not to intervene. She tried to convey that she didn't intend to harm Demeter, but that she had a point to make. Persephone nodded and remained behind her desk, willing to hear Keira and Leo out.

Keira turned her attention back to Demeter once more. "We have spent the last eighty-four days trying to find Hecate. Your daughter has information that will help us find her. I don't want anything from you or from her other than information. But trust me when I say I will get it. You think this is the extent of what I can do? You have no idea. I am under no illusion I'm stronger than either of you. But I am a crafty witch. And a determined one."

She bent down and put her face close to Demeter's. "Look. I know when I let you go, you can squash me like a bug if you so choose. I'm taking a calculated risk here because we need this information, Demeter. We're fighting for our right—and yours—to live. If you take

Hecate's side in this, you will lose. I won't be the one to defeat you, but you will lose all the same."

Keira stared at the goddess for several more moments before straightening. When Demeter fought the bonds this time, Keira let them go.

Demeter rose to her full height. In her heels and with her back ramrod straight, she was taller than Leo's six-foot-three.

And she was ticked.

Leo stepped up next to Keira and took her hand. She looked up at him and he nodded at her in solidarity. Whatever was about to happen, he was with her one hundred percent.

"I have been alive a very, very long time. No one, except Zeus and the rat-bastard who married my daughter, has ever dared to challenge me the way you just did." Demeter's eyes practically spit fire. The sky outside darkened, the clouds threatening.

Keira clutched Leo's hand tighter and prepared to throw up an energy shield to try to mitigate whatever Demeter was getting ready to blast them with.

The goddess looked back at her daughter, who nodded.

When Demeter turned back to Keira and Leo, Keira braced herself. She knew she had taken a gamble, binding the goddess the way she did, but they really didn't have time for all this bullshit. And she was tired of being thwarted at every turn.

"You're lucky I'm one of the nice ones. If you try that with Zeus or Hades, they will end you and make sure your soul is tortured for all eternity. I really should do the same. But I understand where you're coming from and the kind of desperation you're feeling right now. I felt the same when Hades took Persephone. I still feel it every year when she returns to his side. Are your friends as powerful as you are?"

Keira nodded. "In their own ways, yes."

Demeter let out a low whistle. "Okay, then." She sighed. "I'm not happy you're helping Hades. I would as soon see the rat rot in his own world for all time, but I don't want to rot alongside him. I'm inclined to believe you. I can't see someone risking what you have risked on a fool's errand. Persephone will tell you what she knows and help you however she can."

Elation rocked Keira to her core. She wanted to grab Leo and kiss him, but held herself in check.

"Thank you, Demeter."

Demeter waved off her thanks. "Don't thank me. Just stop this. And *never* use your powers against me again. I won't be so forgiving next time."

"Yes, ma'am." Keira let out a sigh of relief. Leo threaded his fingers through hers and raised her hand to place a kiss on the back.

"Come here," Persephone beckoned.

Eager for information, Keira pulled Leo around the desk to Persephone's side where the younger goddess was busy sketching a map. Demeter stood on the other side of the desk and watched.

"This is Hecate's domain. It's guarded." Persephone pointed to a set of crudely drawn gates. "She has her own version of my husband's hellhounds you'll have to get past."

Keira wrinkled her nose. She was not a fan of dogs. Leo's dog, Clyde, was the lone exception.

"Once you're inside, you have to go through a forest. It's got things that go bump in the night. If you're not supposed to be there, they will come after you if you stray from the path. After you're through the forest, you cross a small clearing to get to the house. There are more dogs at the house. She'll likely ward the house as well. I doubt you'll be able to sneak up on her."

"So, we draw her out. Make her come to us," Leo remarked to Keira. "How do we get to her domain?" he asked Persephone.

"You'll need a guide for that. I'll contact Hermes. He ferries souls around the underworld and knows the way."

"He's also Hecate's friend," Keira noted. "Is he really going to help us?"

"I'm her friend and I'm helping you." Persephone shook her head. "I still can't believe this. I'd heard rumors she was planning something. Hades has a hard time keeping secrets from me, and when he asked me if I knew where she was, I knew something was going on. I just didn't know what. I never imagined it would be this, though. She's really gone around the bend and must be stopped. I wasn't around when Hades and his brothers battled their parents, but the repercussions still haunt Olympus and the underworld."

"And that is the only reason you two aren't worm food in my garden right now," Demeter stated from behind them. "I remember the Titanomachy. It nearly destroyed everything. I don't know if the world—either one—can survive that again. Particularly if the battle releases Cronus from his prison in Tartarus."

"He's not the only dangerous thing down there, either," Persephone added. She handed Leo the map. "Once you cross the Acheron, Hermes will guide you to Hecate's territory. But he won't help you once you go inside. He wouldn't be able to do much, anyway. He can fly, that's about all. If your friends are as strong as you say they are, you won't need help. Hecate's power is in her magic. Keira, if you can keep her occupied, your friends should be able to subdue her."

"You also need to talk to the Furies before you go down there," Demeter interjected. "I'm assuming the rat-bastard demanded you four do all the work and bring Hecate to him?"

Keira couldn't hold back a grin as she nodded. Leo barked out a sharp laugh.

"He did," Keira acknowledged.

"Then you need to tell the Furies you're coming. If you waltz past the gates to Hades's palace with Hecate in tow and they don't know what's going on, they're going to side with her and do some unpleasant things to you in an attempt to help her. I'll contact them as well and tell them you're legitimate, so they'll actually hear you out. You can tell them the story," Persephone said.

"How do I contact them?" Keira was genuinely puzzled by that. A seance worked on her dead aunt, but she hadn't a clue how to contact a god not currently on Earth. That was one reason they went after Persephone first. They could actually get to her to talk to her.

"You need to go to the Athens. They have a sanctuary there near the Acropolis. If you make a sacrifice at their altar, they'll talk to you."

Leo frowned. "This isn't going to involve dead animals and shit, is it?"

Persephone shrugged. "If you want to send them a sheep, they won't mind. But they like honey water just as much."

Keira felt her eyebrows rise at Persephone's very matter-of-fact tone. The Greek gods really were of a different breed.

Leo just shook his head. "Glad to hear it. I imagine we'd have a harder time explaining a dead sheep or a container of blood to the guards in the area than a container full of honey water." He laid the map Persephone drew back on the desk. "Now tell me more about this compound. How many dogs are we talking?"

Keira sat back and let Leo pepper Persephone with questions about Hecate's domain. He was in full planning mode and determined to squeeze as much information out of the goddess as possible.

It wasn't until Persephone's intercom buzzed, announcing her next appointment, that she brought the information session to an end.

"Get to Athens. I'll make sure everyone who needs to know about you knows you're coming. I wish you luck."

Finally feeling like they were on to something, Keira and Leo bid Persephone and Demeter a good day and left.

CHAPTER 20

Leo waited until they were in the elevator to pounce. As soon as the doors closed, he grabbed Keira and pulled her in for a scorching kiss. Fire blazed, but Leo kept it banked, cognizant of their surroundings. He pulled back after a few moments.

"That—*you*—were incredible! I can't believe you kept Demeter bound like that. And that she didn't kill us."

Keira smiled. "She wanted to. I could feel it every time she pushed against the bonds." She dropped her head in her hands and released an airy laugh. "I still can't believe I managed to hold her." She raised her eyes to his. "I was just so furious. At the situation, at all the setbacks we've had, at Demeter for being all uppity. It just fed my power and let me control her."

"However you did it, it was impressive. And it got us what we needed." Plans and scenarios had been running through his head from the moment Persephone drew that map. Now that they had solid information, he could see the op taking form. They actually had a chance at stopping the witch-bitch now.

Leo kissed Keira again just before the elevator doors opened, elation making him feel happier than he had since Hades took his soul. The deep, black void was still there, eating away at him, but right now, it was bearable.

CHAPTER 21

B ack at the B&B, Leo made arrangements to get them to Athens while Keira called Penny and filled her in. Leo planned to call Ty later so they could discuss strategy. A new kind of energy filled the room. Buoyant and spirited. Things finally seemed to be moving in the right direction.

Leo looked up from packing when Keira ended her phone call with Penny. She jumped off the bed and went to her stash of herbs.

"What are you doing?" She had that look on her face. The one that said she had a plan, and nothing and no one was going to stand in her way.

"I got to thinking last night and this morning. If I can't reverse the spell Hecate placed on me, I might just be able to throw it off." She picked up several containers, studying their contents.

"How?"

"Well, her spell is tied to my blood, which is why I haven't been able to reverse it and get it to stick. She has an endless supply of part of me through her own blood. She can just keep renewing the spell every time I try to get rid of it."

Leo strode over to stand next to her. "Right. That's the roadblock you kept running into last night."

"Exactly. But what if instead of trying to reverse it, I just disguise my scent? If I can obfuscate my blood, it will confuse her spell, and she won't be able to find me."

That sounded great, but he didn't see how it was possible. "How do you plan to do that? I mean, genetics are genetics."

Keira nodded, sorting the containers. She pulled several forward and set them off to the side. "I know, but I think I can make a tea I can drink that will alter my blood chemistry and confuse her spell."

Alarm bells went off in Leo's head. "Whoa. That sounds dangerous. Keira, you could do some real damage to yourself if you mix the wrong things or make it too strong."

Keira huffed out a breath, fluttering the curls hanging down around her face. She sagged against the dresser and looked up at him. "I know. That's the only thing stopping me. A lot of times, these spells just come to me and I can whip them up with barely a thought. This one, though, is just a vague idea. I know what I need to use, but not the proper proportions."

"Then you're not doing it," Leo declared. They would just deal with Hecate knowing when they were coming for her. There was absolutely no way he was going to let Keira put herself in jeopardy like that.

Keira arched an eyebrow at him. "You know how well the alpha thing works on me, Leo."

He rolled his eyes in exasperation. "You're not putting yourself in danger for something that might not even work. We'll think of something else, or we'll just deal with Hecate knowing our every move."

Keira sighed and ran her hands over her face before clasping them in front of herself. "Do you have a better suggestion? Because I'm open to just about anything at this point."

Something Persephone said niggled at the edge of his brain. He'd recognized the protective nature of it at the time, but hadn't given it much thought until now. "Persephone mentioned that Hecate will probably ward her home. Can you do something similar to yourself?"

Keira's brow dipped in a thoughtful frown before her eyes widened as an idea took hold. Leo loved how expressive her face was. He rarely had to guess what she was thinking.

"That might actually work. Only instead of the ward being an early warning system, I could make it into a shield." She started grabbing containers before she was even finished talking. "Leo, you're brilliant!" She whirled and kissed him quick before pushing past him to the phone.

Smiling at her enthusiasm, he turned to follow her furious movements. "Now what are you doing?"

"Calling for tea." She picked up the receiver and dialed the front desk, requesting a tea service.

She had him confused now. "Why do you need tea?"

She hurried past him again and began opening containers. "I need the hot water. I'm going to make a tea and say the spell over it, then drink it." Grabbing an empty jar, Keira began measuring herbs into. "And before you start in on me, it won't be toxic."

"I'm glad, because I wouldn't have let you do it otherwise. Ty and I are pretty good at battle strategy, even when the enemy knows we're coming. We could have come up with a damn good plan that still took down Hecate, even if she knew exactly when we were coming." Leo settled in on the sofa, content to watch her work.

A half smile quirked her mouth. "Cocky much?"

He grinned. "No cockiness. Just fact. If you could see our military records, you would see they speak for themselves."

"How convenient then I'm not allowed," she retorted, still smiling.

"Very," he quipped.

She laughed and continued to measure.

When the tea service arrived, she was ready to make the tea. She dumped the contents of the jar she filled into the ball strainer, then plopped it into the water she poured into a teacup.

Leo watched, fascinated, as she whispered words to herself while the tea steeped, working out the spell that would hide her from Hecate. He was in perpetual amazement at everything this woman did. If anyone had told him three months ago, he would be half in love with a witch, he would have laughed himself silly.

He let his head fall back against the sofa cushions, enjoying the rare moment of rest and contentment. Life had certainly taken some turns over the last couple months, but he couldn't be too upset with it. It had led him here. With Keira. She brought a joy to his world that helped him deal with the yawning hole where his soul used to be. He physically ached every moment of every day, his body yearning for the piece of himself that was missing. Keira's light helped ease that pain just a little. There wasn't anything he wouldn't do to keep her safe.

"It's ready," Keira said, interrupting his thoughts.

Leo rose and joined her where she had everything set up on the dresser.

"Two cups?" he asked, frowning.

She nodded and held one out to him. "Since she likely knows you're with me now, I made one for you, too. Just in case."

Leo took the cup and sniffed it. It didn't smell like any tea he'd ever had.

"I can't promise it will taste good, but it'll do its job, and hide us from granny-dearest."

He eyed the tea with a healthy dose of trepidation. This was going to be unpleasant. "Okay, then. Bottoms up." He raised his teacup to hers in salute and lifted it to his mouth.

"Make sure you drink it all." Keira lifted her own cup, taking a healthy swig. Her nose wrinkled in distaste. "Oh yeah. That's terrible." She tipped it again, chugging the rest of it.

Leo did the same, doing his best to ignore the extremely bitter, grassy taste of the tea. He swallowed every last drop from the cup, then set it back on the dresser. "Remind me to never let you cook," he teased.

She laughed. "I promise not to put magic potions in our food unless absolutely necessary." She set her cup next to his. "How about neither of us cooks tonight, and we go out?"

"Seeing as the alternative would likely be sandwiches or a microwave meal from the local Tesco? Sure." They didn't have much to pack, and they didn't have to leave for London to catch their flight to Athens until the morning. He couldn't think of a better way to spend the evening than exploring Norwich with Keira.

Keira grinned and grabbed a dress out of her open suitcase on the floor next to her. "Good answer."

She scurried into the bathroom to change, leaving Leo to stare after her swaying backside as it vanished behind the frosted glass doors.

CHAPTER 22

"What the hell is it?" Keira frowned at the plate the waitress had placed in front of Leo.

He laughed and picked up his fork. "Haggis."

She rolled her eyes. "I know *that*. I meant what's in it? It looks like meatloaf." She poked at the mound on his plate with her fork.

"I can't believe you don't know what haggis is." Leo took a sip of his beer, savoring the taste. He had missed English beer. This pub they stumbled upon had some of the best. He glanced around the room, admiring the décor. It was quintessential English. Hardwood floors scuffed from years of use, low doorways, and exposed rafters gave the pub a cottage feel. It was like stepping back in time.

"My parents weren't big on European culture. Probably to keep me from asking too many questions about our family history, now that I think about it. They usually focused on things closer to home, so I grew up with only a rudimentary knowledge of all things European." She waved her fork at his plate once more. "So? What's in it?"

"It's a mix of organ meats and spices." He cut a chunk off and speared it with his fork. "Here. Try it." He held the bite out to her, and she eyed it the same way he had her tea.

"Organ meat? Like liver?"

Leo barely contained the grin that wanted to break free at the look on her face. "Among others, yes. Just try it."

Eyeing the chunk of meat on his fork a moment longer, Keira finally opened her mouth to take the offering. Leo slid the meat between her lips.

She chewed thoughtfully.

"Well?" He watched her face for clues as to what she thought of the dish. It definitely wasn't for everyone. Leo had always had a taste for the offbeat, coming from the bayou. It wasn't unusual for his family to eat gator or snake. His dad liked to trap and hunt, so they often ate whatever he brought home. Some of the best meals Leo ever had came from the bayou.

"It's... interesting," she said, reaching for her water glass as all the flavors hit her tongue. "Spicy." She gulped several mouthfuls before setting the glass back on the table.

He split off another bite and held it out, barely suppressing a grin. He could tell she was fighting the urge to scrunch her face in disgust. The corners of her mouth had tipped down, and she practically glared at the meal in front of him. The flavors were more than she had expected and not to her liking.

"You want more?" he teased.

Quickly, she shook her head, holding out a hand to ward him off. "I'm good. You go ahead. I'll stick to my burger." She picked up the massive sandwich and took a huge bite.

Leo grinned and forked the piece of haggis into his mouth. They ate in silence, both hungrier than they thought. It didn't take them long to polish off their meals.

Leo set his fork down and spared a glance at Keira's plate. He was amazed to see she had eaten all the massive hamburger and most of her fries. Although he shouldn't have been. It hadn't taken him long to learn that Keira liked to eat, and she wasn't afraid to fill her plate.

"Where do you put it all?" She wasn't a twig, but she most definitely wasn't overweight. Her curves were lush and perfect on her small frame.

Leo squirmed slightly in his seat, his body heating at the direction of his thoughts. He squashed them back into their box and did his best to focus on the conversation.

She shrugged. "My mom used to tell me I had a hollow leg. I still do, I guess."

Thoughts of her legs led him to thinking about them wrapped around his waist.

Christ, he needed to get a grip.

Desperate to distract himself, Leo suggested a walk around the downtown area before they headed back to their suite. He wanted to prolong their outing as long as possible. They might have made a breakthrough in their relationship, but neither of them were ready to take the next leap, no matter how strong the attraction. This was all too new, and they needed to get used to the idea of being in a relationship before they slept together.

With a smile and a nod, Keira agreed to his plan.

Leo waved the waitress over to settle the tab, and they were quickly on their way.

Norwich at night was delightful. Music filtered out into the streets from pubs that had bands playing. Light spilled from storefronts and streetlights alike, giving the tight streets a cozy feel. A warm breeze blew, fanning Keira's curls and ruffling Leo's hair.

Leo took a deep breath, inhaling the scent of her shampoo as it wafted to him on the breeze. The agitation plaguing him for the last three months ebbed as they walked. He wasn't exactly content, but he didn't feel like the tension was going to snap him in half either.

Today's events had a lot to do with that. They finally had a lead that would get them somewhere. Now, they just needed to finish planning and laying the groundwork so they could go after Hecate. There was finally an end in sight, and that brought Leo a sense of excitement only the woman beside him had been able to give him lately.

"You look deep in thought," Keira remarked as they continued to stroll. They turned a corner and were headed toward their B&B.

Leo shrugged. "Just thinking about what comes next, I guess. I'm ready to take Hecate down. I just want the next few days to go quickly, so we can get to the underworld and finally end this."

Keira didn't say anything. She simply tucked herself up tighter against him and wrapped both arms around one of his, hugging it tight.

Leo looked down at the curly head tucked against him and felt a wave of emotion hit him. He would do anything for this woman. Not because she was the one helping to get his soul back or because she was trying to stop the destruction of the world, but because she had snuck in and found a little home in his heart and then refused to leave. She had become his everything. Leo couldn't imagine going back to Louisiana when all this ended without her by his side. He didn't want to.

But those were thoughts for another time. Until all this was over, planning for the future in more than just general terms would have to wait. Until he was whole again. He couldn't offer her himself when he didn't have all of himself to give. He didn't even want to think about what it would mean for them if they failed to meet their deadline.

CHAPTER 23

They walked in companionable silence back to their B&B, each lost in thought. Keira was more content tonight than she had been in a long time. Accepting her feelings for Leo had gone a long way to soothing her emotions. She didn't realize just how keyed up she'd been while trying to fight her attraction to him. When this was all over, she needed to seriously think about where she was going to go. Her heart was screaming at her that she should be wherever Leo was. There was certainly nothing for her in Texas anymore.

She had only heard from her father once since her move to South Carolina. He called to beg her to come back to Austin and forget everything. He vowed he was done trying to get the belt. That losing her brother, Greg, made him rethink everything. Keira refused to do as he wished, telling Dominic she couldn't abandon her friends when they needed her most. She hadn't realized it then, but really, she hadn't been able to abandon Leo. He needed her, and she needed him.

Keira sincerely wished her father did exactly what he said he was going to do and washed his hands of the entire thing. She had her doubts, though. Uncle Max could be extremely persuasive. With no one to keep him from folding to the pressure, she had a feeling Dominic was helping Max keep tabs on her, as well as doing whatever Hecate needed them to do. It didn't change anything, though. Keira would still do whatever it took to bring Hecate to Hades, and to get Leo's soul back.

They walked past a small bath boutique, and Keira stopped to look at the window display. She wanted to use the massive tub in their suite. There was no way they could leave the B&B without her trying it out. It would be a sacrilege to women everywhere if she didn't.

Mind made up, she pulled Leo through the doors of the shop. The scents of all the different soaps assailed them immediately. Lavender, jasmine, tropical fruit, coconut, and a hundred other smells, all combined to give the store that aroma unique to bath shops worldwide. To a woman like Keira, who in her previous life was a girly girl of epic proportions, the aroma was like a drug. It immediately lifted her spirits and made her smile. She missed her long baths so very, very much. Even though Penny's house in Charleston had that enormous Jacuzzi tub, Keira had only used it a couple of times. She had been so focused on finding Hecate she had taken to showering quickly so she could get right back to work.

Tonight, though, she was going to take the time to soak and relax. It was going to be heavenly.

"You like all this stuff?" Leo broke into her thoughts.

Keira nodded. "Immensely." She let go of his arm and set off toward the bath bomb display. Fizzies of every color and scent sat before her on the shelf in baskets, just waiting for someone to pick them up and smell their sweet scents. There were so many choices, she didn't even know where to start. She wished she and Leo really were just here on their honeymoon. She would get several of the fizzy bath bombs to take back with them and use at home.

As fun as the bath bombs were, what she really wanted was to take a bubble bath. There was nothing quite like sitting in a bathtub full of fragrant bubbles to help her relax. Keira glanced around the store, looking for bottles of the stress-relieving liquid.

Her perusal didn't go unnoticed.

The woman behind the counter saw her and made her way over. "Hi. Can I help you find something?"

Keira smiled. "Bubble bath?"

"We have lots of that. This way." The woman led them to a display toward the back of the store. Bottles and bottles of the fragrant soap lined the shelves.

"Let me know if you need help with anything else," the saleswoman said before heading back to the counter.

Keira thanked the woman, then grabbed a bottle of cucumber lime verbena off a shelf. She flipped open the lid. "Oh, that's heavenly," she murmured, taking a sniff. She waved it under Leo's nose, and chuckled when he just shrugged.

"It's all just soap to me."

She rolled her eyes and put the bottle back before grabbing another. There were so many good ones to choose from. Again, she wished she could take a bunch home.

Finally, after looking through the entire line, Keira decided on a lavender lemon scent. She was going to double down on the relaxation front. She knew it might be the last time she got to do so until after they confronted Hecate.

Bubble bath paid for and tucked into a cute little flowered sack, they headed back to the B&B.

***

Eyes closed, Keira sank further into the bubbles surrounding her. This felt wonderful.

She had wasted no time once they returned to their suite before she filled the tub and climbed into the warm, scented water. She wished she could stay here all night, but she knew that all too soon, the water would grow cold, and the bubbles would all pop.

But right now? Right now, she was going to savor the warmth and the languid sensation coursing through her body. Between the bubble bath, and the absolutely wonderful time she had with Leo tonight, Keira felt quite content.

Thinking about her evening with Leo brought a new heat to Keira's body, one not caused by the warm bath water. The man had looked good enough to eat in his butt-hugging jeans and tailored dress shirt. She spent a good chunk of dinner wondering what that exposed patch of skin at the base of his neck tasted like.

She sank further into the bubbles, trying to drown those thoughts. They were not helping her to relax whatsoever.

It was useless, though. Now that her mind had turned to Leo, it refused to be dissuaded.

Keira groaned at herself. Her body hummed with the thought of having Leo's hands on it. She could almost feel them running over her, the rough callouses rasping along her soft skin.

Water splashed as she sat up and grabbed a washcloth. She soaped it up and began scrubbing, trying to scour the thoughts away. She was teetering on the edge of jumping out of the tub, waltzing out into the suite and pushing Leo down on the bed. Only the fact it felt weird, and a little wrong, to do something in such opposition to the seriousness of their situation, kept her in the bath.

Keira blew into the cloud of bubbles in front of her face in exasperation. She was so confused.

With a thunk, she let her head fall back against the rim of the tub and dropped the rag into the water with a plop. Eyes closed, she inhaled the lavender lemon aroma of her bath, willing it to wipe away all her stress.

Her thoughts continued to whirl, though, until the water cooled and most of the bubbles dissipated. With a deep sigh, Keira heaved herself out of the water before her warm, relaxed limbs cooled down. She wrapped a towel around herself and pulled the plug to drain the water.

Drying off her legs, her hands froze mid-swipe as she realized that in her haste to get in the tub, she forgot to bring any clean clothes into the bathroom with her.

Keira bit her lip and eyed the door, wondering if she could sneak out quick, grab her bag, and get back in without Leo noticing.

Immediately, she dismissed the notion. Who was she kidding? There was no way the man would miss her coming out of the bathroom in nothing but a towel.

Crap. There was nothing to do but to open that door and go out there.

She squared her shoulders. She was an adult, and so was Leo. They could handle her parading around in a towel.

Hopefully.

Keira clutched the towel in one hand, so it wouldn't inadvertently come loose, and made her way to the door. Why this place couldn't have bigger towels, she didn't know. She felt like she was wearing a hand towel. It barely covered all her bits. She thanked her lucky stars she was small. If she were Penny's size, there was no way the towel would cover her body.

With one more tug on the bottom of the towel, Keira pulled open the frosted glass doors.

Leo looked up from where he sat sprawled on the sofa when the door opened, a book in his hands. Instantly, his eyes darkened and his entire body stiffened.

"I forgot my clothes," she quickly explained before he could say anything. She forced her feet to move toward her suitcase. Squatting down to rummage for a pair of underwear and a sleep shirt, she did her best to keep her towel in place.

Keira heard a thud as his book landed on the floor. She chanced another glance at him. He sat up straight now. Looking away, she quickly grabbed her clothes and stood. Her eyes darted toward him once more.

He stood, his body rigid, and just stared at her. His eyes were dark pools of desire.

Keira felt like her feet had grown roots into the floor. She couldn't have moved if she tried. And she didn't particularly want to. The look in his eyes was enough to make her body hum. That familiar heat only Leo could cause spread through her limbs.

"You should go get dressed."

Keira shivered at the low rumble of his voice. She heard what he said, but she still couldn't make her feet move.

When she continued to stand there, Leo stalked toward her.

"You really should go get dressed," he said again, stopping within touching distance.

More shivers wracked her as his voice washed over her.

"I know," she whispered. She still didn't move, though. She wanted him to kiss her. Her body strained toward his. It was like he had a rope around her, tugging her inexorably closer and closer.

CHAPTER 24

Leo swayed toward her, his brain on autopilot. His hand landed on her waist. Christ, she was so small. He could nearly span her tiny waist from one side to the other. But this petite fireball of a woman had him completely enthralled.

He stared down at her. A yearning shone from her dark eyes he was sure was reflected in his own.

Her hands landed on his chest, and she fiddled with his collar. Electric shocks shot down his torso at each feathery brush of her fingers on his collarbone.

"Why are we fighting this, *chère*?" Leo's voice was barely above a whisper. He was at his breaking point. This thing between them had been building and building over the last several days. Tonight, they had seemed to turn a corner. Having her come out in nothing but a towel when they finally decided to quit fighting what they felt had unleashed the desire Leo kept in such careful check.

"I don't know." Her voice was just as soft as his.

Leo cupped her neck, his fingers stirring the hair at her nape. He stroked the line of her jaw with his thumb as he dipped his head. "Stop me now, *chère*, if this isn't what you want." He wanted to make sure she was on board with this one hundred percent.

She didn't answer. Instead, she reached up and grasped his face in her hands, pulling his mouth down to hers.

Fire immediately blazed a path down all of Leo's nerve endings. He groaned and wrapped his arms around her hips, lifting her into his embrace. He wanted to go slow and take his time to learn every inch of her, but at this rate, he would be lucky to last past the first few moments.

Walking blind, he half walked, half carried her as he headed for the bed. When her knees hit the mattress, he laid her down. Keeping an arm wrapped around her, he crawled up with her and scooted them toward the stack of pillows. Her towel slid, offering Leo a glimpse of her full breasts. Attention caught, he finished loosening the towel, baring her to his view.

"You're so beautiful. How did I get so lucky?" He didn't give her a chance to respond. Wanting to taste that creamy, perfect skin, he bent and dropped feather-light kisses across the tops of her breasts before heading south to take a nipple in his mouth. She let out a long moan, making him grin.

He looked up at her through his lashes. Her hooded eyes stared back at him, begging for more. Not one to disappoint, Leo flicked the tip with his tongue. Her hips bucked against his thigh. Leo could feel how wet she was through his jeans. It was enough to make him groan and push back as she continued to ride his leg.

CHAPTER 25

Keira's hands flew to Leo's chest as he kissed her breasts. She was about ready to come unglued, and he hadn't even touched her anywhere besides her chest yet. She rolled her hips against the rock-hard thigh between her legs, the friction from the rough denim doing wonderful things for her.

Desperate to feel his skin beneath her hands, Keira yanked the tails of his shirt free from his pants and tried to unbutton it. Her fingers, which had worked fine just a few minutes ago, fumbled the buttons until finally, Leo took pity on her and pulled it over his head.

She slid her hands through the smattering of dark blond hair covering his chest. The firm muscles beneath jumped and flexed at her touch. She really wanted to taste him, but he was moving further down her body, completely focused on her. Not that she was complaining, but she really wanted to do the same to him.

He pushed the towel away from her lower half as he went, dropping kisses on her belly and hip bones. He skipped right over her center, and Keira growled at him.

"You're mean," she moaned.

She could feel his smile against her thigh as he kissed and nipped his way down her legs. Never had she been more thankful she was short than right now, as it meant he was quickly kissing his way back up her legs, and heading for that sweet spot that so desperately wanted his touch.

He paused when he reached her hips again, smiling devilishly up at her.

"Leo, you better not stop now," she warned.

His grin only grew. "Or you'll what? Take over? I'm okay with that, so long as we reach the same ending."

Hanging on by a thread, she thrust her hands into his golden locks and tugged him toward her.

A laugh broke from him, but he did what she demanded and settled between her legs. He ran one finger through the wetness coating her, and Keira thought she would explode. Stars swam behind her eyes, and she tingled everywhere as her body strained toward a peak only it could see.

She even heard shrieking. Absently, she hoped she wasn't the one making that noise. It was quite high-pitched and a bit nasally.

Suddenly, Leo pulled away and sat up. Keira's body rebelled at the loss of sensation and she moaned, loud and long, cursing at him.

Before she could do more than utter a few choice words, though, he was hastily covering her with her towel. One look at the seriousness on his face wiped the fog of desire from her brain, and she realized that the shrieking had not been her, but the fire alarm in the hallway.

Keira struggled to sit up as Leo dove off the bed.

"Get dressed," he ordered, his soldier mask slipping into place. A set of clothes landed next to her on the bed. Keira quickly donned the items. Ripples of unease skated down her spine as she searched for her shoes and picked up her purse. It could not be a coincidence that the fire alarm was going off so soon after her uncle and his cohort broke into their room.

Leo took her purse from her and stuffed it down inside his backpack, along with a good portion of their clothes.

He took her hand and towed her toward the door. "We're going outside. We're going to blend in with the other guests and whatever looky-loos are out there, then we're going to disappear."

Keira nodded and followed him down the stairs.

Smoke filled the hallways, but she didn't see any active fires. She hoped that whatever their pursuers had done to flush them out, they hadn't damaged the building too much. She couldn't help but remember the charred remains of Leo's house, or the conflagration that engulfed Penny's parents' house. Keira had certainly developed a new appreciation for the power of fire since all of this began.

They stepped outside into the crowd of guests just as the first fire engine pulled up. The doors opened, and half a dozen firefighters spewed forth, ready to battle whatever blaze caused the fire alarms to shriek.

Leo took advantage of the chaos caused by the firefighters' arrival and led her past the firetruck to an alleyway tucked between the buildings. He ran at a quick jog down the narrow passage to the next street, pulling her along. They made several quick turns and took a few more side streets and alleys before he paused to survey their surroundings and the people milling around them.

Keira bent at the waist and sucked in air. She was fit, but she wasn't a runner by any stretch of the imagination. She was thankful for the adrenaline that kept her going to this point.

"What are we doing?" she asked between gasps.

"We're going to take the night train to London," he said. "Come on."

"Please tell me we're not running all the way to the train station." Adrenaline could only carry her so far, and the train station was a good mile or more away. She didn't think it would carry her *that* far.

He flashed her a quick grin before pointing down the street to where a group of people stood waiting. "We're going to grab a taxi down there at the taxi stand."

She said a silent prayer of thanks and started walking.

Leo kept his head on a surreptitious swivel while they waited. Keira tried to be as casual, but her heart was hammering away in her chest, and she knew her eyes had to be as wide as saucers. Her mind and body were reeling from the abrupt switch in emotions, as well as the rush of adrenaline and endorphins from their quick escape.

Thankfully, they didn't have to wait long for a taxi, and the drive to the train station was fairly short. Once inside, instead of going straight to the ticket counter, Leo pulled them off to the side, out of sight, but in position to watch the doors. The station was busy, even at this time of evening, making it easy for them to fade into the background.

He pulled out his phone. "I'm going to call Ty and fill him in. I think they need to meet us in Athens now. We're not lingering anywhere. I know you messed with Hecate's spell, but it always pays to be cautious."

Keira agreed. They should have moved after Max broke into their room, but it likely wouldn't have made a difference since she hadn't figured out how to block Hecate's tracking spell until earlier that day. She had a feeling Ty and Leo would have them hotel hopping now, though, if they stayed in any one city more than a night or two until they went to the underworld.

Leo was quick to fill Ty in on tonight's events and get his assurances they would be on a plane bound for Athens in the morning. He also learned Ty and Penny had some troubles of their own that day. Ty was attacked out on a call by what he could only describe as a demon. He said it had been supernaturally strong and had a depth of evil in its eyes that put Ty on full alert. Thankfully, it was alone and the only witness to the attack was Ty's partner, Colin Jacobs, who already knew all about their predicament. Penny saw another lurking near the estate, but it quickly disappeared when Ty came home after dispatching its friend.

Keira was glad they were all right, and that they were all going to be together again. Things felt... off. Like something big was coming. She didn't know if it was her own paranoia making her feel anxious, or if she was picking up on something. She just knew she wanted all of them together. That they *needed* to be together.

Their talk with Hermes and the Furies couldn't come soon enough, as far as she was concerned. They needed to stay one step ahead of Hecate and her minions if they stood a chance against her.

CHAPTER 26

Max Artherton leaned on his hands on the counter as he stared at himself in the mirror. Beads of water dripped off of his wet hair to roll down his face. He had returned to his hotel half an hour ago after setting the small trash fire at the B&B where his niece was staying and immediately hopped into the shower to wash away the scent of smoke clinging to his hair.

This whole thing had turned into such a disaster. It was supposed to be a simple thing to take the belt from Penny Dimas. Instead, his sons were dead, his father was dead, his brother hated him, and he was half a world away from home in pursuit of his magical niece.

It really made him wonder if it was all worth it.

But he didn't want to die—didn't want his wife to suffer—and that is what Hecate had promised him would happen if he failed.

So, here he stood, in a hotel in England, wondering what the hell he was going to do next now that Keira had slipped through his fingers once again.

Suddenly, his image in the mirror shimmered. Max stepped back warily.

Hecate's face appeared in the mirror. She did not look pleased.

"I take it from the fact you are still in this establishment, you were unsuccessful?"

Max squared his shoulders, immediately on the defensive. "She slipped through our net. Her companion is more resourceful than we anticipated."

She arched an eyebrow and stared at him silently for a moment before continuing. "And do you know where they went?"

"Not specifically, but we think they're headed to Greece."

Hecate's frown deepened. "Of course they're headed to Greece. That's where they've always been headed. I need to know where in Greece!"

He bristled at her tone. "We're trying to locate them. Like I said, her companion is rather resourceful. We don't know much about him other than he was in the military with Ty Farris. All of his records are sealed at the highest level. I don't have a contact in the government with enough pull to unseal them. Whatever he did, it was beyond top secret. Can't you track them?"

Hecate shifted and looked away briefly at his question. "I was, but my granddaughter seems to be more adept at witchcraft than I expected. Somehow, she has blocked my ability to track her."

The urge to smile hit Max hard, but he swiftly squashed it. He had no desire to get on Hecate's bad side. That was why he was in this predicament to begin with. She had been quite clear about what she would do to him and his wife if he double-crossed her. He couldn't help but feel a surge of victory for his niece, though. She'd done the right thing and fought against the witch currently in his mirror. He wished he had her courage.

"So, what do you want us to do? We've put out feelers to see where they went, but it may be another day before we get anything definitive."

Hecate waved her hand. "Forget your niece for now. I have another task for you."

Dread pooled in Max's gut as she smiled; a cold, hard glint in her eyes. He was not going to like what she had to say.

CHAPTER 27

Sipping her tea, Keira sat with her feet propped up on the balcony rail of the B&B room she and Leo checked into earlier in the day and tried valiantly to relax. Ty and Penny would be in Athens in the morning, and then they could finally put their plan in motion. She hated sitting idle, just twiddling her thumbs. Patience was definitely not her strong suit.

Taking another sip of her tea, she stared out at the city before her, doing her best to shove the restlessness down deep. Athens was gorgeous. It had been pretty during the day when she and Leo went on an excursion to get food and do a little reconnaissance near the Acropolis. At night, though, the city was stunning.

From her vantage point, the Acropolis was front and center. The Parthenon was lit up, a shining beacon to all atop the hill. More lights dotted the city, and the sounds of laughter and conversation floated up to her from below. Athens fairly teemed with life. Keira loved it.

Sighing with a bit of temporary contentment, she reached into the sack on the table beside her and pulled out a loukoumas. Taking a bite of the sweet cinnamon and honey donut, Keira stifled a moan. She liked all pastries, but she had a soft spot for donuts. This trip to Europe was going to be bad for her waistline.

Leo slipped into the chair beside her and snagged a donut of his own from the bag. Keira sent a mock glare his way, and he grinned around the sweet treat.

"I figured I'd better come snag one before you ate them all." Leo licked the cinnamon and honey off his fingers, his eyes twinkling with mirth.

Keira rolled her eyes. "I was going to leave you some." And she was. Like one. Maybe two. She eyed the bag again, resisting the urge to eat another. They were so good, and her sweet tooth screamed for more.

She sipped her tea instead and turned back to the view of the city. "So did you just come out here to steal my donuts or was there something else on your mind?" Keira suddenly had something besides the view and donuts on her mind. Scenes from the evening before in Norwich flashed through her head. She felt a hot blush steal over her body and was happy the lighting on the balcony was dim.

Leo shook his head. "No. I finished sketching my plans to go over with Ty later and thought I'd join you."

A scowl immediately descended over Keira's features at the mention of Leo's plans. He had been inside sketching the area surrounding the grotto where they were going to summon Hermes and the Furies. She'd been trying not to think about it. She just wanted one evening without thoughts of gods and saving the world intruding.

Leo noticed her abrupt mood shift. "You okay, *chère?*"

"I'm fine," she retorted. "I just don't want to talk about anything to do with Hecate or Hades or any other Greek deity. I need a break, Leo. Just for tonight."

Abruptly, Leo stood. Keira stared up at him quizzically.

"I like that plan. We both need a break." He pulled his phone from his pocket and soon, she heard the first strains of a slow song come from its speaker.

He set the phone on the table and held out a hand to her. "Dance with me."

Delighted, Keira took his hand and let him pull her into his arms. She settled in with a sigh. The world melted away as Leo's arms closed around her, and they swayed to the soft music.

She wished she could just stay right here. No more quest to stop the end of the world, no more divine ancestors, no more magical powers. Just this man and the feelings building between them. Keira wanted all their troubles to go away so they could just be together. She didn't think it was too much to ask to have a normal relationship like everyone else.

Loathing for her ancestor and her family filled her, intruding on the pleasant moment. What she wouldn't give to have Uncle Max standing before her right now. She would give him a piece of her mind and probably a piece of her abilities, too. He better never show his face to her again.

And her dad—his betrayal was even worse. She had always been a daddy's girl—had always known Dominic Artherton loved her. She couldn't help but wonder now how much of that love was because she was his daughter and how much was because of what she could do.

"Stop thinking," Leo murmured against her hair.

Keira huffed and looked up, not the least bit surprised he could tell what was on her mind. "I can't seem to help it. I keep thinking about my dad and Uncle Max and how they could do something like this. And to family, no less. It just doesn't make any sense. And it hurts." Her last words came out choked and tears welled in her eyes.

Leo clutched her tighter. His voice was low. "I'm sorry, *chère*. I wish I had answers for you, but I don't."

Keira sniffed. "My dad hurts the most. He turned his back on me. I don't even know what happened to him. I didn't see him at your house that night. Part of me doesn't care if he's halfway to Brazil, hiding like a scared child from Hecate—he wanted to use me. But the other part, the daughter, she wants to know where her daddy is. The man who said he'd always protect her." She choked on a sob. "What happened to that man, Leo?" Her tears spilled over and ran down her cheeks as sobs wracked her body.

"I don't know, *chère*." Leo pulled her close and tucked her head under his chin. "I don't know."

Keira sobbed against his chest, letting out all the hurt and frustration that had followed her around for months now. She hadn't let herself grieve for her old life, for losing her family. Her heart ached for all she'd lost. She missed her brother and her mom. Keira tried calling her mother once, not long after their encounter with Hades, but Sarah just told her that Keira had made her choice and then hung up. Some days, she just felt so alone.

"I swear to you I will never leave." Leo's firm voice was in tune with her thoughts. "As long as there is breath in my body, I will always be here for you. Your father is an idiot for siding with your grandfather over you. He's lost more than just the fight over the belt, and that's all on him, *chère*. You are the true treasure he lost."

Keira clung tighter to Leo at his words. She didn't know how it had happened, especially so fast, but this man meant more to her than anyone else ever had. Losing her family broke her heart, but she had a feeling if she lost Leo, it would completely crush her soul.

Slowly, her tears dried up and an awareness of the man holding her so tenderly seeped in. Her body ignited. She pulled back far enough to look up at him. Leo's chocolatey eyes glittered with the same desire she felt.

"Take me inside." Her voice was barely a whisper. "Finish what we started yesterday."

With only a momentary hesitation, Leo scooped her into his arms and carried her into the room. Keira's heart beat double-time as he laid her gently on the bed, settling her on the stack of pillows. Hovering above her, he threaded his fingers into her curls and stroked his thumb over her cheekbone. Tingles spread outward from the contact, racing along her scalp and down her neck. She covered his hand with hers, urging him closer.

"*Mon coeur*," Leo said softly before closing the distance between them to kiss her tenderly.

Keira's heart took flight at the tenderness of his touch. She knew he meant what he said outside. Whatever the world threw at them, he would always be there.

Hungry for more of him, Keira tugged on his t-shirt and slipped her hands beneath the soft material. Warm flesh over hard, taut muscles greeted her fingers. She ghosted her hands up his back, bunching material as she went. When she got to his shoulders, he pulled back enough to whip his shirt over his head. Keira took advantage of the space between them to remove her own t-shirt.

Leo's hands immediately went to her chest. He hooked a finger in one cup of her bra and tugged it down, exposing her breast. Already peaked, the rosy tip begged for his attention.

Keira held her breath in anticipation.

He didn't disappoint her. Streaks of lightning shot through her with one scrape of his nail over the tight bud. A strangled moan stuck in her throat when he sucked it into his mouth.

He released her breast with a pop and grinned at her. "Like that, do you?"

She nodded jerkily and urged his mouth back to her chest.

He chuckled softly as he released the clasp on her bra. The garment went the way of their shirts. Keira speared her fingers into his hair as he laved her breasts once more. Heat quickly built in her core, and she squirmed beneath him, her body wanting more.

"We're not going to last any longer tonight than we were yesterday, are we?" Leo muttered against her belly as he kissed his way down her torso.

"No," she breathed, her head rolling from side to side.

Leo sat up at her answer and quickly unsnapped her shorts and drew down the zipper. Keira lifted her hips so he could slide them and her panties down her legs.

Completely bare to him, Keira watched him as his eyes devoured her. His face was all hard planes and sharp angles as desire blazed from his chocolate eyes. He looked like the poster boy for virile masculinity in that moment. Heat pooled in her belly and made her limbs heavy with desire.

"So beautiful." Leo leaned down, pressing kisses on her hipbones and down her thighs.

Keira tugged at his hair, trying to pull him back up to where she wanted him most. "Touch me, Leo. I'm still strung out from when you teased me last night."

Leo pulled back, a grin slanting over his handsome face. "Really? Let's see, shall we?"

He slid his hands up her thighs until he reached their apex. His thumbs glided through the wetness coating her there.

Keira nearly rocketed off the bed. Her back arched, and she moaned in delight. That was the spot. "Oh, that feels good," she panted.

"How about this?" Leo slid a finger inside her. His thumb found the little nub at the top of her mound and circled it while he slowly slid his finger through her wet channel.

Keira saw stars. "Yes," she hissed. She bit her lip, eyes squeezed tight. The sensation was almost too much. She was so close to going over the edge, but she wanted him there with her. "You need to get naked."

Her eyes snapped open when his hands abruptly left her body. She watched as he chucked his pants and boxer briefs. Keira couldn't help but stare. He was magnificent. His long, well-muscled body was perfectly proportioned. His erection jutted out at her, ready. Keira felt her mouth dry up as all the moisture in her body headed south to flood her core in anticipation. Her body craved this man like nothing else.

Quickly, he pulled a condom from his wallet and sheathed himself. Keira opened her arms to him as he crawled back onto the bed and settled between her thighs. His mouth landed on hers, hot and hungry. Their tongues dueled. Pleasure skated down her nerve endings. He trailed one hand down her side to wrap around her thigh, lifting her leg. He probed at her entrance, just the tip of him sliding in.

Keira's breath caught, and she wrenched her mouth from his. "Now, Leo. Please." She was most definitely not above begging at this point. Her entire being felt like it was focused in on one point on her body. Fire raged from her core, waiting for him to extinguish it.

He slid a hand beneath her hip to hold her steady and pushed into her in one long, smooth stroke.

A harsh groan broke from him while Keira let loose a shriek of pleasure. She felt so full. Stretched to the max, she could feel every inch of him, and he felt so delightfully good.

"Are you okay?" he asked, holding still. The muscles in his neck and shoulders strained with the effort.

"Yes." She kissed his throat and rolled her hips. "I'm so very okay."

Another harsh groan broke from Leo, and he began to move. Keira felt the first thrust all the way to the ends of her hair. An airy sigh escaped her and it was like the dam broke. Suddenly, he was pumping into her at a rapid pace. Keira met him thrust for thrust, her need spiraling upwards rapidly. Jolts of electricity shot through her with each slide of his hips until she tingled all over.

Within moments, they were both climbing the peak and falling over the edge. Light burst behind her eyelids and intense pleasure jetted through her every nerve ending. Her senses opened to the point she felt like she could see the very fabric of the universe. Energy swirled all around her in more detail than she had ever seen it before as pleasure zinged through her body.

As they rode the wave of ecstasy, Leo sealed his mouth over hers, slowly bringing her down from her high with gentle nips and soft, tender kisses. A warmth, like being bundled up in front of a roaring fire on a cold night, flowed over her, taking the starch out of all her muscles. Keira sank into the mattress, completely boneless. "Wow." Heart thundering in her ears, she sucked in great gulps of air.

Leo placed one last kiss on her neck before rolling to her side and tucking her close. "I concur, counselor." His own chest heaved as his lungs struggled to get enough oxygen.

Keira laughed softly, turning, so she was tucked more snuggly into his side. Contentment washed over her as her body calmed and she relaxed. She practically purred when he combed his fingers through her hair.

She looked up at him to find him watching her, a contemplative yet serious look on his handsome face.

"What? Why are you looking at me like that?" she asked, genuinely curious.

He brushed her curls back once more and ran his thumb over her cheek, eyes roaming over her face.

"Leo? What is it?" She frowned up at him. He was starting to worry her. He looked so serious.

He smiled softly and shook his head. "Nothing. You're beautiful."

A pretty blush stole over her face. Leo pressed a gentle kiss on her cheek and tucked her back into his side.

Eyelids heavy, Keira rested her head on his shoulder. She felt safer and happier than she had in months. A huge yawn overtook her, nearly popping her jaw. She hadn't realized how much of a burden carrying around the hurt from her family's betrayal was until she unloaded it.

The sex played a role in making her sleepy, too, she thought, a satisfied smile ghosting over her mouth. She snuggled closer to Leo's side. Burrowing beneath the covers, she gave the lethargy free rein.

As sleep slowly claimed her, the tension she'd been holding on to melted away. For tonight, secure in Leo's arms, she didn't have a worry in the world.

CHAPTER 28

Leo held himself still, not wanting to wake the sleeping woman in his arms. This was the most relaxed he had ever seen her. She had been a giant ball of tension since all of this began, and it had only worsened the closer they came to their deadline. He was glad that at least for tonight, she could relax and push everything away.

It nearly killed him earlier when she sobbed against him over her family's betrayal. To know she was hurting so deeply cut him to the quick. He wanted desperately to take away her pain and make it his own. It would fit right in with the agony already tearing him apart.

Fury swelled in his chest once more at the thought of how her family had turned their backs on her. This woman deserved so much more than the hand life dealt her.

He pushed a curl of hair away from her face, his fingers lingering on her soft skin. Admiration for this tiny spitfire of a woman shot through him. She was absolutely amazing. Any other woman—with perhaps the exception of Penny—would have given in to her family's demands and left Leo high and dry. He was nothing to her except a pain in the ass when Hades took his soul.

With a huge yawn of his own, Leo carefully turned until he laid comfortably beside Keira. Snaking an arm around her waist, he closed his eyes, thanking his lucky stars for this woman and her beautiful heart.

CHAPTER 29

"You slept with him, didn't you?" Penny asked Keira out of the blue. She and Ty just arrived in Athens. Keira and Leo had come to the airport to pick them up, and they were headed to the car from the terminal.

"Shhh!" Keira's eyes nearly bugged out of her head at Penny's sudden question. She looked around frantically. No one paid them much attention other than to gawk at Ty. Luckily, he was smiling thanks to Leo, and not sending people scurrying away with his frowning cop face.

"You don't need to announce it to the world," she hissed, never more glad than she was right now that most of the people around her spoke a different language. She did not want an audience for this conversation. She might be boisterous and outgoing in most things, but her love life was not something the world at large needed to know about.

Penny stopped suddenly and stared at her wide-eyed. "I was right? Holy crap! I was just guessing."

Keira flushed to her roots. She should have just kept her damn mouth shut. She kept walking. "Why would you guess something like that?"

Penny shrugged and resumed walking, her rolling suitcase clacking along behind her. "I don't know. You guys seemed... closer? I mean, you were arguing and ready to rake each other's eyeballs out when you left Charleston. Now, you're touching each other all the time and smiling. I figured you had either come to a truce or slept together."

"So you automatically went with we had sex?" Keira's tone was incredulous, but honestly, she wasn't surprised. Penny knew her too well.

Penny grinned and shrugged sheepishly. "Can I just say I'm happy for you? If Leo's anything remotely like Ty, then you've snagged a good man."

Keira eyed Leo's strong back as he walked in front of her. A rush of emotion blazed through her as she watched him tilt his head as he listened to something Ty said. He had donned another of his silly t-shirts today. This one had a picture of a dog on a motorcycle on the back and the name of a bar on the front.

Keira certainly couldn't argue with Penny. Leo was everything a woman could want. Genuine, funny, kind, incredibly smart. And utterly gorgeous.

She smiled to herself as she remembered last night. And this morning. He was definitely everything a woman could want, plus a little more. Her body still hummed.

Penny's laugh had Keira snapping back to the present. She looked over at her friend.

"I was going to ask how it was, but I can tell by looking at your face it was amazing."

Keira's face flamed brighter. "It was that, yes."

Penny just laughed.

An inner debate waged in her brain for half a second before she confided in Penny. "He's so much more than I thought he was, Penny.

These last few days… I've really gotten to know the real Leo. He's not the smartass, hard-nosed, ex-soldier he seems to be."

Penny arched an eyebrow, questioning that statement.

Keira rolled her eyes. "Okay, so he is, but that's not all he is, or even the dominant part of his personality. He's gentler. More thoughtful." She shrugged. "He's just Leo."

The clacking came to an abrupt halt as Penny stopped. Keira looked back to see Penny staring at her, eyes almost comically wide.

"Oh my God. You're in love with him."

Keira immediately opened her mouth to deny it, but couldn't seem to get the words past her lips.

Was she in love with Leo? Was that what was rolling around inside her anytime she thought about or looked at him? It seemed much too soon, but then, Penny and Ty had fallen in love—and married!—in less time than she had known Leo.

"Hey! Are you two coming?"

Keira spun around at the sound of Ty's booming voice, bringing her thoughts back to their current predicament. Ty motioned to the car where he stood with Leo, one eyebrow arched in question toward them.

Thoughts of love and marriage would have to wait. They had more pressing matters to deal with.

The clacking resumed as Penny breezed by her, headed toward her husband and the waiting car.

"Don't think you're off the hook. We'll finish this conversation later," Penny tossed over her shoulder.

Keira rolled her eyes and followed. Of that, she had no doubt.

Whether she would have an answer for her friend—and for herself—was another story.

CHAPTER 30

Keira concentrated hard as they moved through the trees toward the ruins of what used to be a shrine to the Furies. After getting Ty and Penny settled into their room at their tiny B&B, Ty and Leo meticulously went over Leo's plan for sneaking into the grotto unnoticed. Once they were satisfied they knew the path they wanted to take, had covered all contingencies, and it was dark outside, the group made their way to the Acropolis.

Now, approaching the shrine, Keira attempted to keep a cloak over them so no one would notice them. It was more to muffle the sound of their footfalls than keep them invisible. Under the thick tree cover, it was so dark Keira could scarcely see a foot in front of herself. She didn't know how Leo managed to move with such stealth and speed through the thick brush without a light. If she had been the one leading, they would have rammed into so many trees by now. Conscious of how very turned around she would be if she lost her grip on Leo, she tightened her hand where it clamped on to the backpack he wore. She did not want to get lost in the woods.

They quickly reached the stone structure hidden in the trees. Keira released her grip and Leo set the backpack down, withdrawing a bottle of water they had mixed some honey into, and a carton of strawberries.

He set them on the altar, then pulled out a small, battery-powered lantern and switched it on. It bathed the surrounding area in a soft glow. Just enough to chase away the dark. Keira double-checked her shield to make sure none of the light escaped. Leo stepped back and nodded to her that he was ready for her to do her thing.

Taking a deep breath, Keira stepped forward and let the magic flow. Tapping into her ability, the words to summon the Furies and Hermes flowed from her like water. Within moments, the air around them crackled with otherworldly energy. She paid it little heed. The world faded away around her as she concentrated on calling the gods.

A wailing reached her ears seconds before three of the ugliest beings she ever laid eyes on appeared before them. Serpents, much like those Medusa sported, spat and hissed from their heads. Putrid yellow eyes glowed from their deeply lined, craggy faces. Huge wings, black as the surrounding night, folded up on their backs as they came to rest near the altar.

Following closely on their heels with a rush of wind was an astonishingly beautiful man dressed in a flowing, sleeveless cream robe made of the finest silk that stopped just above his knees. His dark, curly hair fluttered in the breeze before it settled appealingly around his chiseled face.

He joined the winged creatures, and they all glared darkly at the group of four humans standing in front of them.

"Who has summoned us?" one of the Furies intoned. Her voice rumbled over the landscape, graveled and dark.

Keira gulped and lifted a hand to wave at the hideous being. "I did. We did."

"Why?" another of the Furies fired back.

"Persephone sent us," Leo said, stepping up beside Keira.

A frown settled over the goddess's face, deepening the lines. "You are the humans she told us about."

Ty stepped forward, Penny right by his side. "We need your help."

"Actually," Keira interrupted, "we need his help." She pointed at Hermes. "We just need you three not to smite us for what we're going to do."

"Perhaps you should explain who you are and what exactly is going on. Persephone may have told us to hear you out, but that does not mean we have endless patience for half-truths and riddles," Hermes intoned.

Without hesitation, Keira dove in. She was no fool and knew they were only going to get one shot at this. "My name is Keira Artherton. My ancestor, Hecate, is out to get revenge on the gods for forcing her father to sacrifice her in penance for hunting one of Artemis's sacred stags. Instead of just blaming Artemis, she's blaming all of you. She wants to destroy everything and build again anew, with herself at the helm."

Penny picked up the tale. "Almost three months ago, she sent Keira's family to take this." She pointed at the belt wrapped around her waist. "This is Hippolyta's golden belt. I am Penthesilea Aeolia, descendant of the Amazons and the goddess Thetis. This is my husband and descendant of Hercules, Tyreece Farris." She pointed to Ty, who stood imposing and mountain-like at her side.

Hermes looked at Leo. "And who are you?"

Leo held up his hands in supplication. "Leo Devereaux. I'm just a friend who's trying to help. Hades took my soul as an incentive for us not to twiddle our thumbs. We have *four* of our ninety days left to find Hecate and stop her. After that, Hades gets to keep my soul in his little staff of death for all eternity."

Hermes's glower softened slightly as a thoughtful gleam entered his eyes. "Why do you need my help?"

"You're the courier of souls and know the underworld better than most. We need you to lead us through the underworld to Hecate's domain," Leo replied.

Hermes arched one perfect brow. "And if I don't?"

"Then we still go, but our chances of succeeding drop dramatically. And I don't just mean to get my soul back. I will gladly sacrifice my soul if it means we stop her from destroying everything." Leo inhaled deeply. "I'm hoping it doesn't come to that, though."

Keira's heart clenched at his words. She was determined not to let that happen. Leo didn't deserve any of this. For that reason alone, she couldn't let Hecate or Hades win.

"I cannot help you fight her. You understand that, yes?" Hermes asked.

"We know," Leo replied. "We just need you to get us there. The rest is on us."

"How do we know you tell the truth?" the third Fury asked, squinting at them suspiciously. "You're all human and humans lie."

The same anger that stirred when Demeter tried to thwart them roused in Keira again. Leo's hand landed on her back, giving her the strength to resist the urge to bring some magic down on the Furies' ugly heads.

"You have to take us at our word, and at Persephone's word, that we're telling the truth. Would we really risk her wrath, and yours, for a lie?" Leo arched an eyebrow and stared the gods down.

Hermes was the first to break the silence.

"I will help you. I have known for quite some time Hecate was not happy with her lot and have often wondered if she was planning something. She is a very secretive woman. What you say," he shook his head in a bit of disbelief, "let's just say, I am not surprised. And I know what she is capable of. If she has a plan to bring down Hades, I have no doubt she could easily succeed."

Throughout his speech, the Furies whispered furiously between themselves. It came to an abrupt end when Hermes stopped talking. They straightened, their stoic expressions giving nothing away. Keira held her breath and waited.

"We will not stand in your way," the first Fury intoned.

All four friends sagged visibly in relief at the Fury's words. Relief made Keira's muscles threaten to collapse, and she locked her knees to stay upright. Knowing they had cleared two major hurdles tonight went a long way to boosting her confidence they would succeed in their venture.

"Go to the River Acheron, where it wells from the ground and forms deep pools. There, you will find a cave that is an entrance to the underworld. Meet me on my side of the river when the sun meets the horizon in two days' time. Do not be late. I will not wait for you."

Before any of them could respond to Hermes's declaration, a bright light, accompanied by a deafening clap, exploded in front of them. Keira shrieked and ducked. When she opened her eyes, Hermes and the Furies were gone, along with the offering Leo laid on the altar.

Alarmed voices reached Keira's ears just as a flashlight beam cut through the trees. It missed highlighting Ty's face by inches. Keira hastily threw the energy shield up again. She had lost it when the gods made their dramatic exit, which was also likely what drew the guards to the altar.

"Come on," Leo whispered. He quickly led them away from the guards and toward the road where they left their rental car.

Heart in her throat at the near miss, Keira grasped his hand and followed.

CHAPTER 31

L eo surveyed their surroundings as they headed away from the guards, who were now busy searching the area around the ancient altar. His gaze landed on the Parthenon atop the hill. Something about the large stone structure beckoned him to come closer. It was like the temple had thrown a rope around him and pulled. Hard. It was insistent and demanding.

He paused and stared at it, the unrelenting beat in his head thrumming louder now that he had recognized it. "We need to go up there." He motioned toward the temple.

Keira paused next to him and followed his gaze up the hill. "The Parthenon?"

He nodded, still staring. He could swear he could hear it whispering to him. Calling him to it.

Ty walked up beside him. Leo could feel Ty's eyes on him, contemplating his strange request.

"There are more guards up there," Ty stated. "We don't know where the cameras are or the entrances and exits. It won't be as easy to get in."

Leo kept staring at the temple. "We'll be fine," he murmured, certain down to the core of his being that it was true.

Not waiting for a reply, he started through the trees to the road that separated the grotto from the Acropolis, his strides sure and determined. Only Keira's hand in his and the knowledge she could never keep up with him kept him from running. The closer they got, the louder the call of the temple became, urging him to go faster. At the road, he spared a glance in both directions for traffic before jogging across. Heeding the call slightly, he didn't slow.

"Leo!" Ty whispered fiercely as they neared the edge of the clearing around the Acropolis. "Slow down. The guards will see us, not to mention there are cameras over here. Jail is not on our list of things that will help us bring down Hecate."

"They won't see us," Leo said, voice low. And they wouldn't. Whatever was up there was making sure the group was neither seen nor heard by man or machine.

"Keira, do you know what's going on?" Ty asked when Leo kept moving into the clearing.

"No," she replied, slightly breathless, trying to keep up with his pace. Leo felt a twinge of guilt for pushing Keira so hard. Because of her stature, she was having to take two or three steps for every one of his. Then the whisper in his head would get more insistent and he would keep pressing on. He *had* to find out what was up there.

"Just follow him," Keira said, clinging to his hand. "We'll find out, eventually."

Leo's mouth quirked at that, even as he remained focused on reaching the source of the power pulling at him. The closer they got, the more he could feel it. It hummed through his veins now, tugging him along.

In minutes, they arrived at a gate on the southern slope of the Acropolis. Leo assessed the area, looking for a way over or around the fence when the gate suddenly creaked open.

"Okay, that's not weird at all," Ty muttered, standing a little straighter.

Leo couldn't help but agree. Something strange was definitely happening, and all the answers were at the top of the hill.

"Let's go get some answers." Leo pushed through the gate and started up the staircase along the side of the hill. It eventually gave way to a small escarpment. He hopped the rail, then helped Keira over before heading up the steep slope. The call was becoming louder and more insistent the closer he got to the top. It pounded inside his head now, pushing out everything else.

Soon the group reached the summit of the Acropolis and were staring up at the Parthenon's ancient edifice. Lights shone on the structure, highlighting the sculptures and throwing the interior into shadow. Leo's eyes traveled over the temple before he started forward. The power calling him from inside lit a path only he could see, guiding him through the ruined structure to the eastern end of the temple, where a sacred inner sanctum was once housed.

Leo stopped and closed his eyes. The call was so loud now it pushed against his skull until he felt like it would crack open. A heavy energy settled around them, completely shielding them from outsiders. The call grew even louder. Leo pressed his hands against the sides of his head, trying to ease the pounding.

The collective gasp of his friends reached his ears at the same time the pounding in his skull abruptly ceased.

An unfamiliar voice rang out.

"Hello, Leo."

Leo's eyes popped open at the soft, feminine voice. His hands fell away from his head as he stared at the statuesque woman in front of him. She reminded him a bit of Persephone. Eyes the color of quicksilver gleamed back at them in the light from the moon. Her dark hair and gauzy, cream gown fluttered around her in the breeze as she looked at Leo, a soft smile on her beautiful face.

Keira stepped up next to him and slipped her hand into his. Leo was glad for the contact. It grounded him and reminded him this was far from a dream.

"Who are you?" Keira echoed the thoughts running through Leo's head. He watched the woman silently, waiting for her answer.

The woman's eyes shifted to Keira before settling on Leo once more. "I think Leo can tell you that."

Leo stared closely at the woman, confusion and a healthy dose of trepidation racing through his brain. His mind whirled, and a sliver of memory at the edge of his mind flitted close. Leo tried to reach out and grasp it, but it wasn't until she smiled fully that the memory suddenly became clear.

Her identity hit him like a punch to the gut. Leo sucked in a harsh breath, his eyes growing wide. "Athena."

The others mutter quiet exclamations, but he barely heard them. His focus remained on the goddess in front of him.

Athena's grin grew. "It's been a long time, child. I'm glad you remember."

Ty and Penny stepped up on his other side. Still too stunned to speak, Leo just stared at the goddess.

"What's going on?" Ty asked.

Athena barely spared Ty a glance, her eyes trained on Leo. "It's time, Leo."

Frowning, Leo found his voice. "Time for what? I don't understand why I'm here. Was it you who called me up here?"

She nodded, her smile soft, eyes kind. "Yes. It's time for you to remember your destiny."

Leo's eyes widened at the implications of her words. She couldn't mean what he thought she did. He wasn't one of the special ones. He was just normal old Leo.

Athena laughed. "You are far from normal, Leo," she said, shocking him by reading his thoughts.

Anger flared, and a dark frown overtook his face. He didn't like the idea she could read his mind. His thoughts were his and his alone. He was so done with all the godly bullshit.

"Stay out of my head. And no more games. Explain. Now."

Seeming to sense he was at the end of his rope, Athena was quick to answer. "You, my dearest Leo, are like your friends, but at the same time highly unique."

Keira clutched his hand harder as she sucked in a surprised breath.

Shock froze Leo's muscles. His mind whirled. He didn't want it to be true, but deep down, he could feel it was. Memories from long ago tried to surface. Images of Athena's face looking down at him floated through his consciousness, but quickly escaped his grasp.

"Why do I know you?" he finally managed to ask. "I remember you, but I don't know from when."

"You met me at your birth."

Leo's eyebrows dipped quizzically. "That's impossible. I wouldn't remember anything from then."

"You would if I made sure you did. Perhaps I should start at the beginning."

"That would be a fantastic idea, because I think we're all very confused right now," he growled. This was getting strange. Goddess or not, if she didn't start explaining, he was going to shake the answers out of her.

"When Artemis gave Iphigenia her divinity and the young woman became Hecate, Artemis realized almost immediately she had made a terrible, terrible mistake. The sweet, innocent girl she rescued suddenly became arrogant and smug. And vengeful. Fearing the worst, Artemis consulted the Oracle at Delphi, who confirmed Hecate did indeed have a plan for revenge. One that would destroy both the mortal and immortal worlds. Artemis asked if there was anything that could be done to keep Hecate from destroying everything. The Oracle told her one day, a reckoning would come that would determine the fate of the world. A reckoning between Hecate and four humans: three human descendants of the gods and one unique being. You three," she pointed at Ty, Penny, and Keira, "are the human descendants. You, Leo, are the unique being."

Eyes like saucers, Leo could barely breathe. "Unique how?" he forced out.

"You are human, but Artemis and I gave you a little something extra when you were born. Did your parents ever tell you the story of your birth?"

Confusion lit Leo's eyes once more. "Yes."

"What?" Keira's eyes bounced back and forth between Leo and Athena, concern lacing her voice. "What happened?"

He tore his eyes away from Athena to look down at the petite woman at his side. She stared up at him, curiosity shining from her dark eyes. "My mother didn't make it to the hospital. I was born on the side of the road. A couple of strangers—two old creole women—happened along while my mom and dad were stopped and helped to deliver me." He turned back to Athena. "Was that you?"

She nodded. "And Artemis. In the chaos, your parents didn't notice us anoint you with a mixture of our essence and ambrosia. As a result, you are divine, but not born of divinity. Human, though. Not an immortal god, like Hecate."

Fury surged in Leo as it hit home how he had been manipulated. "How have I never known this? And what gave you the right to mess with my life?"

Athena smiled, looking every inch the goddess she was. "I am a god. I have every right. And you can't stand there and tell me you haven't noticed you are different from everyone else. That you don't see and feel and comprehend things others don't."

Leo frowned as he contemplated her words. He'd always had a unique way of seeing the world. Complex strategies to solve the most intricate problems always seemed to just come to him. It's what made him such a good soldier. But he had always chalked it up to the way his brain worked.

"So, you're telling me I'm a master at strategy and at computer programming because you made me into some sort of hybrid deity?"

Athena nodded, unfazed by Leo's anger. "That's a good way of saying it. You get your affinity for animals from us, too."

Leo's mind turned to Clyde and every other animal he had ever owned, as well as a few he just happened across—like Clancy, the gator that lived in his swamp. Animals had always seemed to like him and listen to him. He hadn't ever given much thought as to why that was. It just was.

It still didn't excuse what she and Artemis did. "Why is it on us to fight your fight and right Artemis's wrong? Can't she fix this? And who's to say we will succeed?"

"The Oracle declared it will be you four and *only* you four. It is just the way it is. As for whether you succeed—you have to. Any other outcome means the end of everything."

"No pressure, then," Ty quipped.

"The Oracle needs to come up with some less complicated plans," Penny muttered. "This is ridiculous."

Athena's smile was genuine. "I agree, but she thrives on complicated. And there's nothing anyone can do to change it, so you just have to follow along. It's easier than trying to fight her. You can't ever win. Even Zeus bows to her prophecies. He fights them tooth and nail, but eventually she always wins."

Frustration tightened Leo's jaw. The idea that all this was preordained millennia ago chafed something fierce. It made life seem cheap. Like it didn't matter what he did, it would turn out however these gods deemed it should.

"Did the Oracle foresee Hades stealing my soul?" he asked, a hard edge to his voice.

Athena's mouth quirked ruefully. "That one... that one took us all by surprise. You were part of this, whether he took it or not. It just sped up the timeline. Hades has always marched to his own drum. I think he just wanted to make things more interesting. He gets bored and every once in a while stirs the pot just to have a little fun."

Leo felt Keira vibrate at his side. Hades better hope she exhausted herself bringing in Hecate, and he didn't balk in giving Leo back his soul. God of the underworld or not, Leo had a feeling Keira could take him if he pissed her off any further.

Athena stepped forward. "It's time, Leo. Time for you to be what you are truly meant to be."

She laid her hand on his arm.

Immediately, searing pain raced up his arm to lance through his skull. Leo dropped to his knees, eyes shut tight. He heard Keira shout his name, but he couldn't do anything to reassure her. The pain running rampant through his head was too great.

He clutched his head as an agony unlike anything he had ever known flowed over him. A white-hot light speared his eyes behind his closed eyelids as the power Athena unleashed surged through his veins.

Leo roared with the pain as raw energy blasted through his muscles. He wanted to writhe on the ground, but was held paralyzed by the energy flowing through him.

Just when he felt like he was going to be ripped to pieces by the power surging through his body, it settled into a steady hum, and the pain receded.

Gasping, Leo felt like he'd run a marathon. When he opened his eyes, the shock at what he saw rendered him speechless. He blinked hard several times to make sure what he was seeing was real.

Sure enough, the world stared back at him in vivid relief. It was like someone turned up the wattage on the moon. Shadows still blanketed the world around him, but he could see past the shadows to what laid beneath. Everything was sharper, more vibrant. Colors he had never seen before flared to life everywhere he looked.

And his body... moving felt effortless. He had a feeling he could lift one of the Parthenon's mighty columns and not come close to breaking a sweat.

"Leo." Keira clutched his arm, a frantic edge to her voice. "Leo, talk to me, please."

He turned to look at her. Her beautiful face was scrunched with concern. Flecks of amber he never noticed before made her eyes glitter like diamonds in the low light. "I'm okay, *chère*," he hastened to assure her. He laid his hand over hers on his bicep and squeezed.

"Truly," he said when she continued to assess him. A sense of rightness settled over him. He still didn't feel whole—that gaping, glaring, black hole where his soul used to be made sure of that—but this went a long way to explaining why he had always felt so restless and edgy. Why being outdoors calmed him so. His body had craved to have its full capabilities, but his mind hadn't understood that anything was missing. Now that Athena had released his true self, his whole being felt settled and ready to go.

Leo rose, pulling Keira with him, and faced Athena.

She grinned. "How's it feel?"

He rolled his neck, smiling back. "Can't say I was a fan of the pain, but the result? This is unreal. Do I get to keep this?"

Athena nodded. "This is what you were meant to truly be. We didn't want to raise any questions among your human family, or tip off Hecate when the prophecy was going to come true, so we suppressed most of your abilities. Now that you have them, unless you want them suppressed again, they are yours to keep."

"What abilities?" Keira questioned. "What is she talking about?"

"I'm like you now, *chère*. Or more accurately, like Ty. Athena unleashed the abilities she and Artemis gave me at birth."

Ty stepped forward and looked Leo up and down. "You don't look any different, but yet you do. I'm going to go out on a limb and say challenging you to an arm wrestling match wouldn't go my way."

Leo grinned. "Probably not."

Keira's hand on his face brought his attention back down to her. She stared hard into his eyes, her gaze searching. Finally, after several long moments, she spoke. "You really are like us. I can see it. There's a depth in there that wasn't there a moment ago."

Bringing his hand up, he covered hers once more. "I am. But I'm not, too. I can feel your abilities now, like they're a tangible thing." He looked up, his words encompassing all three of them. "I can feel all of you. Athena's right. I am the same, but distinctly different. I'm more powerful than any of you, but I'm still human. I can still die, but I have all the powers and abilities of any full-blooded god, plus a few gifts from Athena and Artemis."

Keira stared at him a moment longer before stretching up on tiptoe to place a hard, fierce kiss on his lips. "You're still my Leo, no matter what you can do."

He smiled and kissed her, gently this time. "Always, *chère*."

Athena clapped in delight. "Now that you all know your destiny, go. Hecate is waiting. And Leo?"

He quirked a brow in question.

Her eyes went hard. "If you succeed and get Hecate to Hades—if he gives you any trouble, you call for me. You all have sacrificed enough and proven yourselves more than worthy. He will abide by the pact he made with you or he will regret it."

Leo nodded, glad to know she had his back. Although, if Keira's rigid posture was any indication, Athena would have to get in line for a chance at Hades.

A glow emerged around Athena. "Good luck to you all. The worlds thank you."

Leo watched as she faded away and the heaviness that had settled over them lifted.

"Man, that was nuts," Ty muttered.

Leo agreed. He clenched and unclenched his fists, trying to get used to the way his body felt now. While it felt right, it was still going to take some getting used to.

Movement out of the corner of his eye caught his attention. A guard was headed their way, but hadn't seen them yet.

"Keira, can you put a bubble around us so the guards can't see and hear us? Athena took hers with her."

Rather than answer, Leo watched her eyes go slightly unfocused as she drew on the energy around them. He felt the air shift as she created a cloak, much like the one Athena had used. He watched in amazement as the energy around them shimmered and coalesced over their heads to shield them from view. Seeing what she could do on this level was incredible. She truly was amazing.

Coming back to herself, Keira gave a quick nod. "We're good."

Leo nodded, resolve filling him. He tugged on her hand. "Let's go. We've got a witch to stop."

CHAPTER 32

"Hades said to cross at the Necromanteion. That is nowhere near there," Penny argued a few hours later. They were back at the B&B pouring over Google Maps to find the place Hermes told them to go. What he said and what Hades said did not jive.

"There's no welling of the river there," Ty argued back. "And looking at the map, the site isn't even close to the river's course. It's nearly a quarter mile away."

Penny looked at her husband, exasperated. "Then why would Hades tell us to go there?"

"I have no idea, but that is not the same place Hermes was talking about. This place makes much more sense." He pointed at a different area on the screen.

Keira had been keeping half an ear tuned to her friends' arguments while she did her own search online about the site. Greek history was fascinating, but because of its ancient nature, there was very little written record left of anything. Many times, the history of a site was presumed based on a piece of pottery found there or the name of a nearby town. A tidbit about the Necromanteion leaped out at her as she listened to Ty and Penny argue.

"Guys!" She sat up straight, laptop clutched in her hands. Three sets of eyes swung toward her. "Look at this. There's some speculation the Necromanteion isn't the site they think it is. It may just be an unusual manor house instead of a temple devoted to Hades. They don't know where the actual site is, just that it exists." She looked up at the others who now gathered around her, excitement shining in her eyes. "What if the springs place Ty pointed out is the real Necromanteion? Hades didn't say where it was, only that we needed to go there."

"That's true, he didn't," Penny said, coming over to sit down next to Keira to look at the computer screen.

"That makes sense. Let me see that." Leo sat down on her other side and commandeered her laptop. His fingers flew over the keyboard as he looked for information. Images of a beautiful, aquamarine river flowing through a gorge filled the screen.

"Look! There are little caves and coves carved into the gorge walls." Keira leaned over Leo's shoulder and pointed at the screen. "One of those could lead to the entrance, right?"

Leo rubbed his jaw thoughtfully. "It's certainly possible. I think Ty's right and the area near Acheron Springs is more likely to be the site of the Necromanteion than the historical site that's in question. It's either the springs or the headwaters, but looking at the satellite images and pictures available, the headwaters look to be little more than a trickle. There are no pools, just a small stream that flows down the mountain. The water at the springs seems to come up from below and it's deep in some spots." He tapped the image on the screen. "I vote we go here."

Ty gave a quick, decisive nod. "Works for me. Ladies, any objections?"

Keira and Penny both shook their heads.

"I'm not arguing with his Spidey-sense. Not now that I know where it comes from," Penny said with a grin.

Keira shook a finger in Leo's face, a sudden thought occurring to her. "That does not mean you get to milk this for all it's worth, so you can get me to agree to stuff. I can still tell when you're lying."

Leo nipped her finger, a playful gleam in his eyes. "I have no doubt you will call me on my bullshit, *chère*."

She gave him a cheeky grin. "Always."

He tipped his head down to touch his forehead to hers. The heat that found its way to his eyes brought out an answering heat in Keira. She felt her cheeks flush as desire began to hum through her veins.

"And on that note, Penny, I think it's time for us to say goodnight." Ty held a hand out to his wife.

The couch shifted as Penny took his hand and stood.

"We'll meet here about eight tomorrow morning and head out," Leo told Ty, not taking his eyes off Keira.

"You got it. Come on, Pen. Let's leave the lovebirds alone."

Keira heard Penny's chuckle, but couldn't care less. Alone with Leo felt like a wonderful idea.

CHAPTER 33

T he morning of their journey to northern Greece dawned bright and hot. After a quick breakfast, the group climbed into Leo and Keira's rental and set off for Acheron Springs. They cleared Athens and were curving west and north now through the parched Greek countryside. Mountains covered in scrub brush and dry grass stretched as far as Keira could see to her left. To her right, water dominated where the Gulf of Corinth separated the Peloponnese peninsula from mainland Greece.

Even with the air conditioning in the car on full-blast, it was still warm in the vehicle. Keira dug a hair tie out of her purse and piled her riot of curls on top of her head in a messy bun to try to get some air onto her neck. She wished there were air vents in the back where she and Penny sat. Ty and Leo's massive bodies blocked a lot of the airflow from reaching the backseat.

Resigning herself to being hot, Keira watched the landscape fly by outside the car. Greece was beautiful, but the poor economy showed in the towns they passed through. Away from the bustling tourist attraction of Athens and the coastal towns that drew vacationers, the small inland towns showed the toll the lack of money was taking on the nation. Many of the buildings had peeling paint and chipped brick.

Some had no glass in the windows, sporting weathered boards instead. Ramshackle sheds housed livestock and acted as garages for ancient vehicles. It was depressing.

About halfway there, they stopped at a small gas station to take a break. Keira and Penny used the restroom, and Keira bought some water for herself and Leo. She didn't know about him, but she was parched. After paying the clerk, she made her way back outside. Ty stood next to the car, arms crossed and a deep frown on his face as he stared off into the distance.

She frowned and looked around, expecting to see Leo nearby. Only trees, their thirsty leaves waving in the breeze, and dry grass met her gaze. "Where did Leo go?"

Ty unfolded his arms enough to point behind the gas station. "Over the mountain. One minute we were joking while I pumped the gas, and the next, his head whipped around to stare at that mountain. He said he heard something and that he'd be back in a bit." If possible, Ty's frown deepened further as he spoke. "I don't know if I like the fact he can take off like lightning now. He gets into trouble—or we get into trouble while he's gone—and we're going to have problems."

Keira didn't like it either. The rest of them, while they had special abilities in their own right, couldn't hold a candle to Leo now. He needed to remember Athena said it would take all four of them to bring Hecate down, not just him.

"If he's not back in the next few minutes, I'm going to fly over there and see if I can find out what's going on," Ty told her.

Penny emerged from the little store just then to hear Ty's statement. She handed her husband a bottle of water. "Leo took off?"

Ty nodded and twisted the cap off the water. "His Spidey-sense heard something."

Penny frowned and sipped her water while they watched the mountain.

Keira felt her anxiety ratchet higher the longer Leo was gone. She didn't doubt he could take care of himself, but she was worried he had run into an ambush. The easiest way to make sure they didn't succeed would be to divide them up and pick them off one-by-one.

Movement in the store caught Keira's attention. The clerk peered out the window at them.

As nonchalantly as she could, she straightened from where she leaned on the hood of their car. "Ty. We need to move. We're attracting attention." She motioned with her eyes toward the store.

Ty's head didn't move, and his sunglasses camouflaged his eyes, but Keira could tell by his stillness he saw the clerk watching them. He dug the keys out of his pocket and handed them to his wife. "Babe, there's a picnic spot just down the road. You and Keira take the car down there. I'm going to go in and use the restroom to draw the clerk's attention away, then go after Leo."

Penny took the keys without question and climbed into the car. Keira got in next to her, her heart thundering in her ears. She didn't like that Leo had been gone so long. As fast as he could move, he should have been back.

They pulled into the picnic spot in time to see Ty emerge from the store. He turned their direction and began walking like he was going to join them. Once past the line of trees at the edge of the parking lot, Keira watched as he darted behind them. A quick glance around confirmed no one could see him and he quickly shifted into a hawk and took flight.

"Despite the fact he used those abilities against me when he was trapped in that nightmare, I'm not upset we shared our powers with each other." Penny stared out the windshield of the car, watching Ty fly toward the mountain, before looking back at Keira. "This may not be the last time one of us has to use the other's ability."

Keira had a feeling Penny was right.

CHAPTER 34

Leo heard Ty before he saw him. The flap of a hawk's wings flying with purpose toward him was hard to miss. As was the familiar cadence of Ty's heartbeat. Keeping an eye on his quarry, Leo raised an arm and waved Ty down. He had wondered how long it would be before his friend came after him. Leo hadn't intended to be away as long as he was, but he was trying to see if the creature he heard would lead him to more of its kind.

Ty set down beside Leo and quietly shifted human again.

"What the fuck, man?" Ty whispered fiercely. "Why'd you take off like that? Keira's worried sick."

He'd been afraid of that, but when he had sensed the danger just over the mountain, his first thought was to find out what it was so he could keep them all safe.

"Sorry," he whispered back. "I only intended to see what was over here, but once I found it, I decided to follow it to see if there were more. I was afraid it would vanish if I left to give you an update."

"Found what? What did you hear?" Ty peered around the copse of trees.

Leo could tell the moment Ty saw what Leo had been tracking. His eyes went wide, and he quickly moved back behind the tree to look over at Leo in astonishment.

"Holy hell," Ty muttered. "You're forgiven for worrying us."

Leo nodded and looked past the tree to check on the demon that sat a hundred feet away. The ugly, horned creature had come across some carrion and was gorging on the carcass.

Tufts of scraggly black hair that looked like they'd been singed grew on its sinewy, black body. Six-inch, black horns curled upward from either side of its head. It had the face of a man, but the teeth it sported as it fed were straight out of a horror movie. Leo hadn't needed to take more than a quick glance to realize they were dealing with something sent from the underworld.

"What's it doing up here and not down where we are? And how the hell did it find us?"

"I'm not sure, but I think Hecate's either found a way around the shield Keira put over herself and me, or she's tracking you and Penny now. And I'm betting that beast is just supposed to keep tabs on us while we travel. There's too much of a chance it'll be seen if it tries to attack us in broad daylight. We need to watch our backs tonight."

Ty nodded in agreement. "What are we going to do about this one?"

"I was watching to see if it had any friends, but I haven't seen or heard any others."

"So let's get rid of this one and get moving." Ty began to rise, but Leo grabbed his arm to stop him.

"No. We need to leave it alone. I don't want Hecate to know we're on to her henchmen. She might send a bigger contingent if we eliminate this one. The one thing we have on our side right now is the fact she doesn't know when we're coming for her just that we are. I know we have another day yet before we need to meet Hermes, but my hope is we can fend off whatever attack this thing mounts tonight, and then be across the river tomorrow before Hecate can send something else at us."

Ty stared at him thoughtfully. "That thing is likely just a scout and there's a larger force coming. Hecate is no fool. Even if she doesn't know about you yet, she's not going to underestimate the three of us. Especially not after I defeated one of her surprise demon buddies already. And with ease."

Leo nodded. "I know. We need to get moving. I want to be in as defensible of a position as possible before night falls."

Ty grinned. "Are we camping? Keira's going to love that."

Leo bit back the chuckle that threatened to break free. Leave it to him—the survivalist—to fall for the one woman who relished her creature comforts. "She can use me as her mattress. Come on. Let's get back down to the car before she makes your wife fly her up here."

With a nod and a smile, Ty shifted back into his hawk form and headed back over the mountain. Leo took one last look at the demon still stuffing its face. He had a bad feeling tonight was going to be a challenge.

CHAPTER 35

As dusk fell, the group settled into their little campsite in the middle of nowhere, about a half mile from the springs. They had scrounged some wood from the forest to build a decent campfire to keep the bugs away and provide some light. Much to Keira's delight, they hadn't had to eat over the fire. The hotel in the nearby town also boasted a small restaurant. They stopped there to eat after gathering the few supplies they would need to see them through in the wilderness until morning.

Keira shifted, trying to find a comfortable position on the piece of rock she had parked her butt on. It didn't matter which way she moved; it was still just as hard. Giving up, she sighed and looked around. It was beautiful here despite the hard ground. Rockier than she thought it would be, there was still a good amount of forest. It wasn't the dense forest she was used to seeing in the states, though. Smaller shrubs were scattered around them, growing through cracks in the rock. Spindly cypress trees clung to the ground and cliffs. Keira couldn't help but think it was a mountain goat's paradise.

She glanced over at Leo where he sat, stirring the fire, body on high alert. The relief she felt when he emerged from the tree line at the edge of the picnic area earlier had been enough to nearly bring her to her knees. It lasted only long enough for the fear she felt to turn to anger, and then she laid into him.

He let her rant at him for a moment before kissing her to stop the flow of words. Taking her hand, he apologized for worrying her, then explained what he'd seen and why he was gone so long.

Keira suppressed a shudder as she thought about the demon that had been so close.

Thoughts of the demon had her eyeing their rapidly darkening surroundings with unease. Leo and Ty both seemed to think something was coming for them tonight. She felt slightly defenseless. She left her herbs behind when they fled Norwich, so all she had was her energy-drawing ability to rely on to help keep them safe. She put a shield around their campsite, but she didn't know if it would be effective against a supernatural being. It would be moot anyway once she fell asleep.

Rustling to her left sent her heart into her throat. She had energy balls in her hands, ready to blast whatever showed its face, before she even knew they were there. She heard Leo rise from his seat by the fire just as two golden jackals waltzed out from behind the scrub. Keira scrambled to her feet, hands raised, when the jackals shifted and Ty and Penny appeared.

Shoulders slumping, Keira let the energy go. "Announce yourselves next time, will you? I about blasted you both."

They both grinned at her. Keira just shook her head and sank back down onto her hard patch of rock, heart still pounding in her ears.

Penny sat down beside her. "Sorry about that. We didn't mean to startle you."

Keira looked over and gave her friend a half smile. "It's okay. I'm just a little jumpy after the whole demon thing earlier. Not that I think one would be so bold as to just waltz right into our camp, but stranger things have happened."

Penny nodded, her attention turning to the men, where Ty was no doubt imparting to Leo what he and Penny learned on their perimeter run.

"So have you forgiven him yet for running off on us this afternoon?" Penny tipped her head toward Leo.

"Yeah."

One eyebrow quirked over Penny's jade eyes.

Keira rolled her eyes. "Sort of," she amended. She gave a deep sigh, her thoughts a jumble. Anger really wasn't what she felt when she thought about the time he was gone earlier. "I'm not really mad at him."

The eyebrow quirked again.

"I'm not," Keira vehemently denied. "He scared me," she finally admitted, her voice softer. "I don't know what I'd do if something happened to him, Penny. He's come to mean so much to me in such a small amount of time."

Penny stared at her for several long moments until Keira fought the urge to squirm. She hated it when Penny did that. Keira had never been able to lie or tell half-truths to Penny. The woman had this way of always knowing when she was lying. It was uncanny. And unnerving.

"You need to admit how you feel about that man and tell him," Penny finally said. "Maybe if he understands where you're coming from, he'll be more careful in the future."

Keira had her doubts about that. Leo was a soldier to his core. He would never shy away from danger. Even less so now that he was superhuman. And she didn't want him to hesitate because he was worried about how she would feel. It could cost him his life, superhuman abilities or not.

"Seriously, Keira. Don't wait. We don't know how the next couple of days are going to go. Make the most of whatever time you've got. You don't want any regrets."

As the night stretched on, Keira kept replaying Penny's words over and over in her head. Was what she felt for Leo love? She knew she had a hard time imagining her life without him. She didn't really want to, to be honest. But love?

Keira had never been in love. Not the truly deep, forever kind of love. She'd had a couple of serious relationships, but when they ended, there had been no hurt feelings or intense emotional pain. If she lost Leo, it would crush her so completely she would never be the same.

The fear she would lose him before all of this was over crept back in. Ruthlessly, she clamped down on it, refusing to let it grow. It would do her no good to worry about something that may never happen. But what did it say about how she felt about the man, when the very thought he might die left her a quivering, blubbery mess?

Admitting her feelings would change everything, though. As long as she was in denial, she could fool herself into believing losing him wouldn't be as bad as she knew deep down it would be.

She scoffed at her own thoughts. That made absolutely no sense, but it was true. She didn't want to put a name to it because it made it all too real, with real consequences if something happened to him.

But Penny was right. Keira needed to pull up her big girl panties and face reality.

She was in love with Leo Devereaux.

Now, she had to decide what to do with that knowledge.

Her eyes cut over to where Leo dozed, propped up on his pack. He and Ty were taking turns keeping an eye out for trouble. Ty was somewhere in the scrub with Penny, circling in jackal form once more.

Keira was supposed to be sleeping like Leo, but her thoughts were too incessant to let her relax enough to sleep.

Emotion swelled in her chest as she stared at the man. Now that she had faced her feelings, they refused to be contained. They wanted to remind her she had acknowledged them and they weren't going anywhere.

They also wanted her to crawl over there and snuggle up against him. She hadn't when they bedded down because she needed some time to think. Leo had respectfully not pushed her to rest, seeming to understand she had some things to sort out. Now that they were sorted, she wanted to be over there right next to him.

Scrubbing her hands over her face, Keira gave in and half crawled, half scooted on her butt to where Leo rested, his long legs stretched out before him, arms crossed over his broad chest.

He stirred when she sidled up next to him, an arm coming around her to pull her close. Keira laid her head on his chest, one hand resting on his abdomen, and forced her mind to settle. She didn't know how much sleep she was going to get before the shit hit the fan tonight, but something would be better than nothing.

As comfortable as she could be on the rocky ground, Keira pushed all thoughts from her mind and concentrated on Leo's even breathing and steady heartbeat, praying sleep wouldn't be too elusive.

CHAPTER 36

Dark hair fluttered in the breeze, while the gauzy white gown flowed around her, wet from the knee down from the river. She turned slightly so Leo could see her face. He smiled, love swelling in his chest as he watched her tip her face to the sun. She looked like the demigoddess she was. Beautiful and ethereal.

Unable to resist her pull, he waded through the river toward her. She saw him and scampered away, laughing. Running after her, his much longer legs quickly ate up the ground until he snagged her around the waist and hoisted her against his chest. He smothered her squeal of delight with a fierce kiss. Everything else around them—the breeze, the chirp of the birds in the trees, even the voices of other people around them—faded away as he kissed her.

A voice niggled in the back of his mind that there was something he needed to remember. He tried for a moment before she wound her arms around his neck and threaded her fingers in his hair, making desire race down his spine to pool low in his belly. Whatever it was, could wait. Leo had more important things to worry about right now.

CHAPTER 37

Keira came awake as the hard ground beneath her shoulders registered. Groaning, she sat up, her back aching from the rocky earth.

How had she ended up on the ground like that? The last she remembered, she had been cuddled up to Leo, using his chest as a rather comfortable pillow.

A quick glance around showed Penny and Ty both sleeping, but no Leo. It must have been her turn with Leo to keep watch, and he decided not to wake her. The only problem with that was she now had no idea where he was.

Exasperated, she stood and brushed the dust off her clothes. She wandered the campsite, trying to find him, but he was nowhere close.

Getting concerned something happened to him, or that he heard something and followed it again, she called on the energy around her, waking it. "Okay. Take me to Leo," she muttered softly. Concentrating, Keira asked the energy to point her toward Leo. It buzzed around her briefly before it lit a path down the mountain toward the river.

Picking her way carefully over the rocky ground, Keira followed the energy path. Several hundred yards down the mountain, she began to get concerned because she still hadn't found him.

Keira rounded a boulder, only to find herself at a sharp drop off. Grumbling to herself, she carefully picked her way down to the ledge below. He was so going to get a piece of her mind when she found him. She was going to make him wear something absolutely ridiculous. And in public. She couldn't believe he wandered away so far without telling anyone.

As she hopped down to the ledge, it occurred to her that perhaps he told Ty where he was going and she should have awakened him to ask before she set off on this folly.

Oh well, she thought with a sigh. *Too late now.*

Dusting off her hands, she turned and saw him. He was just below her at the edge of a copse of trees. With a woman.

Eyes wide, she could hardly believe what she saw. He had the woman pressed against a tree and they were kissing. His shirt was in shreds on the ground at his feet, and the top of the woman's dress was loose, exposing her breasts to the moonlight. Leo's large hands squeezed and caressed them.

Keira stared a moment longer in shock.

Wasn't that the waitress from the restaurant?

Barely registering the crazy question, she found herself moving, her feet carrying her down the hill without her telling them to.

"Hey!" she shouted, scrambling over the rocks.

Leo didn't even twitch at her shout, but the woman's eyes snapped open. They gleamed a sickly yellow in the moonlight.

Horror filled Keira as she realized what was happening. The woman was another of Hecate's tricks.

Keira pulled energy into her hand as she ran toward them, hurling it at the woman. The woman shoved Leo away, sending him flying nearly twenty feet. He skidded to a stop on the rough ground. The woman ducked the blast and laughed as she flitted away.

Hurrying toward Leo, Keira looked around warily, waiting on the woman to reappear. He was utterly still, sprawled in the dirt. She landed next to him and shook him.

"Leo!"

He didn't respond. She shook him again, harder. A moan was his only response. A small sense of relief filled her. At least he was still alive.

A rush of wind was her only warning before a hideous, winged creature with flaming hair dropped in on them from overhead. Keira saw it just in time to throw an energy shield around them. The creature hit the shield and bounced off. Its halo of flaming hair whipped out behind it as it backed away.

Keira stared, terror locking her muscles. The same glowing, yellow eyes the woman in Leo's arms sported stared back at her from the face of this monster. Heavy breasts swung freely from its naked body, marking it as female. It flapped just outside her shield with wings that looked like they belonged on a bat.

With a scream like a banshee, the creature dove at her again, its sharp, pointy teeth glinting in the moonlight. Keira pulsed her shield as it hit, sending it careening off into the trees.

Wasting no time, Keira swung around to the still unconscious Leo. "Leo! Wake up! We need to get out of here." She shook him again, but he just kept on sleeping.

Shoving aside the fear threatening to choke her, Keira tried to think what Leo would do in this situation. She didn't know how to fight this creature. She wasn't super strong or super fast, and this thing was obviously both—a monster from the underworld. All Keira had was the energy around her. It made for a good defense, but she wasn't sure about an offense.

So how could she use that to her advantage?

Looking down at the man prone at her side, she realized they needed to get back to the others. Praying she could hold the energy field for what she wanted to attempt, she stood.

You held Demeter at bay with imaginary vines. You stopped a hail of bullets from hitting Leo and yourself. You can do *this*!

Gathering herself, she pulled on the energy field around them and lifted them off the ground. A quick look below had Keira concentrating harder to move them up the mountain faster. The she-creature was struggling, attempting to pull itself out of the tree branches.

Keira made it up over the ledge and part way up the path with Leo in tow before the beast was on them. She dropped them back to the ground just in time to throw her shield back up. The monster screeched at her and dove back at them again. Keira reinforced the shield and held it with one hand while the other gathered a blast of energy and directed it at the beast floating above them. She hit it in the gut, and it went tumbling away again.

Wasting no time, Keira quickly flew them up the mountain. She reached the campsite this time without incident.

"Ty! Penny! Wake up!" Keira laid Leo by the fire, shouting as they landed.

Penny snapped awake, eyes wide. "What? What's going on?" She stood as soon as she saw Leo's unconscious form on the ground.

"Leo was attacked by the waitress from dinner," Keira explained. "I can't get him to wake up."

"What?" Penny's tone was nothing short of completely confused.

"There's something out there! It looked like the waitress. And then it didn't. She put Leo under some kind of spell. He was wrapped around her like a monkey, kissing her. I yelled, and she threw him twenty feet through the air before she changed into some kind of hideous winged beast. Why isn't Ty waking up?" Keira asked, abruptly shifting gears.

Penny whirled around. Ty still laid in the same place, sound asleep. She hurried over and tried to shake him awake. Like Leo, he was sound asleep and refused to wake.

"Keira? What's going on? I can't get him to wake up!" A frantic note entered Penny's voice.

Keira gulped. This was not good. "I don't know. I think we're on our own, though." She had a feeling their "waitress" slipped something into Ty and Leo's dinner that locked them into a dream-state. She could only hope they would be fine until she had time to deal with them. Keira and Penny had a more pressing concern at the moment.

Gathering the energy around Leo like a floating bed, she lifted him and moved him over to lie next to Ty. It would be easier to keep the men safe if they were close to each other.

Something flapped overhead. Keira wished she had Leo's eyesight. She could feel things hiding in the darkness.

Eyes flitting from shadow to shadow, Keira tensed. "Get ready, Pen."

Both women stood, eyes studying the area around them.

The first demon swept in from up the mountain. Flying fast, it dove at them. Hands like claws, it went straight for Penny, talons extended. Penny shrieked and ducked. Keira threw an energy ball at it, knocking it away, but it quickly circled around and came back.

"Can you grab it?" Keira asked. She threw up her shield and pulsed it, repelling the creature once more.

"What? Why would I do that?" Penny asked.

Keira fought the urge to growl in frustration. She loved Penny dearly, but the woman was not a fighter. She was a peacekeeper.

But Keira needed a fighter right now. She had a feeling this guy had friends. And that horrid she-creature was still out there somewhere. "To kill it! Use your super strength. Squeeze it to death, behead it, rip it limb from limb! I don't care, just do something! My energy balls didn't do much."

The demon came back. This time the she-creature was with it. Keira once again pulsed her energy shield as the woman-slash-monster came rushing at her, sending the beast crashing into a pile of boulders.

Penny leaped at the demon, shifting into a mountain lion as she moved. She raked her claws over the demon's chest, tearing its flesh. It wailed an ungodly sound and landed hard on the ground. Black blood oozed from its wounds, but it still quickly rose from where it tumbled to the ground. Teeth bared, it faced Penny in her lion form and dove at her. Neatly, she sidestepped it. Shifting human, she grabbed it around the neck as it passed and twisted as she fell sideways. With a crack and a wet, ripping noise, the demon's head separated from its body.

Penny flung it at the fire with a squeal. "Ugh!" She glared at her still sleeping husband before turning back to Keira. "They are never going to hear the end of this. They should be the ones ripping off demon heads."

Keira couldn't agree more, but didn't have a chance to reply before three demons—one flying and two on the ground—rushed into the campsite. Penny shifted back into the lion and leaped at the flying one. It quickly met the fate of the first, while Keira tried something new on the others. She used her control of the energy around them to lash the two demons together with vines, much like those she used on Demeter. They wrestled and squirmed, screaming out their displeasure with that unholy screeching they made, but could not escape. Keira held them while Penny—human again—dispatched them, the same as their friends.

The she-beast, who had held Leo in her clutches, hovered over them, watching.

Keira glared up at her. "Come down here, hussy, and face us!" She sent a vine shooting upward, attempting to snare the beast and bring it down.

Laughing, the creature moved, and Keira missed.

Done playing, Keira heaved a wave of energy at it and sent a tangle of vines up to snare it as it was pushed sideways by the blast. It shrieked and squirmed, trying to break free.

Keira just grinned and tangled the vines more. Bringing it down to the ground, she set the thing on its feet, arms trapped across its chest and its legs locked together.

"I am The Empusa!" the she-beast screeched. "You cannot do this to me!"

Keira just laughed. "Really? Because I just did." She stepped forward, careful not to get too close, as the flames on the beast's head whipped around wildly, demonstrating the creature's displeasure.

"You messed with my man. Tell me what you did."

"No."

Controlled rage made Keira twist the vines higher, so they snaked up The Empusa's throat, wrapping it. She squeezed. "Tell me."

The Empusa tried to shake its head. Keira squeezed tighter. Its eyes bulged, and it gasped for breath. Keira would make the creature talk or it would die. "How do I fix him?"

Stubbornly, The Empusa still refused to talk. Defiance screamed from its glowing eyes even as they bulged out of its face and it gasped for air.

"Tell me!" Keira practically roared. Red colored her vision. Slowly, she pushed the ends of the vines into The Empusa's face.

Fear finally entered The Empusa's eyes as it felt the vines pierce its skin.

"I will rip you to pieces," Keira growled. "Slowly and painfully. Tell me how to reverse the spell." She was rapidly losing her patience with the repulsive monster in her grasp. Keira was not a bloodthirsty person, but she was feeling zero remorse in making The Empusa bleed. She would not lose any sleep killing this creature.

Another set of four demons landed in the campsite before The Empusa could say a word. Keira quickly hardened the vines, effectively trapping the beast, and spun to help Penny, who had shifted into her mountain lion form once again.

With one quick swipe of her paw, Penny sliced open the belly of one demon before she smacked it hard, sending its head whipping sideways and breaking its neck. Keira slammed two of them together as they tried to attack the sleeping men. Stunned at the blow, the demons staggered several feet apart. Keira didn't let them regain their equilibrium. She hurled them at the pile of boulders at the edge of their camp, rage fueling her powers. Stalking toward them, she made more vines and sent them shooting through the demons' necks, relieving them of their heads.

Huffing with adrenaline and the power coursing through her, Keira turned to see if Penny needed help with the last demon.

She didn't. It too laid at her feet, headless.

Demons dealt with for the moment, Keira turned her attention back to The Empusa. The winged beast held perfectly still, wrapped in the vines, trying not to jar them and send them further into its face.

Body humming and energy swirling all around them, Keira faced The Empusa. "Want to talk now?"

Imperceptibly, the beast nodded. Keira withdrew the vines from its face so it could speak.

The Empusa swallowed audibly in relief before replying. Holes peppered its face and thick, black blood flowed in rivulets down over its neck and the vines trapping it.

"It's a sleeping spell," The Empusa finally said. "Meant to lock them into dreams for the night. Hecate gave me the elixir, and I mixed it in their drinks at the restaurant. It allows me to invade their dreams, but I have to be touching them."

"Is that how you lured Leo away?"

The Empusa nodded. "I snuck up behind him and touched him, sending him into a dream-state, then made him think I was you. He followed me away from camp." The creature suddenly glared at Keira. "His blood smelled so good, and you took it from me! I would have had him if you hadn't come after him." It began struggling again. "You were all supposed to die!"

Cinching the vines tighter, Keira stopped the creature's struggles. She was very glad something awakened her to stop this thing from—drinking—Leo.

Keira cringed. What an awful thought that was. Whether it had been a sense of unease or just a case of missing Leo as her pillow, she was thankful she hadn't stayed asleep.

"How do we wake them up?" Penny asked, casting a worried look at Ty.

"You can't without the proper potion."

"What do I need?" Keira demanded.

The Empusa listed several items, none of which Keira had with them.

Keira was weighing the merits of taking the car and driving to the nearest city to get what she would need when Penny stepped closer to the she-beast trapped in Keira's vines.

She squinted at the creature. "It's hiding something, Keira."

With a trust born from a lifelong friendship, Keira didn't question Penny's statement. She just immediately thrust the vines back into the creature's face. "What? What did my friend see in your eyes that you didn't tell us?"

The Empusa whimpered as Keira dug the vines deeper. She felt no remorse for the creature who had tried to kill them. Who would have killed them, likely painfully, if Keira hadn't stopped it.

She pulled back enough to let the creature talk.

The Empusa inhaled sharply. "It will wear off by morning. Once their bodies have obtained adequate rest, they will awaken and be fine."

Keira studied the creature's face intently, trying to see if it was telling the truth. Even as beastly as it appeared, there was a humanness about its face that made it easier to read. The Empusa just glared back at her. Finally, Keira turned to Penny.

"What do you think? Is it telling the truth now?"

Penny studied The Empusa for several long moments before she shrugged. "I think so, but I can't be a hundred percent certain."

"Well, then." Keira retreated to a patch of rock next to Leo. With a flip of her hand, she spun The Empusa to face her, vines and all. With another quick tick of her finger, the vines edged toward The Empusa's face, enough to touch, but not enough to reenter the holes the others left behind. "I guess we wait until morning to see if you're lying."

CHAPTER 38

Keira and Penny left the dead demons where they fell. They quickly discovered burning demon flesh smelled absolutely awful when the head Penny threw into the fire started to burn. They choked and gagged through that smoke and decided no more.

Now, the sky began to lighten finally as the new day dawned. Keira rubbed her gritty eyes and looked over at Penny, who half-dozed next to her on the ground. Thankfully, no new demons had arrived to try to kill them, and they spent the remainder of the night staring at The Empusa. It continued to writhe and snarl, struggling to break free. Keira finally wrapped vines around its mouth to muffle the sound.

Ty began to stir around mid-morning. Keira heaved a sigh of relief at the sight. She had been getting worried that neither man had awakened yet.

With a groan as he stretched, Ty yawned hard. He opened his eyes, squinting against the bright Greek sun.

As he came awake, Penny rushed to his side. He blinked at her, confused.

"What? What's going on? Why are you freaking out?" He sat up abruptly, eyes wide, and grabbed her biceps, fear stamped all over his face. "I didn't attack you again, did I?"

Penny cradled his face in her hands. "No. You were just sleeping."

Ty's frown showed his deepening confusion.

Before Penny or Keira could explain, Leo woke. Keira held her breath as he slowly blinked and sat up next to Ty.

He yawned, and stretched, arms over his head, before he realized everyone was staring at him.

"What?" Slowly, his arms fell back to his sides. His eyes took in the three people watching him, then traveled past them to the carnage littering the ground.

"What happened?" Leo stood and walked over to the closest demon carcass. He nudged it with his foot.

"Penny and I had some fun last night while you two slept." Keira stood and walked in front of him. She brought her hands up to grasp his face and forced him to look at her. "Are you all right?"

He frowned down at her. "I'm fine. Why wouldn't I be? Although, I'm guessing the reason you're asking me that has something to do with the dead demons all around us and the fact I'm missing my shirt?"

Keira nodded, immensely relieved he seemed to be completely fine. Nothing untoward lingered in his eyes from his dream-filled night.

"You remember our waitress from dinner?"

He nodded, a perplexed frown on his handsome face.

"Turns out she was that thing." Keira pointed at the nearly unrecognizable being near the fire. Still wrapped in vines, it looked like a gnarled tree trunk. "Called herself The Empusa. She slipped one of Hecate's potions into your drinks and they locked you both into a dream-state. Then she lured you down the mountain to try to drink your blood, while Ty slept like a baby all night."

Ty cursed.

Leo stared at her wide-eyed and rubbed a hand along his jaw. "I'm almost afraid to ask how she got me to follow her."

Keira grinned mirthlessly. "You thought she was me. I'm glad to know how thoroughly irresistible I am, but I would have preferred to find out a different way." She shook her head to rid her mind of the images permanently burned there. "Seeing you with your hands and mouth all over another woman—even if it turned out to be a trick—is not something I ever want to see again."

"*Jesus*." He swiped his hands down his face. "I'm so sorry, *chère*."

Keira shrugged. "It wasn't your fault. Hecate's a powerful witch, and she apparently still has some loyal friends. Speaking of," she turned her attention to the creature, silently watching their exchange, "we need to figure out what we're going to do with that thing."

"Whatever we do, *I'm* not the one ripping off its head. I had my fill of that last night, thank you very much," Penny quipped.

"Did you two really kill all these demons by yourselves?" Ty asked, turning a circle.

Penny and Keira simply nodded.

Ty looked at Leo, amusement in his eyes. "I feel a bit redundant right about now. How about you?"

Leo only grinned. "I see they did leave us to clean up, though."

Keira patted his chest. "We figured you could put that strength of yours to good use." She looked over at The Empusa. "You can deal with your girlfriend there, too."

He groaned. "You're never going to let me live this down, are you?"

A wicked grin spread over Keira's face. "Nope. Even when we're ninety, I'll be reminding you of the time you made out with the she-demon under the starry Greek sky."

Ty and Penny laughed, while Leo smiled ruefully.

Keira stepped forward and looped her arms around Leo's neck, suddenly overwhelmed. "All joking aside, I'm so glad you're okay, and that I found you before she—it—managed to sink its teeth into you.

Literally." She blinked furiously, trying not to cry. All the events of the last eight hours were hitting and hitting hard.

Leo brushed her curls back and palmed the back of her head, holding her close. "Hey. I'm okay. You kicked ass, and I'm okay."

A watery laugh was her only answer.

He dropped a quick but intense kiss on her lips before releasing her. Keira stepped back as the god-but-not-a-god mask slipped over his face, and he surveyed the mess she and Penny made overnight.

"We need to dispose of these things. Did you really leave the mess for us or was there another reason you left them all where they fell?"

"Mostly, we left them for you," Penny replied. "But we also discovered they smelled terrible if we burned them. I threw the head of the first one I killed into the fire, and we gagged through the smoke until it was all burned up. Thankfully, it didn't take too long."

"No burning, then." Ty scratched his head, staring at the carcasses. "What if we buried them? I know we don't have any shovels, but with our abilities, we could probably dig a deep enough pit with some branches."

"Burying them works for me," Leo said. He spun toward the bound creature, watching them warily. "Now. What to do about you?" Leo walked toward The Empusa. Defiance shone from its eyes as he got closer.

"*Chère*, can you unwrap its mouth so it can talk?"

Keira removed the strands of vine over The Empusa's face. Momentary shock coursed through her as she gazed at The Empusa's unencumbered face. The holes she put there yesterday were completely healed. This creature was more than just a mere demon from the underworld.

It bared its teeth and snarled. "Let me go!"

Leo laughed mercilessly. "Not a chance. Do you want to be useful and give us some insider information on your friend, Hecate, or should I just kill you now?"

"I will never tell you anything about her. Her vision for the future *will* come to pass. Zeus, Hades, and Poseidon *will* fall and she will be queen! And you'll never kill me. I am a demigod! Not some paltry demon that even the like of those two can kill." The Empusa tipped her head at Keira and Penny. It snarled at Leo, then spat at him. "What are you? Nothing. Only a mere human. No match for me."

Keira glared at the creature. She may not be able to kill it, but she could sure make it hurt. Only Leo standing there, so tall and confident, kept her from thrusting the vines back into The Empusa's face and breaking some bones.

Absently, Keira noted she had become rather violent since all of this began. It was slightly unnerving, but warranted, considering the situation, she thought.

"See, that's where you're wrong," Leo retorted. "You are right that *they* can't kill you."

Without warning, moving so fast his arm was nothing more than a blur, he plunged his hand through the stiff vines holding The Empusa hostage and into its chest.

"But I can."

A look of horror washed over The Empusa's face. The vines crumbled away with Keira's shock at his actions, leaving him holding The Empusa upright by its spine. Ashen, the creature's breathing labored thanks to Leo's blow. "This... isn't possible," it gasped. "You're... *human!*"

"Not quite. I am a mortal god, created by Athena and Artemis. Hecate's vision for the future will never come to pass so long as there is breath in my body." He stared hard at the dying demigod. "You, however, will not be around to see her fail." As violently as he plunged his fist in, he pulled it back, ripping the creature's heart from its chest and breaking its spine, leaving a gaping, oozing hole in its chest.

Clutching the wound, body contorted from its broken back, The Empusa's eyes glazed as death took hold. It stared at him a moment longer before crumpling to the ground. Thick, black blood pooled in the dirt beneath it. The flames circling its head flickered and died as the creature took its last breath.

"Holy shit, Leo," Ty breathed.

Leo let The Empusa's heart drop onto its fallen body. He looked down at the black sludge covering his hand and wrist, then over at his friend, a pang of misgiving shining in his eyes. "Sorry. I didn't have any other weapon, and with the flaming hair it seemed like the best option."

Ty held up his hands. "I'm not judging. I'd have killed it with my bare hands too, given half the chance. I'm just impressed. That's the first time we've really seen you in action since Athena unleashed your abilities."

Keira appeared at his side with a bottle of water and started pouring it over his hand to wash off the creature's blood. "I, for one, am glad you killed that thing, no matter how you did it. After what it tried to do to you,"—Keira shook her head. "The bitch deserved to die."

Hand clean, Leo framed her face, concern shining in his eyes. "I didn't scare you? The vines vanished pretty quickly when I punched through them."

She shook her head. "No. You startled me just because you moved so fast. I figured you were going to do something. That thing needed to die. I just didn't know what you were going to do or how quickly you would move."

He pulled her into a hug and kissed the top of her head. "Good. The last thing I ever want to do is cause you to look at me like *I'm* the monster."

Keira smiled into his chest and hugged him back. She could never look at Leo like he was a monster. He was too good and kind to ever be something so evil. Love exploded in her heart for this man. He was so worried about her, she feared he wouldn't worry about himself. She hugged him tighter. She would just have to worry about him for him.

CHAPTER 39

The group made swift work of disposing of their dead friends. Leo, Penny, and Ty dug a pit while Keira sent a targeted breeze at the loose dirt, sweeping it up and over the side of the deepening hole to pile it off to the side. Once Leo deemed it deep enough, they tossed all the carcasses into the pit—including The Empusa's—and Keira swept all the dirt back over it, erasing all traces of the demon attack.

"We need to get something to eat and then get in the river if we're going to find that entrance before sunset." Leo wiped the sweat off his brow. He was feeling the push now to find the Necromanteion. Because they slept so late due to the potion, it was already nearly noon when they started digging the demon grave. Now, it was well past that. Sunset would be upon them before they knew it, and he did not want to miss their rendezvous with Hermes. They would be on their own, traversing the entire underworld without him.

They made a quick trip into the nearby small town for a late lunch after packing up their campsite and heading down the mountain. Instead of taking the chance on another restaurant, they found a small grocery store and bought sealed packages of lunch meat and bread to make sandwiches, and more bottled water.

A package of Oreos landed atop the other items in the basket. Leo looked over to see Keira offer him a rueful shrug.

"Today calls for some chocolate therapy."

Leo rolled his eyes and smiled, while Penny offered her an enthusiastic high five.

He wasn't going to argue with her. After what she and Penny did while he and Ty were incapacitated—well, they deserved something stronger than chocolate. If it was chocolate they wanted, chocolate they would get. Hell, he'd buy them all the chocolate in the store if it made them happy.

They made quick work of eating—Oreos included—before heading into the public restrooms to change into the swimsuits they bought before leaving Athens. Not knowing what they would be up against, they all bought short-sleeve swim tops and swim shorts along with water shoes, so they wouldn't have to walk barefoot once they crossed over to the underworld. Penny looped Hippolyta's belt around her waist under her clothes. Leo strapped a slim, waterproof pouch around his waist, containing things he thought they might need, as well as the coins from Hades to gain them entrance to the underworld. Ty had a similar one wrapped around his own waist, minus the coins.

Clothes changed, they stowed their belongings in the car and headed for the river.

It was a hot summer day, and it definitely showed. Leo stared at the crush of people inhabiting the river. It was chock full of locals and tourists alike, taking advantage of the cool, clear water of the Acheron. Locals congregated and chatted like magpies in the shallows while tourists wandered, busy snapping pictures.

Not wanting to attract undue attention, Leo and the others waded into the throng and floated around a bit. The water was actually very refreshing. He had been in hotter places than Greece, but the Greek heat was no joke. It felt nice to get a little relief before they stepped into the pits of hell.

Leo let his mind wander a bit as they floated idly, waiting for the interest in them to wane. His eyes strayed to his left, where Keira floated lazily on her back, her hands making circles in the water. Her ponytail fanned out behind her, an inky cloud on the otherwise aquamarine river. A soft, serene smile sat on her face as she rested in the water with her eyes closed to the bright sun streaming through the trees.

The look on her face brought back memories from the night before last. She'd had the same expression on her face after they made love again.

That experience had to be one for the record books for Leo. With his heightened senses, he felt like he touched the very heart of the universe during their lovemaking. When he had come, it was like a bomb detonated inside his head. Sensations overwhelmed him from every direction. Colors he hadn't known existed, the sound of their breathing, the touch of her skin on his, as well as the taste and smell of her honeyed essence, all bombarded him until he was a limp, sweaty, sated version of himself.

The one thing that still stood out to him was how fragile Keira seemed. He had been so afraid he would hurt her now that he was superhuman. She felt so delicate in his arms. It made him highly aware of how easy it would be to break her. It had been like holding a delicate baby bird. Thankfully, his body adjusted to his newfound strength, instinctively trying to protect the precious woman he cradled in his arms.

His eyes traveled over her floating form. She was so tiny. He was very conscious now of just how easily one of Hecate's minions could rip her from him if they weren't prepared. Keira had her magical abilities to defend and protect herself, but she didn't have the strength to fight back like the rest of them did if she were ambushed. He was terrified of that very thing.

Scenario after scenario ran through his head constantly to make sure she was always protected. It bugged the hell out of him he failed at that last night. She and Penny shouldn't have needed to face those beasts alone.

A burst of laughter from the crowd around them drew Leo out of his thoughts. He perused the crush of people. No one paid them any attention anymore.

Standing, he motioned for the others. "I think we can slip away now." Slowly, so they didn't draw looks from the crowd, they edged away and headed upstream.

They went east, away from the tourist attractions on the river. Leo was fairly certain humans would steer clear of an entrance to the underworld. Its dark energy would subconsciously repulse anyone who got too close.

Aware of the potential for another attack, Leo put his head on a swivel as they moved through the shallow water. He opened his heightened senses and took in as much information as possible.

Sunlight filtered down through the leaves of the cypress trees, dappling the aquamarine waters of the Acheron. Animals scurried through the underbrush along the banks of the river and birds flew lazily overhead. He could hear their steady heartbeats, assuring him—for the moment—they were safe.

Even as idyllic as the river seemed, a sense of danger lurked in the air. It felt heavy with an ominous presence. They had been swimming for nearly an hour now and had wandered far enough from all the people enjoying the river that Leo believed one of Hecate's minions would feel comfortable attacking them without fear of being seen or heard.

"Do you feel that?" Ty asked, echoing Leo's thoughts. He stopped, muscles coiled, ready to spring should the danger show its face. "The hair on my neck just stood straight up."

Leo came to a halt as well and scanned the riverbank once more. Still, nothing leaped out at him. All the animals still seemed calm and the insects still chirped happily. But Ty was right. Something felt off.

"Keep moving. Hopefully, we can get to the entrance before whatever is out there shows itself." Leo continued upstream, the others following.

The sense of foreboding didn't dissipate as they moved further upstream and into deeper water. The canyon walls rose higher as the water deepened. Either there was something coming, or the Necromanteion entrance gave off stronger "no go" vibes than he believed it would.

A splash in the water was their only warning before Penny shrieked. Leo turned in time to see her get yanked off her feet and disappear under the water.

"Penny!" Ty dove for the spot where his wife vanished, Leo and Keira on his heels.

Ty turned a full circle, looking for her. "Penny?" He spun again, searching. "Do you see her? Penny!"

Leo scanned the water, but the river's sun-dappled surface offered no clues.

Just as Ty prepared to dive under to look for her, she surfaced. Laughing.

She was also riding a large fish-dragon creature. It had the head of a dragon, but the body and tail of a fish.

Water sprayed over them as the monster slapped its tail.

Leo stared in shock. He blinked hard, sure his eyes were playing tricks on him. What the hell was going on?

Ty was the first to recover. "Penny. Sweetheart, why are you riding a—a dragon fish?"

Water dripped off of her as she smiled radiantly up at her husband. "This is Ketl. Hecate sent him, but she apparently didn't realize these creatures are loyal to Thetis."

Ketl snuffed loudly, spraying more water.

Penny patted the creature on its head. Leo could swear the damn thing purred.

"As soon as he grabbed me and got a taste of my blood, he realized who I was, and he let me go."

"Blood? You're bleeding?" Ty moved forward, concern written all over his face. "Let me see."

Ketl growled and moved back, Penny still on his back.

Ty held up his hands and stopped. "Whoa, there big guy. I just want to check on Penny's wound."

Penny stroked the creature's head soothingly and murmured to it. Ketl snuffed again and bobbed his head, soft clicks emanating from him.

"I'm okay, honey." She sat up and addressed her husband. "It's more a scratch than anything. And Ketl promises not to hurt you. I told him who you are to me."

Ketl snorted at Ty.

Ty gave the creature a skeptical look and stayed put.

"How can you talk to it?" Keira asked, moving slightly closer.

The urge to grab Keira and pull her back behind the safety of his bulk hit Leo hard. He resisted, though. Keira posed a valid question. Leo hadn't heard anything that remotely passed for words from the beast.

Penny stroked Ketl's head once more, a soft, delighted smile on her face. Ketl rolled his eyes back in apparent ecstasy and a low rumbling emanated from his throat. The creature looked like he had found his long-lost best friend.

Penny shrugged. "It's crazy, I know. He does this series of clicks and grumbles as a form of communication. I guess since he and the others of his kind are so connected to Thetis, the knowledge of their language was passed down to me as well."

"And he can understand you back?" Ty took a step closer to his wife and the creature she sat astride.

Penny nodded. She motioned him closer. "He can understand all of us. Come say hi. He won't hurt you. Not now that he knows you're with me."

Leo caught Keira's eye, and they shared a disbelieving look. Still, Penny seemed sure of the creature's gentleness. Keira slipped her hand in his and they waded forward to greet Penny's new friend.

Ty put his hand out like he was greeting a dog and let Ketl sniff him. Ketl nudged his hand and Ty stroked the creature's scaly head.

"This is unreal," he muttered, still stroking the beast. It seemed to enjoy the attention.

Leo reached out his own hand to greet their new friend. Its skin was bumpy, much like that of an alligator. It didn't act like an alligator, though. An almost human intelligence shone from its golden eyes. Leo had a feeling this creature was very much aware of what was happening in the world around them.

"So, what do we do with him?" Keira asked, petting the creature. "Is he just going to follow us?"

Pulling back, Leo surveyed the monster before them. "I think a better question is, can he lead us to where we need to go?"

Immediately, a series of clicks and low grumbles burst from Ketl.

"What's he saying, Penny?" Leo asked.

She listened a moment longer before looking up. "He says we're still a ways from the entrance. He'll show us the way."

Leo felt victory surge. He had been getting concerned at how low the sun had dipped in the sky. Now, they had a fast track to the Necromanteion. Hecate made a fatal error in sending this creature to take them out.

He reached out and stroked Ketl's head once again, looking at the beast with new eyes. "Thank you, Ketl."

Ketl snorted and tossed his head, clicking at him. Leo could swear the damn thing said you're welcome.

CHAPTER 40

"Penny, can you ask Ketl if we're getting close?" Leo looked up at the sky with trepidation. The sun was rapidly growing closer to the horizon. Long shadows fell over the river now, giving the water a silvery gleam in the waning light. They had traveled much further than Leo thought they would need to go.

"He says we're nearly there and not to worry," Penny relayed.

That was easier said than done. They had traveled against the current of the river for over two hours now. Leo was very glad they had a guide. There had been several points where caves opened out of the rock face, rising out of the water. Without Ketl to show them the way, they would have wasted valuable time exploring the caves for the Necromanteion entrance. Gliding through the water behind Penny and Ketl, Leo did his best to trust that the creature would get them to the entrance soon, and to ignore the ticking clock in his head.

The river widened, and the water deepened again. Ketl gave a loud snort and began clicking in earnest. Leo's heart thundered in his chest as he waited for Penny to interpret the beast's clicks.

"He says the entrance is there." She pointed to the rock face on their right.

The blank rock face with no cave.

Leo swam over to the wall and placed his hand on it, hoping it was just an illusion and he could pass right through. It was solid, but a dark energy shimmered through the rock to seep into his fingers. He spun back to Ketl.

"How do we get through? It's solid."

More clicks ensued. Penny looked up and grimaced.

"The entrance is underwater. We have to dive down and swim through."

"How far?"

"It's only a few feet down, but the passageway is completely underwater for a hundred feet or more," Penny interpreted.

"We'll never make that," Keira said, her shoulders slumping even as she treaded water.

"Not human, we won't," Ty said, looking pointedly at his wife.

Leo caught their meaning immediately. "Can you two do it? Can you hold on to us and still swim that far?" Keira was right—they would never make it through that length of passageway human without some form of supplemental oxygen.

"Only one way to find out." Penny climbed off of Ketl.

"A lizard of some kind might be best, babe," Ty said, swimming toward Leo. "That way they can hold on to our tails with one hand."

Water splashed as Ketl twitched his tail and swam toward them at the wall, clicking as he moved.

"He says he'll guide us through the passage to where it opens up. After that, we can walk through the water in the passage to get to the underworld."

Leo nodded, liking the plan. "Let's go, then."

With a snort, Ketl dove. His tail slapped the water before he disappeared.

Ty swam over. "Grab on." He turned his back to Leo and motioned to his shoulder.

As soon as Leo touched him, he felt a tingle go up his spine. He knew he shouldn't be surprised by anything at this point, but it was still awe-inspiring to look down and see the hand and arm of an iguana attached to his body.

Iguana-Ty dove beneath the gently moving water. Leo let his hand trail along Ty's back before grasping firmly to the tail now protruding from Ty's body, and followed his friend beneath the surface. Penny and Keira were ahead of them. Ketl's tail disappeared into a crack in the rocks. The women followed, Ty and Leo hot on their heels.

The tunnel through the rock was narrow—much narrower than he and Ty would have been able to fit through in human form. The significance of Penny and Ty's ability to shapeshift, and the necessity of it at this stage of their journey, was not lost on Leo. He understood everything Athena said about their destiny when she unleashed his abilities, but it had not hit home until now.

Renewed determination flowed through Leo as they continued to traverse the passageway. Whatever Hecate threw at them, he knew they could handle it. Fate had made sure of that.

CHAPTER 41

Keira kept a death grip on Penny's tail as they swam through the cool, dark water behind Ketl. What was only minutes felt like hours in the darkness.

How much further could the cavern be?

Their pace slowed as the passageway narrowed even further. As big as Ketl was, Keira was amazed he could fit through. There were a couple of spots barely wide enough for her tiny iguana body.

Suddenly, Penny made an abrupt turn toward the top of the passageway, towing Keira behind her. The body of water felt bigger, the walls further away, as they rose.

Head bursting through the surface, Keira gasped in a breath and let go of Penny's tail, shifting back to human. Ty and Leo surfaced behind her.

Keira's eyes strained in the absolute darkness. Calling on the energy, she created a soft glow, illuminating their surroundings.

"Wow," Penny breathed.

Wow, was right.

Stalactites hung from the ceiling of the cavern, their pearly surface gleaming in the low light. There had to be thousands of them in the small cavern. Some of them were so long they nearly touched the surface of the water.

Beyond them on the cavern walls, drawings covered the surface, all of them depicting what Keira thought was likely Hades and his kingdom.

"This place must have been dry at one time," Ty remarked, turning in a circle to look at the cavern walls. "Some of this artwork is incredible. The stories depicted here are amazing." He looked down at Penny. "I wish Dad was here to see it. He would love this."

Ketl's clicks echoed off the rocks, bringing their attention back to the water. The cavernous space made it sound like Ketl had his entire family with him.

"What did he say?" Keira asked.

"The passageway continues through there," Penny pointed opposite where they had entered. A hole in the wall yawned, dark and menacing. "He says there are some narrow spots, so we may need to shift again."

More clicks echoed off the walls.

"He says we need to hurry. We still have a ways to go and the sun is dropping."

The clicks dropped in volume, but were no less earnest.

Penny smiled and stroked the creature's head. "He wishes us luck and that he was happy to serve a member of Thetis's family."

She hugged the beast tightly. "Thank you for your help, Ketl. I hope I see you again one day."

The big beast snuffled and nuzzled his nose on her cheek before diving beneath the water, a ripple the only sign of its path through the water back to the hole from which they emerged.

Heeding Ketl's warning, they hurried through the water toward the dark hole. Their feet hit the ground beneath them as the water grew shallower until Keira was waist deep when they reached the void.

Shoulder to shoulder, they stood, staring into the dark space. Keira's hand found Leo's. Trepidation coursed through her as she tried to look past the darkness. It was no use, though. The light she made seemed to stop at the entrance to the tunnel, refusing to go further.

"Do you see anything?" she asked him.

"No," he replied, voice low. "It's complete darkness."

He squeezed her fingers and released her hand. "Let's go. We're running out of time."

Sucking in a deep breath, Keira stepped forward into the abyss.

Leo's eyes strained in the darkness. Keira's light couldn't penetrate more than a few feet in front of them, no matter how bright she made it. The darkness swallowed it whole. Even with his heightened vision, Leo couldn't see past the shadows. So far, only rock had greeted them in the dark.

Rock and silence.

As quickly as they dared, they moved through the waist-deep water. Ketl had been right about the narrow spots. There were indeed times when Ty and Leo were forced to shift to fit their bulk through. Penny squeaked through in places, while Keira's small form let her squeeze through with few problems. Only one place required them all to shift. It bottlenecked to a space of only about three feet tall and about a foot wide. They simply shifted to their iguana forms and swam through.

Leo peered at his dive watch. They were getting close to sunset. In September, the sun hit the horizon around seven-thirty. It was three minutes past seven. Anxiety skated up his spine. They were cutting this close.

They traveled several more minutes before a new sound reached Leo's ears. He paused and motioned the others to freeze so he could listen.

"What?" Ty asked. "What's wrong?"

Leo held a finger to his lips and listened intently.

"Running water. Like rapids." He looked at his friends. "Be ready. This could get bumpy."

They began moving again, more urgently this time, sensing an end to the claustrophobic tunnel.

"I hear it now, too," Penny said.

The sound of the rushing water was getting louder. There was definitely some sort of whitewater ahead of them.

Again, Leo bemoaned the darkness. He didn't like walking into danger blind.

Another hundred feet had the current pulling at their legs. Leo grabbed Keira's hand, knowing if she lost her footing, the rapidly increasing flow would sweep her away.

Water rushed around them as the current increased. Whatever was causing it was getting closer.

Twenty feet later, Keira lost her footing.

"Leo!" She clung to him as she slipped on the wet rock. Using his strength, he lifted her out of the water and swung her behind him.

"Get on." He motioned to his back. "Just don't choke me."

She quickly leaped onto his back and wrapped her legs around his waist. Her tiny hands clutched fistfuls of his swim top.

Leo dove into the water and let the current carry him forward, swimming with it as the pace continued to increase. The sound was deafening. What was once a distant rumble was now a rushing roar.

"Get ready!" Leo shouted back at the others. He pulled Keira off his back, but held on to her. They were all at the mercy of the current now. Wherever it went, they were going, too.

The glow Keira created hit on a wall of rock in front of them. Leo's eyes widened as he realized they were headed straight for it.

Penny and Keira screamed. Leo grabbed Keira, wrapping his body around hers, and turned so he would hit first.

The impact never came. Instead, the bottom dropped out of his stomach as they plummeted straight down.

CHAPTER 42

Water roared around them as they fell, their shouts of surprise and fear echoing off the rocky walls. Leo gasped for breath as water sluiced over his face. He clung to Keira's hand, terrified if he let go he would lose her when they finally reached the bottom of the waterfall.

They plunged several hundred feet through the darkness before an orange glow appeared below them. Leo tried to make out what lay ahead, but the cascade of water around them was too great. It kept dousing him as they fell, forcing him to concentrate on keeping his head out of the flow.

The walls narrowed. Leo took a deep breath just as he was completely submerged in the torrent. He bounced off the wall. Pain lanced through his shoulder, but still he clung to Keira's hand, determined not to lose her in the raging water. He threw his free arm up to protect his head.

The strange glow got brighter. As the tunnel widened and flattened out, they passed through an invisible barrier that made goosebumps break out on his skin and shivers race up his spine.

Leo's head broke the surface on the other side of the barrier, and he inhaled deeply. He managed a quick peek at his surroundings before the torrent pushed him under the water again.

What he saw in that quick peek was enough to curl his toes.

They were in hell.

CHAPTER 43

Panic gripped Keira in its icy grasp as the water churned around her, pushing her down the tunnel. Only Leo's crushing grip on her hand kept her oriented to anything.

When the glow from beneath got brighter, she nearly sobbed in relief, knowing they were almost out of the washing machine the river had become.

Like a champagne bottle, the four of them popped free in a cascade of water from the narrow passage and into the wide expanse of the underworld Acheron River.

Limbs heavy, Keira floated for a moment to catch her breath before she made her way to the river's edge. Coughs racked her body as she expelled the river water that made it into her lungs. Exhausted, she let Leo pull her into the shallows where she sank onto her butt.

Chest heaving, she rested her head on her knees. Leo sank down next to her with a groan, Penny and Ty not far behind.

"That," Ty croaked, "was intense."

A hysterical laugh bubbled up in Keira's throat. She squashed it back and took a deep breath instead. Lifting her head, that breath got stuck in her lungs.

Across the river, an eerie mist swirled, backlit by a flickering orange glow. Towering gates made of iron rose high above the river, set into a stone wall several stories high. It stretched along the river's bank as far as the eye could see.

In front of the gates, a solemn line of souls stood waiting for entrance into the afterlife. At the head of the line, a giant three-headed dog with the tail of a dragon towered above everyone, a sentry to Hades's dark kingdom. Keira shuddered at the sight of the dog. Somehow, she had to find the courage to walk past that thing.

Maybe she could put a funny hat on its head to make it look less threatening, she mused, then immediately scoffed at herself. Knowing her luck, that would make it angry and it would eat her.

"Holy shit." Ty's soft epithet echoed what the rest of them were thinking. They had truly landed in another world.

From the dock across the river at the base of the gates, a boat pulled away and headed toward them. As it got closer, Keira could see it was roughhewn, made of the darkest wood she had ever seen. It vaguely reminded her of a Venetian gondola, the ends sweeping up into a point. It was wider, though, and without ornamentation.

Seated at the helm of the boat was a cloaked figure; his head bent as he slowly rowed the craft across the flowing river.

Fear tightened Keira's chest as the boat came closer. A feeling of menace and dread flowed off this being more than any other they had met so far, including Hades and The Empusa. Its presence was heavy, like a wet blanket on a hot, humid summer day.

Keira stood, feeling vulnerable sitting in the river.

"Charon," Penny said quietly at her side.

Hot wind blew down over the wall, stirring the fine hairs around Keira's face as they waited for Charon to make his way to them. Apprehension twisted in her gut. Now that they were actually here, the magnitude of what they were trying to accomplish came crashing down on her.

This was insanity. How could four humans—demigod abilities or not—think they could compete with what was on the other side of that wall? She could only imagine the things that lived over there. What horrors awaited them on this journey?

Only her love for Leo kept her feet rooted in the river. She wasn't doing this to save the world. It was never about that for her. No matter what reasons Leo tried to get her to do this for, she couldn't do it for anything other than to save his soul. Saving the rest of the world and the world of the gods was just a bonus.

Looking at their surroundings, she could just imagine the things Hades would do to Leo's soul if it was his to do with as he pleased for all eternity. There was no way she was going to let that happen. Even if it killed her, his soul would not stay locked in Hades's staff.

But she had to admit, looking at the underworld, the task to capture Hecate seemed impossible.

The roughly carved boat bumped into the shallows in front of them. Keira stood shoulder to shoulder with Penny, Ty, and Leo, and faced Charon as he stepped from the vessel.

Her heart raced as the immortal being came toward them. At least nine feet tall, he was covered in a dark cloak that looked like it had been dipped in oil and dirt. He stopped in front of them and raised long, pale, spindly fingers to the hood covering his head and face. When he pulled it back, Keira fought not to recoil from the sight.

Every inch of his gaunt face not hidden by the long, dirty, tangled black beard, was covered in streaks of filth. What skin she could see underneath looked pasty and sallow. His lengthy, curly dark hair hung in hanks, as filthy and tangled as his beard.

But it was his eyes that were truly horrifying. Flames rippled in the sockets where eyes should be.

He pointed a thin finger at them.

"You must pay the ferryman to cross." His voice rasped and snapped like his fiery eyes.

Leo stepped forward, one fist outstretched. He unfurled his fingers to reveal the coins given to them by Hades.

"Our fare, ferryman."

The coins clinked as Leo dropped them into Charon's hand. Keira held her breath as the monster stared down at the coins for several long moments.

Curling his fingers around them, Charon put the coins in a pocket on his robe and motioned them toward the boat.

"Come." Charon turned and walked back to his vessel.

"Goddamn," Ty exhaled and rolled his shoulders as the ferryman walked away from them. "He is one scary fucker. Hades knew what he was doing when he made Charon the ferryman."

Keira agreed.

Silently, they followed Charon to the boat and climbed aboard. Keira huddled close to Leo, hands clutched around his. Charon pushed the boat off the river bed and slowly began to row them across to the other side.

CHAPTER 44

T he wall loomed ever closer as they neared the opposite bank. Leo stared up at it and the towering gates. This place was beyond imagination. He knew going into this the Greek underworld would be dark and eerie, but in reality it was like death personified. Silent and absolute.

He didn't know what he expected, but the sense of silence down here was not it. It was spine-chilling. The waterfall made noise as it crashed into the river, but even that was muffled.

It didn't echo, he realized. His gaze swung to the cliff that stretched up so high he couldn't see the top. It should echo, but for some reason it didn't.

Beyond the noise of the waterfall, there was nothing. Just silence.

Shaking off his unease, Leo turned to peruse the line of souls standing so somberly outside the kingdom's gates; their vapid countenances statue-like until they had to shuffle forward as another soul made it through to the other side. It was like watching a silent movie. No noise accompanied their movement.

"I don't see Hermes," Ty said, leaning forward. "Think we missed him?"

Leo looked at his watch. They still had five minutes until sunset. He showed Ty the time. "Only if he has a different clock than us. I just hope he keeps his word and shows up." More than likely, Hermes waited for them on the other side of those massive gates.

The boat docked a minute later, and the four friends wasted no time clamoring out of the vessel. Their feet thudded as they ran up the dock to the gate, loud in the thick silence. They by-passed the long line of souls waiting to get inside.

Without warning, the three-headed sentry at the gate lunged at them, snarling, its jaws snapping only feet away as it came to the end of its chain.

The group skidded to a halt. Keira screamed and hid behind Leo, her hands clutching his shirt. He could feel her trembling.

Ty pushed Penny behind him, and he and Leo faced the beast.

"That's Cerberus," Ty told him. "It's his job to keep the living out of the underworld."

Wonderful, Leo thought. His mind raced as it ran tactics, trying to come up with a way past the beast still snarling at them. He could easily leap over the wall, carrying Keira, while Ty and Penny could fly, but they risked landing in the depths of Tartarus if they went over blind. They could also miss Hermes if they didn't go through the gate.

Something Athena said gave him an idea.

Not bothering to think about what he was doing too much, Leo stepped forward within Cerberus's reach.

"Leo!" Keira whispered fiercely. She grabbed his hand, frantically. Her fear was palpable. "What are you doing?"

"Trust me, *chère*." He tried to reassure her with a look, but her eyes were still wide with abject terror. He wished he had the time to really talk to her and calm her, but they were down to their last couple of minutes.

Disentangling his fingers from hers, he took another step forward. She grabbed his shirt again, but didn't interfere. Leo started talking.

"Hi Cerberus. We've come at the behest of your master. My name is Leo."

Cerberus snarled again, but not as viciously.

Leo stood his ground in the face of the enormous jaws, dripping saliva only feet from his face. Cerberus was every bit as tall as Charon, each of his three heads the size of a man, all filled with long, pointy teeth.

"We know your duties are to keep the living out. We don't intend to stay. We don't intend to take anything from behind the gates except my soul—"

That statement elicited a flurry of barking and snapping. Keira whimpered behind his back. Leo held up his hands in supplication, but didn't step back.

"Hades took it, Cerberus. He promised I could have it back if we stopped Hecate and brought her to him for punishment."

The snarling quieted slightly. Hope surged through Leo. Cerberus was listening.

Leo took another careful step forward and reached out a hand toward the beast. His shirt pulled tight as Keira refused to let go. He had a feeling she was ready to yank him back if Cerberus suddenly decided he wanted Leo for dinner.

The growls increased again, and Leo froze momentarily. He heard Keira suck in a breath behind him, but thankfully, she continued to stay quiet.

When Cerberus calmed once more, Leo edged forward again. He drew on all of his military training to keep his heart rate calm as he crept toward the giant animal.

He stopped twice more before Cerberus finally allowed Leo to touch him. Leo couldn't stop the quick double thump of his heart as his hand landed on the nose of the animal's center head.

Cerberus's growls quickly stopped as Leo slid his palm up and over the beast's nose. His sleek fur was soft under Leo's fingers, surprising him. After seeing Charon, Leo thought Cerberus would be as horrifying as the ferryman, but he felt like a regular dog.

The beast bent its center head and Leo ran his hand up, scratching the animal between the eyes.

A low rumble came from Cerberus, and his eyes rolled as Leo continued to scratch the colossal beast's head. The other two heads turned and butted Leo's arm, wanting pet as well.

Disbelief rolled through him. And no small measure of delight. This was incredible.

"Jesus Christ." Ty murmured. "Athena wasn't kidding. You're the fucking animal whisperer."

"That's right," Leo crooned, speaking to both Ty and Cerberus. He kept scratching all three heads as he spoke. "We're going to go meet Hermes now, Cerberus. I promise that the only thing we will take with us when we leave is my soul."

Leo's words seemed to penetrate the bliss his hands wrought. The animal stepped back. All three heads eyed him warily, but the beast did not try to stop Leo when he stepped around him. Keira clung to him, using him as a shield between herself and the creature.

Not looking back, Leo motioned Ty and Penny to follow and made a beeline for the gate. They had only seconds to get through that doorway.

He pulled Keira forward and wrapped her in his arms. The world around them became a streaky blur as he darted for the gate, using his newfound speed. The large, towering gate had a smaller doorway set in it through which the souls passed. Leo dove through it just as the alarm on his watch beeped.

He twisted, so he didn't land on Keira and hit the ground hard on his back, knocking the wind out of himself.

Keira rolled off and immediately bent over him, concern written all over her pretty face. "Leo! Oh my God, are you okay?"

He wanted to reassure her he was fine, but all he could do was lie there staring up at the strange sky, struggling to breathe.

"Quite the entrance, human," Hermes intoned.

He looked up at the god standing over them. An amused smiled quirked one side of Hermes's mouth.

With a gasp, Leo finally filled his lungs. He sucked in another breath before managing to speak.

"But we're here," he croaked out. He pushed up onto his knees and stood. *Oh, that hurt.* He cradled his aching ribs, hoping he hadn't broken any.

Footsteps sounded as Ty and Penny caught up with them.

Tiny hands grasped his face as Keira forced him to look at her. "Are you all right?" Her eyes raked over him, looking for damage, and lingered on his chest where he clutched his ribcage.

Her rich, chocolate eyes met his once more. "You landed so hard. And with me on top of you."

He took her slight wrists in his hands, noting the fine tremor running through her. "I'm fine, *chère.* Just knocked the wind out of myself."

She studied him a moment longer before nodding. Leo watched a calmness settle over her. Her spine straightened and her eyes hardened, the tremor in her hands gone. The badass prosecutor was back.

Before Leo could do more than admire her spirit, she spun around to face Hermes, moving almost as fast as he had darted through the gate.

"Hello, Hermes. Can we go now?"

Hermes laughed. "Hello, witch. I like your spirit."

Leo bit back a smile as Keira frowned up at the god. She was most definitely not amused.

"That's nice. So, can we go?" She propped her hands on her hips and stared Hermes down.

The god's mouth twitched again, but he wisely didn't comment further. Instead, he bent and picked up one of the four backpacks at his feet. He held it out to Leo.

"Persephone left provisions for you all. More than anyone, she is aware of what life is like down here and what is necessary for survival. I have a pack for each of you. It will get you through your journey here."

Leo took the pack, rifling through it, while Hermes passed out the others. He had enough food and water to get through at least a day, as well as some rope, a knife, a set of gloves, and a lighter. It looked like standard survival gear.

"Come. We must be going." Hermes spun on his heel and marched off into the fields.

Following along behind the god, Leo studied their surroundings. The other side of the wall was like looking at the Earth, only on a condensed scale. Grasslands, lush fields, vast areas of water, and mountains were all within view. As much as it was the same, it was still vastly different. Leo couldn't really put his finger on why. It was just a feeling that pervaded. There was an otherworldliness about the underworld that marked it as unique.

Inside the wall, the strange glow persisted, but the sky was bright, if a little off in color. Giant birds circled high overhead. In the distance, Hades's palace stood high on a hill. Past the palace, the same green fields they walked on now flourished, flowers dotting the lush landscape in what Leo surmised to be the Ancient Greek version of heaven.

The shimmer of water was just visible at the edge of the fields. From the information Jack gave them, Leo knew there was an ocean in the underworld that contained some of the scariest creatures he hoped to never see.

Bordering the field to their right as well as slightly off to their left were mountain ranges, rising sharply from the ground. The jagged peaks hid behind the dark clouds that boiled on the edge of the fields.

Directly to his left, the clouds boiled black. The fields beneath were brown and barren. Desolate. They disappeared into a gray fog of smoke. Leo didn't want to know what laid beyond the fog.

Ty walked up beside Leo. "I hope we don't run into any problems, or we're going to be cutting this close."

Leo nodded. He had the same thought when he first saw the landscape. "If we get down to the wire—and we have Hecate—I'm going to use my speed to get her to Hades before the deadline."

"Why don't you do that, anyway? We can catch up."

Immediately, Leo shook his head. "I don't want us to split up unless it's absolutely necessary. We don't know what dangers lurk here. Besides, I think we *need* to stay together. It hit me when we were following Ketl through that passageway just how important each one of us is to this journey. We wouldn't have made it through the passage if Penny couldn't shift and if she hadn't shared the ability with you. We have to work together to make it through this. I think it's part of the prophecy. And why the four of *us* were chosen to fulfill it."

"And we wouldn't have made it past Cerberus without your animal whispering," Ty concluded. "All right. We're a team through this.

But that means you can't just take off like you did at that gas station yesterday."

"Agreed. I definitely won't do that here." Leo looked out at the foreign landscape and the imposing castle in the distance. Getting lost or separated here could mean more than the loss of his soul. It could mean the loss of all their lives.

CHAPTER 45

The group moved quickly through the field and into Elysium, the long grass swishing softly as they walked. Keira stared in wonder, marveling at the beauty surrounding them. Elysium, at least, was magical. A soft, golden glow permeated the air. It felt like she was walking through a dream. The edges to everything were softer, less defined. Occasionally, they would walk past a soul who wandered blissfully unaware through the wildflower fields.

Keira embraced the peace pervading the field, letting it soothe her frazzled nerves and calm her racing heart. The last few hours had been stressful, to say the least. She was glad to finally have a bit of a respite. All too soon, they would be back in a place where things went bump in the night and weren't afraid to attack them.

Here, though, in the heart of heaven, they were safe.

"You holding up okay?" Leo asked, coming up beside her.

"Yes." She smiled at him and looped her arm through his. "I'm trying not to think too much about what lies ahead and just relax for a bit. Recharge my batteries."

She took in his still tense face and the rigid set to his shoulders. "You should try to do the same, you know. We're in heaven." She gestured at the glory around them. "Literally. Trouble will come soon enough."

He rolled his shoulders. "I know. But this place—it's just weird. Even though I know we're in Elysium, it still feels off. Living beings aren't meant to see all this. To be here. It's so out of the norm it's throwing a wrench into my strategic thinking abilities. My brain is telling me one thing, but my instincts are shouting this place isn't normal, like a bright neon sign flashing, 'DANGER.' It's just keeping me on edge."

Keira could understand that. She agreed that even as beautiful as it was, Elysium felt strange. The air was thick, almost tangible in feel, but it wasn't heavy like a summer day ripe with humidity. Because they were still alive, they were straddling two planes of existence and wading through the barrier between the worlds.

"Well, we'll be back in the danger zone soon enough and then your tactical abilities won't be confused anymore."

"Hopefully, they won't be overwhelmed. My brain doesn't think in magic, and I have a feeling Hecate is going to throw the book at us."

Unease skittered down Keira's spine at Leo's words. She agreed with him on that front. Hecate would use everything she could think of to stop them. They would need to be on their toes if they wanted to make it out of this alive.

She hugged Leo's arm just a little tighter, seeking something normal in their currently bizarre world.

Elysium soon gave way to the River Lethe. Murky, it lazily flowed past them, in no hurry to go anywhere. Taking their cue from Hermes, Penny and Ty shifted into birds and flew across the river, Leo and Keira in tow.

Safely on the other side, the Asphodel Fields greeted them. Similar to Elysium, souls milled in grassy fields, seeming oblivious to the mortals walking among them. It lacked the golden glow of Elysium, however, appearing much more mundane. This was the heaven of the ordinary man.

The group plodded through, fatigue pulling at their bodies. Keira's shoulders drooped as she walked. It was an effort to put one foot in front of the other with every step. It had to be close to midnight. She really hoped Leo planned for them to sleep before they went after Hecate. After fighting off The Empusa and her cohorts, and then their long trek through the Acheron and the underworld today, she was running on empty.

Keira glanced over at Leo, who didn't seem any worse for wear.

She smothered a snort.

Of course he didn't look any worse for wear. *He* had slept well the night before. Not to mention he was in top physical condition and could probably run on nothing but adrenaline and sheer determination for days.

She wondered if he got tired now that he was superhuman.

Mind occupied with her thoughts, Keira didn't see the dip in the ground. Her foot rolled off the edge of it and she went flying, landing hard on her knees.

"Keira!" Leo came running. "Are you all right, *chère*?"

Rolling onto her back, Keira laid there and stared up at the strangely glowing underworld sky. Now that she was down, she had no desire to get up again.

"*Chère*?" Leo kneeled next to her.

Weakly, she waved a hand at him. "I'm fine. Just tired." She turned her head to look at him. "We're going to get to sleep soon, right?"

His smile was quick and bright. "For a few hours, yes. But we need to get closer first."

Keira groaned loud and long.

Leo chuckled and held out a hand. "Come on. We aren't far."

With another groan, she took his hand and let him help her to her feet. He kept hold of her hand as they started off across the grassy plain once again. Keira's knees ached from where they slammed into the ground, but she trudged on. With each step, she just kept reminding herself she was getting closer to the chance to rest.

Finally, Keira looked up to see the green grassy plains of Asphodel Fields giving way to a gray, desolate landscape that rose sharply into jagged peaks. A narrow pass cleaved the mountains in two.

Hermes pointed at the pass. "This is where I leave you. Go through there and you will see Hecate's palace." He turned to look at them, his expression serious. "Stay alert once you reach the outer walls of her fortress. Expect the unexpected. Things will not be as they seem. Do not stray from the path. Good luck to you."

"Thank you, Hermes," Leo said.

Hermes gave a small nod, his expression turning slightly sad. "You know, she has been my friend for a very long time. I'm sorry it has to end this way."

A small pang of remorse struck Keira. She felt for Hermes. Losing a friend was never easy.

Keira briefly laid a hand on Hermes's arm. "We appreciate you helping, especially knowing what she means to you."

His nod this time was quick, and he wiped his expression clear so the stoic god-mask was in place once more. "Thanks are unnecessary. Just stop her." Without further ado, he took two running steps and flew away, back toward Hades's palace.

"So, now what?" Keira turned back to Leo.

"Now, we rest."

Keira groaned and sank to the ground. "Gladly."

Penny flopped next to her. "You two can keep an eye out." She slid her pack off and laid it on the ground. Not bothering to even take off her shoes, she stretched out, using the pack as a pillow. "I'm sleeping."

Keira followed suit, ignoring the chuckles from the men. Her body was officially done. She didn't care that she was lying in the middle of the open on the rocky ground in the Greek version of the afterlife. She was going to sleep and nothing short of another demon attack would keep her awake.

CHAPTER 46

T he alarm on Leo's dive watch woke him several hours later. He and Ty decided they were safe enough where they were to get a few hours of rest themselves. Not long after Keira and Penny drifted off, both men laid down. Leo wrapped himself around Keira and quickly fell asleep.

Shaking off his morning brain fog, Leo sat up and looked around. This place was eerie. The sky was continually bright and had an odd orange glow to it. Even colored blue over Elysium and the Asphodel Fields, it had an orange cast. Like the fires of hell couldn't be contained to Tartarus.

He turned to look over his shoulder at the pass they needed to travel through to get to Hecate. A few more hours and he would have the answer to his problems in his hands.

Leo rubbed at the persistent ache in his chest. It had been his constant companion for the last eighty-eight days. The sad thing was, he had started to get used to it. Oh, it still hurt and he was constantly aware of it, but it was background noise more often than not.

His eyes traveled down to the woman still sleeping beside him. She, more than anything, made him not notice the pain. When he was with her, he focused on something other than the deep, black abyss where his soul used to be.

But soon, he would be whole again. Hecate wasn't going to win, and neither was Hades. Athena and Artemis didn't give him all of this power just so he could fail.

Knowing time was short, Leo shook Keira awake. "*Chère*. Hey, it's time to get up."

She grumbled and swatted at his hand.

Leo bit back a grin. He knew she was tired, but they simply couldn't afford to stay put any longer. There were too many unknowns ahead for them to linger.

"Baby, wake up. We need to go." He shook her gently again.

This time, her eyes opened into slits, and she glared at him. "I hate you right now."

He grinned at her. "Come on, *chère*. We have a witch to stop, and I need you."

Groaning, she sat up. "We get home and I'm sleeping for an entire day." She tugged at the hairband holding back her hair. "After a long, hot shower. That river water was gross. My hair is crunchy." With a grimace at the texture, she rewound it into a more secure bun.

His was a little too. The water through the tunnel had been full of sediment, and it had dried into a fine coating on their hair and skin. They all needed a good bath.

"Do you have any pain pills in that little pack of goodies you brought? My muscles are killing me."

Leo dug into the waist belt he wore. It contained mostly first aid items, including pain killers. He handed her two tablets. She dug a bottle of water out of her backpack and washed them down.

"Eat something, too. You're going to need the energy." Leo pointed at her pack.

Keira did as he said and rummaged through her bag. Leo took his own advice pulled out two protein bars from his backpack. He peeled the wrapper off of a chocolate chip bar and took a bite.

Chewing the sticky bar, Leo walked over to Ty and kicked his foot. "Wake up, Farris."

Ty grumbled obscenities at him as he came awake, but quickly rolled to a sitting position. Penny, jostled by her husband waking, looked up at them both with the same glare Keira gave him just minutes earlier.

"You are entirely too perky for getting so little sleep." Penny sat up and rubbed her eyes.

Leo just grinned. His adrenaline was pumping, erasing all traces of fatigue. The end of their journey was through that pass. He was ready for this to be done.

They all made quick work of breakfast and soon were heading toward the yawning gap between two towering peaks, Leo leading the way.

The journey was tedious and difficult. The rugged path through the mountains made their progress slow. After they walked for several hours, taking occasional small breaks to rehydrate, Leo glanced at his watch and grimaced. They weren't making the kind of time they needed to if they were going to have Hecate by the end of the day. The rocky ground made keeping a smooth, even stride nearly impossible. Coming back through here with Hecate in tow was going to be quite a challenge.

They needed a new game plan.

He turned to Ty. "I hate to say it, but we need to fly." He pointed at his watch. "It's getting late."

Ty glanced at his own watch and nodded. He looked over at his wife, who had stopped at Leo's words. "What do you think, babe? Eagle?"

She frowned. "For us, but I don't know how we'd carry something that big that far." She eyed her husband speculatively. "Do you think you can split the change? I know I can. I did it when Keira and I escaped the fire at my parents' house. We could fly over as eagles with them riding as some kind of animal. A small monkey, maybe. Something that could hold on and not fall off."

Ty shrugged. "Let's try it."

Leo barely had time to register Ty's words before Ty reached out and touched his shoulder. A tingle ran over Leo's body as Ty shifted him. Within seconds, he was only a foot tall, staring up at Penny and Keira, who towered above him. Ty stood next to him in eagle form.

Leo held out one hand to see it covered in fur, not feathers. It still amazed him every time they shifted. To see Ty shift to one animal and make him another just blew him away.

Ty let go, and they both shifted human again.

Penny smiled at them both and nodded. "That answers that. Do you think you can hold the split through the pass?"

Ty nodded. "Yeah. Holding the split was the easy part. It was getting the split to happen that took some concentration."

"The packs didn't shift again, so we'll have to carry them just like we did across the river," Keira stated. "Thankfully, they aren't that heavy."

Leo nodded and shrugged out of his backpack. This was the only problem with their method of travel. Their clothes and the things closest to their bodies shifted with them, but not anything with any bulk to it.

"Put your hands on my shoulders," Ty instructed. He set his backpack on the ground next to Leo's. "You can hop right on then once we shift."

Doing as he was told, Leo moved behind Ty and in moments, he was a small monkey clinging to an eagle. Leo couldn't help but shake his head in disbelief. His life had become surreal in the last few months.

Ty and Penny took flight, backpacks clutched in their talons, two small monkeys clinging to their backs. They winged their way through the pass, traveling much faster than they had on foot. It would not be long before they reached the other side.

CHAPTER 47

Keira peered over Penny's feathered head as they flew between the mountains, the rocky terrain sailing past far faster than Keira found comfortable. She clung tightly to Penny's eagle body and prayed it would be over soon.

They rounded a particularly sharp bend in the pass and popped free of the mountains. A dark valley spread out beneath them. Tall pines covered it in its entirety, jagged edges of rock poking through. It was desolate and depressing in its bleakness.

In the center of the valley sat a massive stone fortress. Its high walls surrounded a large colonnaded house and its gardens. It too held a bleakness and an isolation that seemed absolute. It was like a black hole that sucked in all the happiness and wonder in the world and refused to let it escape. Keira suppressed a shiver. It still amazed her how badly Hecate had fooled everyone. For centuries, she had been cast as a benevolent goddess, when in reality she was anything but.

Penny followed Ty's swooping form down to skim the tops of the trees, and Keira clung tightly to her back.

Could it be so easy as to fly right over the fortress walls? Keira's eyes darted all around, watching for danger. It could not be this easy to get to Hecate. Even if she didn't know exactly when they were coming, she wouldn't be unprepared for the eventuality.

Heeding Persephone and Hermes's warnings, they flew over the narrow path through the trees. Keira could see things moving in the pines below. They were big enough to make her glad they had been warned. She hoped the things stayed hidden.

A thousand yards from the fortress, Ty hit an invisible wall. Penny saw him hit and quickly tried to pull up and turn away, but it was too late. She and Keira hit at nearly full speed. The impact was enough to knock Keira loose from her seat on Penny's back, and she went plummeting toward the ground.

CHAPTER 48

Trees and mountains whirled in and out of her vision as Keira tumbled toward the ground. Heart pounding frantically, she closed her eyes and called on the energy around her to slow her descent.

She felt the air press against her as she tried to slow herself and stop her end over end tumble. Grunting with effort, she managed to stop the tumble, but she was still falling.

The impact had knocked her sideways off the path. The tree tops rushed up to greet her. Pine needles slapped her face, making her wince. She threw everything she had into putting a bubble around herself and pushing air up from below in an attempt to stop her descent.

She bounced off of a tree branch before she finally gained control.

Slowly, she lowered herself to the forest floor.

As soon as her feet touched the ground, she let go of her bubble and collapsed in a boneless heap. Heedless of the dry pine needles poking into her skin, she laid there for a moment, panting from the exertion and adrenaline.

That was quite the ride.

Awareness of where she landed slowly sank in as she laid there, catching her breath.

Abruptly, she sat up, adrenaline kicking back in as she realized she was in the trees.

Off the path.

Where the scary shit lived.

Scrambling to her feet, she looked around, trying to get her bearings. She had tumbled and twisted so much in the air she wasn't sure in which direction to go to find the path. The trees were extremely dense. She could be only a few yards from the edge of the woods and never know it. If she went the wrong way, she would end up further into no-man's-land and the territory of those gigantic shadowy shapes she saw from the air.

An eagle's cry from above had her whipping her head up to stare at the gray sky peeking through the trees.

Penny!

Keira waved frantically. "Here! I'm here!"

Penny turned abruptly at Keira's shout.

Keira waved again. Penny spotted her and dove through the trees.

She landed at Keira's side and quickly shifted.

"Are you all right?" Penny grabbed her in a tight hug. "Thank God you can do what you can do. I tried to dive after you, but by the time I righted myself you were already passing into the trees." She pushed back and ran an assessing eye over Keira. "You *are* okay, right?"

Keira nodded. "Yes, I'm fine. But we need to get out of here." She gestured to the dense forest. "We're off the path."

Penny's eyes widened almost comically as she realized they were indeed deep in the forest. Quickly, she pointed to her right.

"It's that way."

Both women scooped up their backpacks and dashed in the path's direction. They only traveled a few yards when the ground shook and a loud rumble sounded through the forest.

Keira skidded to a halt next to Penny and looked around anxiously. That sounded like footsteps.

Giant, booming, belonged to something enormous, footsteps.

The trees to their left swayed as more footsteps echoed through the trees.

An eagle's cry overhead had them looking up. Ty circled the tree-tops, while Leo leaned over his side, still in monkey form, and pointed frantically in the direction of the path.

Penny and Keira's eyes connected briefly before they both took off running as fast as they could for the edge of the trees.

Heavy footfalls echoed behind them, closer than before. Keira chanced a glance back over her shoulder.

What she saw made her heart stop. Fear skated down her spine to jumpstart her heart. It beat wildly, fueled by adrenaline.

"Oh my God! Penny, go faster!"

Behind them, a three-bodied giant stomped through the trees, eyes locked on Keira and Penny. Fused at the hip, the three bodies stood back-to-back, enabling the creature to see in every direction.

He charged at them, knocking down trees. Keira and Penny shrieked and ducked as the giant ripped a tree out of the ground—roots and all—and sent it sailing over their heads. The huge pine crashed ten yards ahead of them, blocking their way.

Penny veered right to go around the tree, and Keira followed.

"He's gaining on us!" Keira cast another glance over her shoulder. "We're not going to make it!"

Another tree landed in front of them, forcing them to veer away again.

Penny halted and grabbed Keira's hand. "Hop on!"

Keira leaped onto Penny's back even as they shifted. Penny morphed into her tried-and-true mountain lion with Keira as a monkey again, and took off, using every bit of the big cat's speed.

The giant roared as they sprinted for the path. The sound of his footfalls increased as he ran after them.

Keira chanced another glance over her shoulder. He still gained on them.

She whipped her head back around, searching for the break in the trees. Only towering pines met her eyes.

More trees landed in their path. Penny zigzagged through them. Keira closed her eyes and held on for dear life, listening as the giant's breath huffed out ever closer as it ran after them.

CHAPTER 49

Leo peered down at the action below with increasing worry. The giant was gaining on the women, even though Penny raced away in lion form. He kept throwing trees at them, forcing Penny to slow down and turn back several times to go around the fallen trees.

Waving his little monkey arm, Leo motioned Ty to go down into the pines. They quickly swooped down until they were just above the giant's reach.

Ty let out a screech to get Penny and Keira's attention and let them know they were there to help. As soon as Keira looked up, Leo jumped, knowing Ty would understand what he intended to do.

He fell smoothly between the branches, shifting human mid-air to land in a crouch between the women and the giant.

The beast skidded to a halt and glared down at the human now blocking his path.

Ty's big wings beat the air as he landed next to Leo. He shifted human.

"That's Geryon," Ty informed him. "He's supposed to be dead. Hercules killed him."

"Great." Leo stared up at the creature studying them. Hecate was either bringing dead giants back to life now or had released him from Tartarus. It made Leo wonder what else she had revived or released.

"You have a plan, I hope."

Leo's mouth quirked. "I always have a plan."

Ty shot him an impatient look.

Leo's grin grew, and he shrugged. "We'll use our strength and my speed."

"To what? Knock him out? He has three heads."

"We're going to bury him."

Ty's eyebrows shot up. "Bury him."

"Yep. In the trees. We need to get him on the ground and then we just knock a bunch of trees over on him." Leo's mind raced as he calculated how many trees they would need to bring down and how long it would take to do it.

Quickly glancing over his shoulder, he spotted Keira and Penny hovering several feet behind them, human again.

"Keira, Ty and I are going to bring him to the ground. Once we get him there, you need to keep him down until the rest of us can topple enough trees to keep him from getting up again."

"More vines. Got it."

Leo turned to Ty. "I'm going to disorient him. You knock his feet out from under him."

The giant, tired of being ignored, yelled something in Greek, bringing everyone's attention back to the problem at hand.

Face menacing, Geryon reached forward, making a swipe at the men. Ty jumped back, but Leo did the opposite. A second before Geryon's hand reached him, Leo leaped onto his fingers and scampered up the giant's arm. He was at the center head in moments.

Geryon hollered and spun, all three heads trying to get a bead on Leo, but he moved too quickly.

Racing around the giant's shoulders, Leo made him spin, pulling him off balance.

"Now, Ty!"

A jolt rocked the giant's body as Ty rammed his legs. Leo slammed his fist into the temple of the center head just before another jolt shook the beast. He glanced down to see Ty and Penny tag-teaming the giant's legs. They had both shifted into muskox and were ramming Geryon's legs with their hard heads.

Leo leveled a few more strikes to Geryon's many heads until the giant wobbled.

"Hit him hard!"

Ty and Penny backed up and ran at Geryon, striking him at the ankles on two different bodies. Finally, the giant began to lose his balance.

"Again!"

They rammed him once more, and Geryon spun wildly. Vines shot from the ground to wrap around the giant's arms and tug him toward the forest floor. Leo rode him like a surfboard as he went down. With a mighty boom, Geryon hit the ground.

More vines quickly grew over Geryon's body, preventing him from getting up.

Leo jumped off and headed for the trees. He, along with Ty and Penny, toppled tree after tree while Keira kept Geryon pinned to the ground. In minutes, they had him buried beneath a mountain of pine trees.

"Will that hold him?" Penny asked as they regrouped.

Leo eyed the pile critically. It didn't budge. "I think so. And he only needs to stay that way long enough for us to get into the fortress."

"Well, I don't want to stick around to see how long our little game of pick-up sticks works. Let's go." Ty grabbed Penny's hand and headed toward the path.

Leo agreed. He wanted to be long gone when that giant worked his way out of the pile of trees.

CHAPTER 50

"So, what the hell did we run into up there?" Ty rubbed his head where he hit the invisible wall. They were finally out of the woods and headed down the path toward Hecate's fortress.

"Some kind of warding spell." Keira looked up at the sky. "We need to see if it extends all the way to the ground."

Hand out in front of herself, she began walking. Twenty yards down the path, she ran into the wall.

Crap.

"Leo, can you see the wall?" If he could see it, it could tell her a bit about how Hecate made it.

He stared at it for a moment, a slightly unfocused look in his eyes, before he shook his head.

"What does that mean?" Penny asked.

"It means," Keira frowned, "that she didn't make the wall with an energy field. She used a spell."

"So, how do we get around it?"

Everything Keira knew about warding spells flew through her head. Unfortunately, she didn't have the things she needed to break the spell. That meant she needed to find a way around it.

She poked the wall with her finger. It felt pliable, like they *could* pass through it. *If* she could make a hole.

"I wonder if it keeps everything out or just us. I wish Hermes hadn't deserted us. If he could walk through it, it would tell me whether this is specific to us."

Mind churning, Keira could only think of a couple of options. "There are a couple of things we can try. First, I can put a bubble around us that 'shields' us from the spell. If that doesn't work, we can try digging a tunnel and going under it."

"Dig?" Penny gave her a dubious look.

Keira shrugged. "Without candles and herbs, there isn't much else we can try."

"Well, let's try your bubble thing first. I had enough digging when we buried our demon friends. If we could avoid that, that would be fantastic," Ty remarked.

"All right." Keira motioned them all closer. "Let's give this a whirl." She focused on building a bubble around them, much like the one she put over them in Leo's garage to deflect the bullets flying through the walls.

Cautiously, they crept closer to the ward. She really hoped this worked. She didn't want to dig that tunnel any more than Ty did.

The bubble glowed bright where it contacted the ward, but it didn't meet resistance. Ever so slowly, they moved forward. The true test would come when one of them tried to breach the ward.

Hand out slightly, Keira led the way as they approached the threshold. She watched the glow come closer to her hand.

Please, please let this work.

Keira held her breath and pushed her hand toward the threshold.

She met no resistance as she crossed to the other side of the barrier.

"Holy crap, it worked." Elation soared through her, and she stepped fully inside Hecate's shield.

The others quickly followed. Keira let go of the bubble.

"You are amazing, *chère*." Leo took her face in his hands and kissed her soundly.

She felt pretty amazing. Hecate kept throwing obstacles in their path, but they just kept knocking them down one-by-one. They were working as a team, utilizing each other's strengths, and kicking butt. It gave Keira hope they could keep pushing on through anything.

"Come on." Leo stepped back and took her hand. "Let's go figure out a way over that fortress wall."

The group jogged down the path, eyes peeled to the trees for any new dangers. Just because Hermes and Persephone said the creatures stayed in the trees didn't mean something intent on doing them harm wouldn't be on the path.

Keira sent up a silent prayer. They were due a little luck.

Two harrowing minutes later, they reached the wall. They all let out a sigh of relief as they regrouped against the tall stone structure.

"So, what's the plan, Oh Master-of-Strategy?"

Keira laughed as Leo leveled a dark look on Ty before he smiled.

"You can fly your ass up there and take a peek." Leo pointed to the top of the wall high above their heads.

One black eyebrow quirked on Ty's face. "Seriously?"

Leo's grin only grew. "Pick something small so she doesn't see you if she happens to be watching."

Ty muttered obscenities under his breath. "You suck, Devereaux." With a leap, Ty shifted mid-air into a tiny sparrow and flew up the wall.

Keira took a deep breath and leaned against the wall, enjoying the temporary reprieve from their hurried pace. She could feel her adrenaline ebbing now that they were past the giant and the shield. There was more danger to come, she knew, but at the moment it was quiet.

Taking a long draw of water, Keira used their momentary break to regroup. She shoved all thoughts of the giant and their harrowing escape from her mind and focused on what came next. She would love to be able to plan what was to come, but until Ty came back down to report what he saw, they were stuck in idle.

Mind adrift, Keira yelped when Ty suddenly landed in front of them, his enormous frame filling her field of vision.

Expression serious, he grabbed Leo's forearm.

"You need to see this."

Before any of them could react, Ty was taking off again as a sparrow, Leo a tiny lizard clutched in his feet.

Keira looked at Penny and arched a brow. She wanted to see what made Ty so anxious.

Penny shrugged and took Keira's hand. "I guess we should take a peek too."

In moments, they were soaring up the wall and landing atop it next to Ty and Leo. Penny and Ty kept Keira and Leo's tiny tails clutched in their feet to keep the connection as they stared out over the interior of the fortress walls.

A giant maze greeted them. And it wasn't an ordinary maze either. The walls shifted and changed position, seemingly at random. Dark shapes moved in the passageways. There was something lurking within the maze's walls. From the way they moved, they looked like dogs. Keira really hoped they weren't dogs. She would be walking through the maze in an energy bubble if they were.

Her little lizard body shivered at the thought of encountering that many of the four-legged, fanged beasts. She hated dogs.

Except Clyde. She actually missed the big mutt. She might even give him a hug when they got back to Charleston, and they picked him up from Colin.

A lizardy smile crossed her face. Leo would probably think she had lost her mind.

Ty motioned for them to head back to the base of the wall. Penny picked Keira up in her feet and flew down, the men right behind them.

"That's going to be tough to get through. We'll have to find a way around it. Or over it," Ty remarked once they were all human again.

"So we fly?" It seemed like a no-brainer to Keira. It was faster, and they avoided all the scary stuff in the maze. It was a win-win as far as she was concerned.

"We can't fly. She has sentries posted on the gables," Leo chimed in. "Some dragon-type thing."

Ty frowned fiercely. "I didn't see any creatures on the roof."

Leo just cocked an eyebrow.

Understanding dawned in Ty's eyes. "Super-sight. Right." He clapped his hands together. "So, no flying. How do we get through that crazy-ass maze?"

"The shifts in the walls were random, so there's no way to predict a path through it. I think it'll be safe for you or Penny to fly up and poke your head over the top long enough to help guide us. It's just going to take some patience and some fast moving."

Not one to waste time once a plan was made, Keira laid her hand on Penny's arm. "Let's get to it, then. We're burning daylight."

Leo nodded and touched Ty's shoulder. "You heard the woman. Let's go."

Ty grinned. "Hang on to your ass, Devereaux." In a blink, Ty was a small hawk, Leo a rat dangling from his talons. Like a shot, they were headed up the wall.

Keira watched them ascend and could understand why Ty chose the hawk. It was much faster and more maneuverable than the sparrow.

Following her husband's lead, Penny shifted them into the same creatures and took off. The wind whistled through Keira's little rat whiskers as they sailed to the top of the wall and dove over. The ground rushed up to meet her as Penny plummeted full speed toward it.

Keira closed her eyes tight. She trusted Penny not to slam her into the dirt, but that didn't mean she wanted to watch it rush up to meet her.

With an abrupt jerk, they slowed, and Keira's tiny feet touched the ground. Penny released her, then landed several feet away.

Keira shook off the shift and went to stand next to Leo. She stared at the towering greenery in front of them. It had to be two or three stories tall and at least two feet thick. She had never seen anything like it.

Feeling like her feet were rooted to the ground, she stared at the gap, yawning menacingly in the hedge to their left. Her heart thumped in her chest. Her brain yelled at her not to go in there. Whatever lurked within the maze's walls was sure to be frightening.

But it was the only way to get to Hecate.

Keira straightened her spine and took a deep breath. The witch better be in her fancy house on the other side. Screw Hades. Keira was going to kill the goddess herself if they had to go chasing her all over the underworld. It wouldn't matter at that point if they delivered her to Hades, dead or alive. They would be past the deadline to save Leo's soul. That alone would fuel her abilities enough to let her blast Hecate into oblivion.

Taking Leo's hand, she reminded herself she was with the animal whisperer, and headed for the gap.

As they crossed the threshold, the light seemed to disappear. The interior of the maze was gloomy, the atmosphere oppressive. *Dark.* In more ways than one.

Creaking from behind had Keira turning quickly, only to see the hedge rapidly grow across the gap, trapping them inside the maze.

"I guess there's no turning back now," Ty remarked, staring at the now closed gap.

"There was no turning back before the hedge closed." Leo headed left down the path, pulling Keira along. "Let's go get Hecate and end this."

Keira studied Leo as they walked. There was an edge to him now that wasn't there before they walked into the maze. It was a bit scary, actually. Her mild-mannered survival guide had suddenly morphed into the god that he was. The way he carried himself and the icy edge to his voice reminded her of Hermes, and even a bit like Hades.

She walked a little faster. The sooner they found Hecate, the sooner she would get the real Leo back. Keira couldn't help but wonder what was going through his head right now. Based on how hard he concentrated, she had a feeling he was using his abilities to guide them through the maze. How, she wasn't sure. He was following some path only he could see or feel.

Snarling pulled Keira from her thoughts. She barely had time to register the dark shape barreling down the corridor at them before Leo thrust her behind him and held a hand out to stop the beast.

It skidded to a stop a foot from his hand, still snarling and snapping, saliva dripping from its massive jaws.

Penny and Ty huddled with her behind Leo as he faced off with the beast. It was a dog straight out of her nightmares. Twice the size of Clyde, its skin was pitch black and rippled as it moved, highlighting the power in its muscles. Its teeth gleamed bright even in the dim light.

Red eyes with fathomless black pupils watched Leo warily. Leo stared right back.

This dog terrified her more than the three-headed Cerberus. This one was loyal to Hecate.

Leo inched forward. The snarling increased, and the dog released a warning bark.

Keira jerked along with the sound. She and Penny clung to Ty, who stood solid and unflinching just behind and to the left of Leo. Her nails dug trenches in Ty's bicep as she watched Leo approach the animal.

"You don't want to hurt us," Leo told the dog, keeping his voice soft. "*We* don't want to hurt *you*." He took another step forward. The dog snarled, but didn't bark this time.

"We aren't your enemy. We're friends." His voice was soothing, almost like he was speaking to a small child. The dog quieted. Leo stepped forward again.

Keira held her breath. He was only inches from putting his hand on the beast's nose.

"That's right. We're friends." Another step.

Keira wrapped her arm tighter around Ty's, fighting the urge to run forward and knock Leo away from the danger.

But Leo wasn't in any danger. As she watched, he took the last step forward and slid his hand along the dog's head to scratch it behind the ear. Immediately, the dog's face relaxed and its tongue lolled out. It leaned into Leo's hand, begging him to keep scratching.

"That's a good dog," Leo crooned, continuing to scratch. He glanced back at them, still huddled together.

"We're good. You can relax now."

Ty relaxed from his battle stance and gave a soft chuckle. "The animal whisperer strikes again."

Keira forced her frozen muscles to release his arm. Hesitantly, she took a step forward. She wanted nothing to do with the dog still leaning into Leo in ecstasy as he continued to scratch its head. But she did want the security Leo's presence provided.

Inching closer, she slipped her hand into his.

"You okay, *chère*?" He looked down at her.

Keira nodded and let out a pent-up breath. "Yeah. Just don't ask me to touch it."

Leo grinned. "He won't hurt you now." He turned back to the animal, rubbing its ears. "Will you? You're just a big softy."

The dog whined pitifully and leaned into Leo's hand.

Keira rolled her eyes and smiled. "Still not touching it." She edged around the animal, tugging gently on Leo's other hand. "Let's get going."

Leo gave the dog one last scratch before they started jogging down the path.

They only went a few yards when Ty noticed they had company.

"We have a tagalong."

Keira looked back to see the dog trotting along behind them, tongue still lolling happily from the side of its mouth.

Leo shrugged. "If he wants to follow us, that's fine. It might actually help when we come across others." A contemplative expression suddenly crossed his face. He turned and walked back to the dog.

"I wonder..." Crouching down in front of it, the dog wagged its tail and nudged Leo's hand. Leo obliged and scratched it behind its ear. "Can you show us the way through this maze?"

The animal cocked its head. Keira could swear it understood him.

Leo stood. "Show us, boy. Show us to your mistress."

To her amazement, the dog barked and took off down the corridor.

"Are we following the dog?" Ty asked.

Leo nodded. "We're following the dog." He took off after the animal. Keira held on for dear life as he towed her through the maze.

After several twists and turns, Keira's lungs burned from the fast pace.

"Can you ask it to slow down a little?" she panted.

Leo whistled sharply, and the dog slowed.

Keira just shook her head. His abilities were freaky.

At a steady jog now, the dog led them through the maze, easily navigating the shifting walls. They collected more furry friends as they moved through the hedges. Ty flew up to the top of the wall several times to check their progress. The dogs lead them on an unerring path toward the house in the center of the maze, and they soon broke free of its confining walls.

Several yards of completely open ground stood between them and the house. More dogs milled in the yard. The dragon things Leo saw from a distance were now clearly visible perched on the roof of the house.

Keira's shoulders slumped. She had no idea how they were going to cross the expanse without those sentries seeing them.

"Do you think you can make that bubble of yours make us invisible?" Leo asked, answering the question floating through her mind.

She wanted to slap herself. Why hadn't she thought of that?

"Yes." She waved them all closer. "Stay close and keep a steady pace."

Energy coalesced around them as she formed the bubble, making it mirror their surroundings. All the sentries should see was the ground around them.

Before they could move from the relative safety of the maze, her eyes caught on the pack of demon dogs watching them, confused now about where their new master had gone. She lowered the bubble.

"Leo, you need to send the dogs back into the maze. They're going to bark and give us away since they can't see you."

Quickly, he did just that, then nodded at her.

"We're good, *chère*. Take us in."

Pulling the energy cloak around them once more, Keira took Leo's hand and let him lead them across the open expanse.

CHAPTER 51

As quick as they dared, they crossed the yard to the side of the house. Keira kept the bubble in place as they huddled against the wall.

"This place is like Fort Knox," Ty grumbled, his voice low. "How the hell do we get her out of there?"

A wicked grin split Leo's face. He held up the lighter from his backpack. "We're going to burn it down."

"Hell, yeah." Ty immediately pulled his backpack off and unzipped it, digging for his own lighter. "Payback's a bitch."

They made a circuit of the yard in their bubble, gathering sticks and other materials to burn, and placed it in piles at different points around the house as inconspicuously as possible.

Studying the sentries keeping watch, Leo realized they were going to have to light these fires in rapid succession if they wanted to get them all lit before the sentries noticed.

He eyed the area around the house. A small alcove caught his attention. He guided them all toward it.

"Ty, Penny, you two stay here. These fires need to be lit quickly." He took off his backpack and handed it to Ty. "Hop on, *chère*." He pointed at his back.

Keira arched an eyebrow at him, making him smile. He loved her expressions. It made it easy to tell what she was thinking.

"I need the bubble still, but we need to move fast."

She dropped her backpack next to Penny. "Fine. But don't drop me."

He crouched, and she jumped on his back, then locked her ankles around his waist. "I got you, baby. Hold tight."

As soon as he felt her tiny hands clutch fistfuls of his shirt, he took off for the first pile. Praying it would light quickly, he touched the lighter to the dead grass in the pile. Flames quickly leaped up to lick at the wood.

Confident it would soon catch the rest of the pile on fire, he took off for the next and repeated the process all around the house. By the time he made it all the way around, the first pile was a full conflagration and spreading.

Returning to the alcove where Ty and Penny hid, he stood back and surveyed the flames. The fires burned brighter now, and the sentries had noticed. Several of them now flew overhead, sounding the alarm and searching for whoever set the fires.

Leo grinned as he watched them fly right over their heads, oblivious because of Keira's bubble. Again, he marveled at how well the four of them worked together.

"It's not burning fast enough," Keira remarked.

Before Leo could reply, she directed a breeze at the flames, urging them to burn hotter and higher. Fire surged up the walls to lick at the windows. Ty picked up a rock near his feet and hurled it at the glass. It shattered and the flames immediately licked into the opening, catching the heavy drapes on fire.

"Come on." Leo stepped to the right. "We need to do that to all the windows."

The sentries squawked overhead as the flames burned higher with each window they broke. The creatures dove and flew faster, trying to find the source of the trouble, but Keira's bubble kept them well hidden. Leo made sure the windows and doors at the back of the house were fully engulfed. They couldn't split up and all of them still stay invisible. Hecate needed to come out the front.

Within minutes, flames burned brightly inside all the ground-floor windows and at the doors on the rear of the house.

But it wasn't enough. The house was large. Burning small fires around the perimeter was going to take too long to create enough smoke and heat to flush the goddess out.

Another sentry flew overhead, drawing Leo's gaze to the roof. They needed to come at it from the top.

He led the others around the yard once again. They had used most of the branches and dead grass littering the lawn for the smaller fires, so he began pulling pieces from the hedge maze and hurling them onto the roof.

"You're driving the dragon things frickin' crazy," Ty remarked, hurling his own section of the hedge onto the rooftop.

A wide grin spread over Leo's face. He really was. No sooner would they rip out a section of the hedge and toss it, than a sentry would fly down and snap at the air where they had just been. Sometimes they were only a few yards away. The creatures were too stupid to realize they needed to snap a few feet to the side if they wanted to catch anything.

"Okay, I think that's enough." They had amassed quite the pile of branches and leaves atop the house. More than enough to at least create a tremendous amount of smoke and force Hecate outside.

"Let's go light it up."

Ty and Penny quickly shifted them, and they flew up to the roof.

"Keira, make the bubble bigger. We all need to light this at the same time."

She nodded and withdrew the lighter from her pack.

"Spread out." Leo pointed at the pile. "Light it."

He touched the lighter to the branches and waited for the foliage to ignite. It was very green, so it wouldn't burn well without an accelerant, but it would make a lot of smoke and eventually catch the roof on fire.

Lighting several areas, he stood back and eyed their handiwork. The vegetation smoked heavily in quite a few places now, small flames peeking out between the leaves.

"Let's go back down." He wanted to be ready when Hecate finally gave up and came outside.

On the ground, the fires had spread, engulfing several rooms now. Smoke billowed from the windows.

"What's the plan when she comes out?" Ty asked.

Leo stared at the heavy front door, still shut tight. That oh-so-wicked smile spread across his face once again as the idea he had been tossing around in his head finally materialized. If it became necessary, and they could pull it off, Hecate would never know what hit her.

Three sets of eyes widened as he outlined his idea.

"That's insane!" Penny cried. "You can't ask her to do that!"

Leo glanced at Keira, who watched them silently. He had just laid a hefty burden on her. If she couldn't do this, then his entire plan was shot.

"No, it's not," Leo countered. "We just have to work as a team. Just like we've been doing all along. If we can accomplish that, we will be fine."

He turned his full attention to the woman who had been by his side since this started. "Can you do this, *chère*? I know it's asking a lot. You'll really have to concentrate."

"I can do it, Leo."

The hard, determined glint in her eyes told him she was dead serious. He didn't doubt her abilities. If she said she could do it, she could. Admiration for this tiny sprite of a woman flared in his chest once again. She never ceased to amaze him with her grit and willingness to try the impossible.

He clapped his hands together. "All right. All we need now is one pissed off goddess."

CHAPTER 52

C amped out in their bubble just yards from the front door, Leo was getting anxious. The house was really burning now and Hecate had yet to make an appearance. He did not want to go in after her, but if she failed to show her face soon, they wouldn't have much of a choice. Time was growing short.

"Come on, granny. Come out," Ty muttered behind him.

"God. Don't call her that. I don't want to claim her," Keira complained.

"Sorry." Ty crossed his massive arms. "She still needs to hurry the hell up, though."

No one could argue with him there. After the pace they had kept for the last several days, just sitting and waiting was irritating. Leo did his best to tamp down the urge to run into the house and drag the goddess out.

It was almost anticlimactic when the front doors finally opened. A tiny woman, smaller than Keira, stepped outside, coughing delicately. Dressed in a long, dark, sleeveless dress that brushed her ankles, she shut the door softly and walked sedately down the steps into the yard.

Leo couldn't help but stare. She acted like nothing was wrong. It was as though she didn't care that her house was burning down around her, or that four people hid somewhere nearby, ready to trap her and take her to the god of the dead.

He could understand now where Keira got some of her moxie. But he would deny he ever entertained that thought until his dying day. She would skin him alive.

As they watched, Hecate calmly surveyed her burning house before she turned and stared right at where they stood, supposedly invisible to all.

"Uh-oh. I think she can see past your bubble," Penny whispered.

Hecate grinned and walked forward until she was an arm's length from the shield surrounding them. With one finger, she reached out and touched the bubble.

It shimmered brightly, then fell away, leaving them exposed. Leo pushed Keira behind him slightly. Hecate would have to go through him to get to her.

The goddess laughed. The tinkling sound surprised Leo. She was much more delicate—and beautiful—than what he imagined she would be.

"Aren't you cute? Trying to protect your lover from me. Humans are so noble. Always fighting for what's right, even when they know they'll lose."

Leo shook a finger at her. "Now, see, that's where you're wrong. We won't lose."

The goddess cocked one perfect eyebrow at him. "I have to agree that the four of you have been a thorn in my side for the last several months. But you're on my turf now. What you have encountered so far is a mere pittance compared to what you'll experience for the rest of eternity in Tartarus."

"Wow." Ty stepped forward before Leo could respond. "The history texts have you all wrong. They paint you as this protector of mankind. Kind and benevolent." He scoffed. "Someone got their translations wrong."

"You are as snarky as your ancestor. He annoyed me too. Mostly because he was so good. And *kind*." She said it so distastefully, like she had stepped into a chicken coop that hadn't ever been cleaned.

Ty grinned at her, unaffected by her tone. "Good. I live to annoy people. Ask him." He nudged Leo's shoulder.

Leo gave her a wicked grin.

Hecate just glared at them both. "You're also rather cocky for someone who is about to die."

The smile immediately fell off of Ty's face. Leo tensed as Ty stepped forward to tower over the tiny goddess, his expression dark and menacing.

"Not today, I'm not. You tried to kill my wife. If anyone is going to die, it will be you. That's not me being cocky. That's a damn fact." He jabbed his finger at her chest.

She just laughed. "Don't you have orders to 'bring me' to Hades?" She put air quotes around the words. "He will end your worthless existence and send you to the pits of Tartarus if you don't do as he asked."

"I didn't say we would be the ones to kill you. I'm fine with letting Hades do the deed. I don't have the time or the inclination to make you suffer enough for all the pain you've caused. That's his specialty, and he's welcome to it."

Hecate arched an eyebrow. "No, you're just too weak, *human*."

Ty's mouth tilted. "If you say so."

Leo waved a hand to get them back on track and moved up next to Ty. The day was rapidly waning and they still had the long trek back to Hades's palace *after* they captured the goddess. He was not going to miss their deadline because Ty and Hecate got into a spitting contest.

"So, are you going to try something? Or are we just going to stand here and jaw all day?" Leo looked down at his watch impatiently.

Satisfaction surged as anger flared in the goddess's eyes. He tamped down the urge to smile. Her temper would be her downfall. The angrier he made her, the more she was going to drop her guard. She was like any pissed off animal he had ever dealt with. Poke at her until she left an opening and then pounce.

She didn't disappoint. Ropes, much like the vines Keira created, shot out to pin his arms to his sides. Leo clenched his teeth as she squeezed.

While painful, the bonds weren't terribly tight. Not wanting to give away that he could break free rather easily, Leo let her believe she had him subdued.

"Leo!" Keira stepped out from behind him to face her ancestor. "Let him go!"

Hecate laughed. "Give me the belt."

"No, Keira," Leo bit out. He tried to convey with his eyes that he was all right and just pretending he wasn't.

More vines grew from the ground to trap the others. Hecate let out a sharp whistle. All the dogs milling around the yard ran toward them. Those Leo sent back into the maze poured out to race across the lawn. The sentries, circling overhead, landed on the lawn behind the dogs.

Hecate laughed evilly, the sound strange coming from such a delicate being. "You four really are weak. I was so hoping after the fight you put up in the mortal world, you would be a more formidable foe in person. My *dogs* are going to be able to defeat you."

Leo tensed against his bonds, ready to break free of them if necessary.

"*Epíthesi!*" Hecate gave the order to attack. As a whole, the dogs turned to look at him, heads cocked, perplexed. The sentries, sensing the dogs' confusion, hopped nervously from foot to foot, squawking.

Confusion colored the goddess's face. Leo fought to squash his grin.

"*Epíthesi!*" she ordered again.

The dogs whined, their eyes shifting from the goddess to Leo and back again. Leo could tell they were unsure about to whom their loyalties should lie. It was time he reminded them.

He made eye contact with the dog from the maze. "Sit!"

Immediately, the dog sat. The other dogs quickly followed suit. The sentries eyed him warily, but didn't attack. Leo could only hope they followed the dogs' lead. He didn't have time to sweet talk them.

"Guard!"

The dogs scurried to position themselves between Hecate and Leo. Much to his surprise, the sentries joined the dogs.

This time, Leo couldn't stop the smirk, quirking his lips when Hecate's gaze snapped to his. Her glare was something to behold. It was a good thing she couldn't kill with a look.

She stalked forward, only to be stopped as the dogs growled collectively in warning. Wisely, she came to a halt.

"How are you doing this?" she demanded harshly.

Leo attempted to shrug in his bonds. "They just like me better, I guess."

She rolled her eyes at him. "I would torture it out of you, but I'd rather just watch you sit there until your deadline to get your soul back has come and gone."

Surprise made his eyes widen imperceptibly.

Hecate grinned mirthlessly. "Yes, I know about that. I watched Hades take it from you. It was rather unfortunate for me, because it spurred my dear great-granddaughter to throw her all into finding me." She shrugged. "It has only been a minor inconvenience, though."

Silently, Leo fumed. He would show her inconvenience. He was done being toyed with.

"I think since the four of you have ruined my plan for your deaths, I'll just wait you out." She shrugged again. "I've had centuries of practice. A few days until you all dehydrate is nothing." With a wave, she turned and walked away.

Enough of this bullshit. He turned to look at Ty. "Can you get free?"

Ty flexed and pushed against his bonds. "I think so."

"Good." Leo gave a quick nod. "It's time to catch a goddess."

He let loose a sharp whistle. The dogs turned to look at him. Leo flexed and pushed against the vines holding him. They shattered into hundreds of pieces, freeing him. The time for hiding what he was had passed.

Making eye contact with the dogs, he pointed at Hecate—who stood mouth agape thirty feet away—and uttered one simple word.

"Fetch."

The dogs took off after their former mistress.

Confident they would corral the goddess and keep her occupied for the moment, Leo turned to free Keira. Ty burst from his own bonds and ran to help Penny.

Furious barking brought his attention back to Hecate. She stood surrounded by her dogs as they herded her toward Leo, snapping at her legs to force her to move.

The goddess fought back, using her powers against the animals to push them away. In the first redeemable quality he had seen in her, he noticed she didn't hurt the animals to keep them at bay.

He doubted she would show him the same mercy.

Leo called the dogs to a halt when Hecate was within a few feet of him and the others.

She glared at him, chest heaving as she huffed in exertion.

"Who *are* you?"

"You know that prophecy the Oracle proclaimed a few thousand years ago? The one about the three demigods and the unique being who would come to defeat you?"

Hecate's eyes widened.

Leo's grin was devilish. "That's right. I'm the unique being."

"No," she breathed. "You're only human!"

"I am human, but I'm *super* human. You can ask Athena and your dear friend Artemis. Thirty-five years ago, they created me." His grin faded, his face turning deadly. He stepped closer until he was within her reach. He towered over her.

"Hades may want to end you himself, but don't think for one second I won't do it for him if you hurt one of my friends. I can rip you to pieces with my bare hands and not lose a wink of sleep over it."

To his surprise, she laughed.

"Oh, I like you. Are you sure you want to stay in the mortal world with my great-granddaughter? We could do so much together down here." She trailed a finger down his chest. Leo fought the urge to shudder. She was utterly revolting.

Quick as lightning, his hand shot out to grab her finger. He bent her wrist back until she squawked in pain.

"Do not touch me, witch."

Her free hand shot up. A blast of energy hit him square in the chest. He tightened his hold on her hand as it knocked him backward. Leo knew if he let go, they wouldn't catch her again.

His ass hit the ground, sending shock waves of pain up his spine. He ignored it and rolled to his feet, still holding the goddess's hand.

She tugged against him once more. "You are bothersome." With a flick of her wrist, a sword appeared in her hand.

Oh, shit. Leo threw up his free arm to block the blow coming at his head and braced himself for the pain sure to come. He squeezed his eyes tight. This was going to hurt.

A clang was all that greeted him.

He opened his eyes to see a shield strapped to his arm. Hecate stared at it, eyes wide. Her sword rested against it.

Leo glanced over at Keira. She grinned in triumph.

"That's right, *grandma*. You aren't the only one with some mojo."

Leo couldn't hold back his smirk. "You woefully underestimated us, Hecate. It's going to be your downfall."

Thoroughly enraged now, the goddess pulled the sword back and swung again. Leo did his best to block it while still maintaining his hold on her.

"Let go, you annoying little rat!"

The goddess twisted, trying to break his hold. Leo twisted with her. He struggled to keep up with her. She was like a cat—all flying limbs, claws out, ready to rake across his flesh. Except she used a short sword and continually tried to stab him with it.

Having had enough, Leo flipped up and over her head. He landed behind her and wrenched her arm up behind her back. She stood on her toes, trying to alleviate the pressure. Leo just pushed her arm higher.

"I don't know if a god's bones will break, but I'm sure as hell game to try. Are you?" Leo growled. He pushed her arm even higher.

Hecate cried out and calmed slightly.

"Yo! Devereaux!"

Leo looked up. Ty immediately flung a piece of the hedge at him, a loop tied in one end.

Smoothly, he caught it one-handed, and quickly cinched the loop around Hecate's wrist.

"You really think that a *twig* is going to hold me?" Hecate snarled angrily. "Who has underestimated whom?"

Keira strode forward before Leo could reply. With a wave of her arm, the vine whipped free of his hands. Leo jumped back and watched the foliage wrap around the goddess.

"Not alone, but it will with a little help."

Hecate struggled fiercely in her bonds. Keira kept pulling them tighter.

"If I can hold Demeter, I can hold you."

Hecate laughed. "You can hold me, but you can't stop my magical abilities."

Dread punched Leo in the gut. She was right. So long as she was awake, she could still fight back.

The air around them crackled. Hecate's eyes glowed silver as she let loose her abilities. Flames from the house fire behind them roared higher. With a loud crash, the roof gave way, sending smoke and flames billowing. A fierce wind whipped through the valley to sweep over the flames, bringing them straight toward where the group stood.

Muscles coiled, Leo prepared to dive for Keira, but moments before he leaped, Keira's energy shield shimmered bright around them.

"Keira, no!" Trying to stop the full force of Hecate's powers could kill her. She barely survived the bullets Victor's mercenaries fired through his garage.

But he was too late to stop her. The words barely left his mouth before the flames reached Keira's shield. They swept over, clashing violently with the energy fighting to protect them from certain death.

Just outside the bubble, Hecate stood in an energy circle of her own, eyes still alight as she attempted to turn them to ash.

Blood began to trickle from Keira's nose as she held the shield against Hecate's assault. Leo grabbed her hand, willing her to draw some of his strength if possible.

Her hand was limp in his grasp momentarily, before she latched on tight. When she did, it was like she flipped a switch. Her spine straightened, and the shield shimmered brighter. Leo looked down at their linked hands. Energy flowed off him and into her. From the ground, energy swirled up her legs to flow out of her hands and into the shield.

He swept his gaze over her, looking for signs she was weakening. To his astonishment, he saw the opposite. His strength had galvanized her. The trickle of blood from her nose had stopped, and like her ancestor, her eyes glowed silver.

Leo held tighter and focused on sending her all the strength he could. She continued to hold the shield and keep Hecate tightly bound.

When the last of the flames from the fire passed over the shield, Hecate let out a roar of frustration. "This is not possible! You are human!"

CHAPTER 53

Keira rolled her shoulders to relieve the tension from the last few moments. She lowered the shield but kept her connection to Leo. She wished she had figured out how to draw strength from him days ago. It would have helped tremendously.

She wiped the blood from her face. "We might be human, but there are four of us. And we are very determined."

To prove her point, she tightened the bonds holding the goddess and grew the ends into sharp points aimed at Hecate's face, much like she had with The Empusa.

"You might have all your magical abilities still, but I can make it damn hard for you to use them."

Hecate tried to make the points disappear. Keira just brought them back.

The goddess eyed the vines inches from her face.

"You really should let me go, granddaughter."

Keira scoffed. "Not a chance, *grandma.*"

The goddess attempted to shrug. "Fine. But it's his father's life on the line if you don't." Her eyes cut to Ty.

That gave Keira pause. Anxiety settled ominously in her stomach and alarm bells went off in her head.

Leo's eyebrows slammed down into a frown at the goddess's words. "What?"

Hecate smiled like a cat that ate the canary. "Did you forget I had humans working for me?" She arched an eyebrow. "Did you think they just disappeared when you fled England? I sent them on a new mission. Just in case." She looked past them, directly at Ty.

Keira turned to look at him, her eyes growing wide as the meaning of what Hecate was saying dawned on her. Ty stared back, just as stunned.

She swung back to Hecate. "What did you do?"

Hecate just smiled.

Fury had Keira squeezing the bonds tighter until the goddess gasped for breath. "Tell me!"

"I... don't... need to... tell you... I can... show you."

Keira immediately freed the goddess's feet so she could walk and attached a leash so she couldn't run off. She handed control of it over to Leo, knowing he was far stronger than she could ever hope to be.

"Show us."

Hecate led them to the well in the center of the courtyard.

"I need my hands."

"You get one." With a flick of her wrist, Keira freed one of Hecate's hands.

Hecate waved it over the surface of the water, then stepped back.

"See for yourself."

Ty was the first one to step forward and peer over the edge of the well. Keira and Leo stayed back to keep control of the goddess.

"What?" Leo asked. "What do you see?"

Fury morphed Ty's handsome face into a thundercloud. He didn't answer Leo's question, his sole focus on Hecate. "How do we know what you show us is real? Prove it's not just another trick."

Hecate sighed in irritation, but waved her hand over the water once more. "Look again."

Ty glared at her another moment before turning back to the water, Penny next to him this time.

"Son? Penny?"

Keira didn't need to see into the water to know what Ty and Penny saw. That was Jack Farris's voice.

Hands clutching the side of the well, Ty leaned forward. "Dad?

"Son, don't do what she wants. I'll be f—" His words cut off abruptly with a gurgle.

"Let him go!" Ty yelled into the images in the well. Penny grabbed hold of his waist to keep him from leaping into the water.

"Ty, no! You can't fight them from here."

"What's going on?" Keira demanded.

"Max has Jack," Penny said quietly after a brief hesitation. Unease settled in Keira's stomach at the hesitant note in Penny's voice. She was holding something back.

"What aren't you telling me, Penny?"

Penny opened her mouth, then closed it again. Keira's anxiety ratcheted higher.

"Your dad is there too," Penny finally replied.

For the first time, Keira's concentration faltered. She thought her father had gone to ground and distanced himself from the whole situation now that Victor was out of the picture and her brother, Greg, was dead. She had guessed wrong. Horribly, terribly wrong.

Hecate took advantage of Keira's momentary lapse and broke free of her bonds. Twin swords immediately appeared in her hands.

"Shit!" Keira backed up and reached for Leo. She spared a quick glance at his face. "I'm sorry. I lost my concentration. I never thought Dad would be involved again."

"It's all right, *chère*." He laid a hand on her shoulder. "We have a contingency plan, remember?"

She did. Thankfully, that part of her role in this whole thing hadn't faltered. They'd really be up a creek without a paddle if she tipped that hand.

Ty stalked toward the goddess, diverting her attention. Murderous intent was etched all over his face. Blue flames licked in his eyes. "Let my father go." His voice rolled like thunder across the courtyard.

Hecate brandished her swords to keep him back. "Give me what I want."

"Not going to happen, witch."

She cocked one eyebrow at him. Her eyes flashed silver. "Careful, grandson of Hercules. I'm quickly losing my patience for you four."

"The feeling is mutual. Now let my father go."

The goddess tipped her head. "No." She ticked a finger.

Screams burst from the well.

Keira's heart leaped into her throat while the bottom dropped out of her stomach. She rushed to the well along with the others. What she saw when she looked inside made her feel physically sick.

A demon had joined her dad and uncle. It held Jack by the head, its black skin glowing like embers from a fire. Wisps of smoke curled up from between its fingers, its fiery hands burning Jack's flesh.

"Stop! Please!" Penny cried. Tears streamed unchecked down her face.

"Give me what I want," Hecate said once more, irritatingly calm. Keira wanted to shake her until her cool façade broke.

"I—I can't!" Agony made Penny's voice rough. She clung to Ty, both of them openly distraught as they watched Jack writhe in agony. Ty clutched the edge of the stone well with one hand so tightly, Keira was amazed the rock didn't disintegrate under his fingertips.

Keira's heart thudded hard in her chest, and tears trickled down her cheeks. They couldn't let Jack die. Especially not like this. She tugged on Leo's arm, her gaze imploring. They *had* to do something.

His jaw worked as he contemplated what she was asking. Keira waited several agonizing seconds while he ran the idea through that computer brain of his. She didn't need him to tell her this was it, though. It was time to play their final hand.

Finally, he nodded.

"What's the plan?" she asked quietly.

"Just follow my lead."

Keira let go of Leo's hand as he stepped forward.

"Hecate."

The goddess looked Leo's way.

"If we give you what you want, you'll let Jack go?"

The goddess stood a little straighter, her swords dropping slightly in surprise. She squinted at Leo, trying to decide if he was serious.

"Yes," she finally replied.

"Leo, no!" Penny cried. "We can't!" She looked up at her husband. "As much as I want to, we just can't. Too much is at stake."

"We'll find another way," Leo argued. He attempted to convey with his eyes that he had a plan. "I can't stand by and watch *anyone* die over this, especially not Jack."

"Don't do it!" Jack yelled from the well. "My life isn't worth it!"

"God, Dad! Don't say that." Ty's gaze swung to Leo, his eyes searching those of his best friend. "Leo, tell me what we do," he said, anguished. "I can't make this call."

"We give her what she wants." Leo's voice was firm. "No one needs to die."

His gaze swung to Penny. He took a deep, steadying breath. "Give her the belt."

Penny's eyes searched his, trying to decide whether to trust the look he aimed her way. Keira knew how she felt. They had talked about this being a possibility, but talking about it and doing it were two different things.

"It's okay, Penny." Keira coaxed. She trusted Leo. He had been made for this very moment. If his plan didn't work, it wasn't meant to be.

Keira closed her eyes briefly and grabbed Leo's hand as Penny slid the belt from around her waist. Tears trickling down her face, Penny stepped forward, a trembling hand outstretched.

One of the swords in Hecate's hands vanished, and she took the belt from Penny's grasp. Keira's stomach dipped when the goddess's hand closed around the thin, golden belt. She clutched Leo's hand tighter.

"It really is a work of art, isn't it?" Hecate studied the belt, her eyes alight with wonder and victory. "It's hard to believe this little belt can take down the most powerful gods. I need to remember to thank Ares and Hephaestus before I throw them in Tartarus." She gave a wicked laugh.

Keira stared at her ancestor, appalled. How could she come from the same bloodline? It just didn't make sense.

"You got what you wanted. Let my father go."

Hecate's second sword disappeared, and she quickly strapped the belt around her waist. A purely evil smile spread across her face. She flipped her wrist.

"I lied."

Screams of agony erupted from the well.

Horror weakened Keira's grip on Leo's hand. He immediately tightened his fingers around hers, keeping their connection. Keira fought to maintain her concentration even as the screams of her father and uncle joined Jack's.

"No!" Penny cried, peering into the well. Sobs wracked her body, and she sank to the ground, her face buried in her hands.

Rage like Keira had never seen came over Ty's face. Blue flames leaped to life in his eyes. He fairly vibrated with the power and fury coursing through him.

Hecate brought her swords back.

"You should not have done that," Ty growled.

The goddess brandished her swords. "Take your best shot. Human."

Channeling some of Leo's strength, and her own fury, Keira cloaked Ty in a suit of armor just before he was within striking distance of Hecate's short swords. A massive clang echoed throughout the courtyard as her swords struck the metal, glancing off harmlessly.

Before he could land a blow, the goddess flitted out of his reach.

Ty turned with military precision. "Hades is going to have to be content with your corpse, because I am going to finish you for him."

Hecate had the gall to laugh.

Keira just shook her head. The goddess's arrogance was incredible. She was so sure she would win.

"You cannot defeat me. I am a goddess. And I have Hippolyta's belt now. If you surrender, I will make your deaths painless." She twirled her swords. "One quick slice. You won't even feel it."

Keira finally had enough. Before Hecate could make a move, she literally rooted the goddess to the ground.

Hecate struggled mightily to free her feet. Keira made sure the bonds were as solid as concrete, then snaked them up the goddess's legs. Like a whip, the ropey vines shot out to grab her wrists to control the swords in her hands.

"You cannot defeat me!" Hecate cried. "You are only making your deaths more painful."

Keira didn't reply. She was using the entirety of her concentration to hold all the illusions she had created. She felt the blood trickle from her nose, but refused to give in to the weakness she could feel stealing over her limbs.

Ty stalked forward until he was nose to nose with the goddess. Keira really hoped he didn't kill her. She wasn't too sure Hades would give Leo back his soul if they brought him a dead witch.

Leo seemed to read her mind. "We need her alive, Ty."

"She doesn't deserve to live," Ty snarled.

"And she won't. But her death belongs to Hades. We promised him that in exchange for my soul."

Hecate began to laugh. A soft, slow chuckle that quickly morphed into a full belly laugh.

Penny rose from her position next to the well, having calmed down. She walked forward to stand next to her husband, who had backed up several paces.

Keira released the illusion cloaking him in armor.

"Why are you laughing?" Penny asked. "We've caught you again. Hades is going to kill you. You've lost."

"No, I haven't. I still have the belt. You can do whatever you wish to me, but I will still win." Her laughter increased.

Penny's grin was swift. "No. You won't." She looked over her shoulder. "Keira?"

Keira stepped closer, pulling Leo with her. Hecate's laughter calmed at the cat-ate-the-canary grin on Keira's face. It was a chilling sight with the blood that trickled from her nose.

Not wasting anytime, Keira dove right in. "That belt you're wearing? It's a fake." She waved her hand over Leo's waist. The black, waterproof pouch strapped tightly around his middle immediately transformed into Hippolyta's golden belt.

Hecate's eyes widened briefly before they narrowed in suspicion. "No. *That* is the fake. You are just trying to trick me. I felt the power in this when I put it on."

"You felt what I wanted you to feel. And probably a little wishful thinking. We told you we were determined. You didn't seem to believe us, and now you're going to pay for your arrogance." Holding the illusion on the belt and on Leo's pack they gave to Hecate had been ridiculously easy. It was all linked to Leo, and she had been practicing holding illusions on him since the moment she discovered her powers. Once she had made the illusion, she simply shoved it into the back of her brain, where it could run on autopilot. The hardest part had been imbuing it with a feeling of power, so Hecate would believe it was real.

Rage turned Hecate's eyes silver. They swirled violently. "You will pay for your insolence!" Pieces of the house rose from behind them as Hecate prepared to attack.

Keira backed up a step, her eyes wide. They might still have the belt, but that didn't mean all of them would survive. Just that they would ultimately win. Some of those chunks of the house were massive.

Ty flew forward. His fist slammed into the side of the goddess's head. She immediately went limp, held up only by her bonds. The pieces of the house she had lofted into the air crashed back to the ground with a boom.

He spun around to face the three of them and shrugged as they just stared at him. "I got tired of fighting her off. Be thankful I didn't rip her arms off. Or worse." His jaw clenched as he spared a glance at the well where the screams had gone quiet.

Leo was the first to shake off his surprise. "*Chère*, detach her from the ground. We need to get moving before she wakes up."

Keira quickly severed the roots holding Hecate's feet and lifted her. Ty walked forward to take the root end. Keira added handles at each end to make it easier to carry her. Leo walked around to Hecate's shoulder on the other side and grabbed hold.

"She wakes up, I'll just bash her again. I still have plenty of rage left to knock her out." Pain pierced Ty's face, and he swiped a tear off his cheek. Penny ran her hand over his back before lacing her fingers through his free hand, tears flowing down her face.

Keira fought her own tears. She didn't want to cry. It would just turn her into a blubbery mess, and she needed her faculties about her to keep the bonds on Hecate strong, just in case the goddess awakened.

Sniffing hard, Keira took up a spot next to Leo. He commanded the dogs and sentries to stay. With one last look around, hearts heavy, they headed away from Hecate's smoldering house.

CHAPTER 54

Compared to their trip to Hecate's fortress, their trip back was a breeze. Ty had to knock Hecate out twice more on the return trip, but it was otherwise uneventful. It also took them a fraction of the time. With Hecate unconscious, all of her illusions disappeared, so they were able to move through the valley quickly.

They also decided not to stop to sleep, fearful it would be too difficult to keep a close eye on the goddess and their surroundings without all of them awake to watch for danger.

Keira helped make the journey easier by "floating" the goddess, so all Leo and Ty had to do was push and guide Hecate's prone form. Penny flew overhead, keeping an eye out for danger.

Nearing midnight, they reached the gates to Hades's palace.

Leo stared up at the tall iron gates in trepidation. His gut churned mercilessly. He knew they had done everything Hades asked, but the pessimistic part of his brain refused to let him believe Hades would actually give him back his soul. After all, Hades wasn't known for releasing souls from the underworld. He had only granted that right to a handful of individuals over the centuries, and those had all come at great cost.

The gates swung open to reveal a stone path and the massive structure behind the wall. The palace was like something out of a dark fairy tale. It was beautiful, but immeasurably frightening at the same time. Tall turrets spiked high into the air like spear points. Ornate stone carvings framed every door and window. The eerie light in the underworld reflected off the light gray stone walls, casting odd shadows all around. Leo's eyes flitted from one shadow to another, looking for threats as they passed through the gates.

Silently, the group walked up the long path leading to the castle. They moved at a steady clip, eager to hand over their bounty, and soon reached the staircase leading to the palace's massive front doors.

Without breaking stride, they ascended the stairs. As they reached the top, the giant, black lacquered doors swung open to reveal the interior of the palace. Hades stood just inside, waiting, his tall staff in hand.

Leo barely spared his opulent surroundings a glance as his eyes locked onto the staff. He could see his soul swirling in the scrollwork on the long iron shaft. Its golden light pulsed and moved as it realized Leo was there. The ache in his chest intensified at his soul's proximity. He could feel it. So close, but just out of reach.

With a titanic struggle, Leo tore his eyes away from the staff and focused on the god holding it. Rage tightened his muscles at the sight of Hades. If he didn't know he would get his ass handed to him, he would lay into the god here and now for daring to take his soul. Leo might have the abilities of a god, but he didn't have the abilities of *this* god. Hades would wipe the floor with anyone, save his brothers.

"Welcome," Hades intoned. "You made it with a just under a day to spare."

Leo sucked in a deep breath and stepped forward, unconscious goddess in tow. "We did, and we brought what you asked. Now it's time for you to hold up your end of the deal."

Hades hummed softly and stepped forward until he was only a few feet away. He tilted his head and looked down at the goddess, still wrapped tightly in Keira's bonds.

"Is she alive?"

"Unfortunately," Ty muttered darkly.

"I have to say, I am impressed. I never thought the four of you stood a chance against her." Hades frowned down at them. "How did you do it, anyway?"

"Determination," Leo said. He pulled Hecate forward and flipped her around one-handed until she was upright, hanging limply from her bonds. He thrust her toward Hades. "Here. Take the witch-bitch and restore my soul. I'm ready to go home."

Hades eyed the goddess Leo presented before glancing at the staff in his hand, the soul inside it now swirling ever more excitedly. He ran his tongue over his teeth and indecision lit his dark eyes.

"You have a truly unique soul. It has been eye-opening to be its caretaker these past weeks."

Before Leo could do more than realize Hades was going to put up a fight over his soul, Keira was marching around him, her eyes ablaze. Fury rolled off of her in waves.

"You promised, you bastard. Either give Leo back his soul or I swear on all that's holy, I will let granny-dearest go and I will help her bring you down." She smiled smugly. "Don't forget, we still have the belt."

Hades's jaw clenched, and his eyes flashed. "Don't threaten me, human."

Keira propped her hands on her hips. Leo bit back an amused smile. She was cute when she was pissed.

"I'm merely stating facts." She glared up at the god. "Now, give Leo back his soul."

To their surprise, Hades laughed. The sound echoed off the marble floors and stone walls.

"You're cute. But belt or not, I am infinitely more powerful than your great-grandmother. You may win, but it will be at tremendous cost. Are you prepared to pay that cost?"

Leo grabbed Keira and pulled her back before she could claw Hades's eyes out as she so clearly wanted to do.

"Enough playing around, Hades. You and I both know you're going to give me back my soul, so just do it."

Hades cocked an eyebrow. "Really?"

Leo nodded. "Other gods are watching you. No matter how much you try to make yourself look like a loner down here in your dark kingdom, you still have contact with those on Olympus. You count on those contacts to get you what you want, to form alliances. If you go back on your word to me, how are they ever going to trust you again?"

Hades scoffed. "They will not care if I double-cross a mortal. You are beneath us all."

"Even a mortal who is your equal? One who could potentially kill you and take over your kingdom? I have all the powers of a god, Hades. I just have to be more careful about how I fight so I don't die. I would think a deal with me, someone who is a threat to any god, would hold some weight with your brethren above."

Leo stepped forward until he was toe-to-toe with the god. "I don't want your kingdom, Hades. I just want to go home and live my life. Do you really *need* my soul? Will having it as part of your collection really be worth the fight? The potential that you will lose?"

Emotions crisscrossed the god's face as he contemplated Leo's words. Finally, he shook his head and took a step back.

"You have more grit and honor than many gods, Leo Devereaux. Athena and Artemis knew what they were doing when they chose you for this fight. I will not renege on our bargain." He pulled the unconscious Hecate to his side before tipping his staff forward and touching it to Leo's chest.

The golden light flowed eagerly from the staff into Leo's body. Elation soared through Leo, along with a warmth that filled the aching darkness inside him. He closed his eyes and embraced the light. All the energy he had been putting into keeping the darkness at bay dissipated, easing the line of tension in his shoulders. His body and mind welcomed his soul back with open arms, giving him a sense of peace he hadn't felt in months.

When all the light had flowed back into his body, Leo opened his eyes to see Hades staring down at him, a calm, relaxed expression on his face.

"You are whole now, Leo. I wish you and your friends all the best. Thank you for all you've done."

Leo held his tongue. He had so many things to say to that, but he had gotten what he wanted and didn't want to rock the boat. Now, he just wanted to go home and get on with his life. He had a lot to look forward to.

He glanced down at the woman at his side, his feelings for her welling up, ready to burst free. He had so much he wanted to say to her, but standing in front of the god of the underworld was not the place to say it.

Particularly when she looked like she was ready to give Hades a piece of her mind.

Leo slapped his hand over her mouth just as she opened it and pulled her back into his chest before she could utter a word. She twisted her head to glare up at him.

He bent low to whisper in her ear. "Let it go. I got my soul. Let's just go home."

Her eyebrows dipped in a fierce frown before her face relaxed and she nodded. He let her go and took her hand. Ty and Penny stepped up to his other side.

"Hades, I'd say it's been fun, but it hasn't, really. You want to tell us how the hell we get out of here?" Ty practically growled.

Hades barked out a laugh. "I wish humans could know the kind of fearless defenders they have in you four." He motioned them forward. "Form a circle and hold hands. I will send you home."

Without a word, the four of them did as he said.

"I thank you again for all you've done. I'm sure the other gods thank you as well. You have saved us all. And Ty?"

Ty looked up with a curious frown.

"I am truly sorry about your father. If it's any consolation, he will spend eternity as a very happy soul with your mother and sister."

Ty's jaw clenched, and tears shimmered in his eyes. He offered Hades a small nod. "It is. Thank you."

Hades tipped his chin, then took a step back. "Safe travels, friends." He struck his staff to the ground.

Just as when Hades appeared in Leo's yard, the wind began to swirl and coalesce around them. Energy crackled as the portal formed. In moments, they were swept into the torrent. Wind rushed past their faces as they flew through the gateway. Leo held tight to Keira's hand. Logically, he knew they would all make it to the other side, but he didn't want to take any chances.

It felt like minutes, but in reality was only seconds before they slowed and their feet hit the ground again. The wind slowly stopped swirling.

As the dust settled, Leo realized they were back in Greece. Hades had dropped them at their rental car.

Ty let out a snort. "The bastard could have at least sent us and our things back to South Carolina."

Leo didn't care where they were. They won. They defeated Hecate, he had his soul, and they were back on Earth.

He pulled Keira into his arms and kissed her. Every emotion he had been holding back when they were in Hades's palace surged forward. Leo let it all loose. He poured everything into the kiss, trying to show Keira what he had been unable to say.

She clung to him and kissed him back just as fiercely. It took everything he had to pull away.

He rested his forehead against hers, his chest heaving with emotion.

"We did it," he whispered.

She beamed up at him. "We did. You're whole and Hecate can never hurt anyone ever again."

He held her head in his hands, brushing tendrils of her hair back from her face. "I love you, *chère*. I've wanted to say that so many times over the last few days, but I couldn't. I couldn't offer you all of me when I only had part of me to give. But you get all of me now. For as long as you want me, I'm yours."

Tears trickled out of Keira's eyes. "My Leo. I love you too."

He placed another fierce kiss on her soft lips before pulling back. "Let's go home."

He took her hand and turned to find their friends. Ty and Penny stood next to the car, beaming at them.

"It's about damn time. Never knew you to be such a slow mover, Devereaux."

Penny slapped her husband's arm. "Ignore him. We're just happy you two are finally happy."

Leo's smile was quick and bright. He was too.

"Come on." He tucked Keira close to his side and started for the car. "We've got a plane to catch and I have a house to rebuild."

Her delighted laughter was music to his soul.

***

Keep reading for a sneak peek of book 3 in the *Hecate's Rebellion* series, *The King*.

CHAPTER 1

"**M**aster."

Hades looked up from the missive that just crossed his desk to see one of his house servants standing in the doorway to his office, eyes downcast. He clutched his hands together in front, the sinewy muscles twitching beneath his black as night flesh.

"Yes, Peilas?"

The demon looked up, his red eyes flitting to his own briefly. "They have arrived, sire."

An evil smile spread over Hades's face. Peilas bowed, backing quickly from the room and darting away.

It was about time. He had been waiting for this for the last eighty-nine days.

He slid his chair back and stood, grabbing his staff from where it leaned against the bookcase behind him. The light that filled the intricate scrollwork swirled angrily at his touch. Distaste soured his mouth as he thought of having to give up the soul it contained. Not only did it go against the grain to release a soul from the underworld, but this particular soul was one of the most unique and intriguing he ever had the pleasure of holding.

As if it could sense his hesitancy to return it to its owner, the soul pulsed again within the staff.

"Yeah, yeah," he muttered, striding towards the door. "I know. I promised."

Making his way down the long corridor toward the front of his house—castle, really—his thoughts turned to what was coming his way. If those four humans had actually captured Hecate alive, it would be worth relinquishing his hold on Leo's soul. He was looking forward to making the goddess pay for her attempted mutiny.

As he reached the foyer, the large black-lacquered doors swung open to reveal the humans he sent to retrieve Hecate.

His eyes roamed over the quartet, noting the fatigue and sorrow etched on their faces, before his gaze caught on Leo Devereaux, the owner of the soul currently contained in his staff. The man looked pissed. He sensed Leo wanted to pummel him to a pulp, but wisely kept the urge in check. Hades couldn't really fault him. He would want to murder him, too, if he had taken his soul.

Mentally, he shrugged. He knew he was an asshole and didn't care. Came with being the god of the dead.

Planting his feet, he stood just inside the door, trying to keep his own expression blank as he noted the prone goddess floating next to Leo. He could hear her heart beating. They *had* taken her alive.

"Welcome," Hades intoned. "You made it with just under a day to spare."

Leo sucked in a deep breath and stepped forward, unconscious goddess in tow. "We did, and we brought what you asked. Now it's time for you to hold up your end of the deal."

Hades hummed softly and stepped forward until he was only a few feet away. He tilted his head and looked down at the goddess, still wrapped tightly in Keira's bonds.

"Is she alive?" he asked, stalling for time. His hand tightened on his staff, sending the light into violent swirls yet again.

"Unfortunately," Ty muttered darkly.

"I have to say, I am impressed. I never thought the four of you stood a chance against her." Hades frowned down at them. "How did you do it, anyway?"

"Determination," Leo said. He pulled Hecate forward and flipped her around one-handed until she was upright, hanging limply from her bonds. He thrust her toward Hades. "Here. Take the witch-bitch and restore my soul. I'm ready to go home."

Hades eyed the goddess Leo presented before glancing at the staff in his hand, the soul inside it now swirling ever more excitedly. He ran his tongue over his teeth and indecision lit his dark eyes.

"You have a very unique soul. It has been eye-opening to be its caretaker these past weeks," he hedged. He really didn't want to give up Leo's soul. It might be worth reneging on his bargain with this human. He was a god, after all. What could this man do to stop him? Nothing.

His eyes snapped back to the group in front of him as the little one—Keira—marched around Leo, her eyes ablaze. Fury rolled off of her in waves. He resisted the urge to smile. She was cute. Like a mother hen, pissed at the fox for messing with her flock.

"You promised, you bastard. Either give Leo back his soul or I swear on all that's holy, I will let granny dearest go and I will help her bring you down." She smiled smugly. "Don't forget, we still have the belt."

Hades jaw clenched and his eyes flashed. Cute or not, she needed to watch her tone. "Don't threaten me, human."

Keira propped her hands on her hips. "I'm merely stating facts." She glared up at the god. "Now give Leo back his soul."

Hades laughed. The sound echoed off the marble floors and stone walls. Humans never failed to surprise him with their pluck. They let their emotions rule, which often led them to taking on more than they were capable of.

"You're cute. But belt or not, I am infinitely more powerful than your great-grandmother. You may win, but it will be at tremendous cost. Are you prepared to pay that cost?"

He couldn't hold back the grin as Keira's face morphed into one of rage. Leo grabbed her and pulled her back before she could claw his eyes out, as she so clearly wanted to do.

"Enough playing around, Hades. You and I both know you're going to give me back my soul, so just do it."

Hades cocked an eyebrow. "Really?" He studied the man in front of him. This one differed from his lady friend. He most definitely thought things through. Hades had learned that and much more about the facets of Leo Devereaux these last weeks. This man was not only thoughtful, but methodical and had a strong moral compass. He was also extremely powerful. More so than he knew. Hades had Athena and Artemis to thank for that, unfortunately.

Leo nodded. "Other gods are watching you. No matter how much you try to make yourself look like a loner down here in your dark kingdom, you still have contact with those on Olympus. You count on those contacts to get you what you want, to form alliances. If you go back on your word to me, how are they ever going to trust you again?"

Hades scoffed. "They will not care if I double-cross a mortal. You are beneath us all."

"Even a mortal who is your equal? One who could potentially kill you and take over your kingdom? I have all the powers of a god, Hades. I just have to be more careful about how I fight so I don't die. I would think a deal with me, someone who is a threat to any god, would hold some weight with your brethren above."

Hades frowned. Maybe Leo was aware of how powerful he was.

He straightened as the man stepped forward until they were toe-to-toe.

"I don't want your kingdom, Hades. I just want to go home and live my life. Do you really *need* my soul? Will having it as part of your collection really be worth the fight? The potential that you will lose?"

Hades weighed the man's words. He knew Leo was right, but he wasn't too keen about being called on his bullshit, especially by a human. He had smited lesser men for the same offense.

He searched the man's eyes, which stared at him unwaveringly. Determination, resignation, and a strength that surpassed any Hades had ever seen in any other human looked back at him. What was shockingly absent was fear. This man did not fear death.

It suddenly dawned on him that Leo knew he was destined for heaven, but could only achieve it if he had his soul. He essentially had nothing to lose by taking Hades on in a fight and would react accordingly. If Hades continued down this path and insisted on keeping Leo's soul, he would have quite the battle on his hands. One he may not walk away from.

A shiver of unease skated up Hades's spine. Apparently, he was the one who underestimated the power Leo held.

Shoving aside his anger at being called out by this man-god as well as his desire to keep the soul swirling angrily in his staff, he finally shook his head and took a step back. "You have more grit and honor than many gods, Leo Devereaux. Athena and Artemis knew what they were doing when they chose you for this fight. I will not renege on our bargain." He pulled the unconscious Hecate to his side before tipping his staff forward and touching it to Leo's chest.

The golden light flowed eagerly from the staff into Leo's body. Hades watched elation cross his face as he embraced his soul. It was nice to see someone appreciate what a precious gift the soul was.

When all the light had flowed back into his body, Leo opened his eyes and smiled.

Hades nodded once at him. "You are whole now, Leo. I wish you and your friends all the best. Thank you for all you've done."

A tinge of anger marred Leo's smile, but he wisely held his tongue. Grateful or not, Hades would not hesitate to defend his kingdom if pushed. Especially by a human, even if he was, technically, an equal.

Keira let out a little growl and lifted a hand, ready to give Hades a piece of her mind. He lifted an eyebrow at her just as Leo slapped his hand over her mouth and pulled her back into his chest before she could utter a word. She twisted her head to glare up at him.

He bent low to whisper in her ear. "Let it go. I got my soul. Let's just go home."

Her eyebrows dipped in a fierce frown before her face relaxed and she nodded. He let her go and took her hand.

Hades looked down at the tiny woman. She would be a good companion for Leo. Strong and independent, but wise, like the man at her side.

Ty and Penny stepped up to stand beside Leo and Keira.

"Hades, I'd say it's been fun, but it hasn't, really. You want to tell us how the hell we get out of here?" Ty practically growled.

Hades barked out a laugh. This one was cut from the same cloth as his friend. "I wish humans could know the kind of fearless defenders they have in you four." He motioned them forward. "Form a circle and hold hands. I will send you home."

Without a word, the four of them did as he said.

"I thank you again for all you've done. I'm sure the other gods thank you as well. You have saved us all." Hades's mind flashed to the note that had come to his attention shortly before their arrival. His eyes landed on the taller man who looked so much like the face Hades saw in the mirror every day. "And Ty?"

Ty looked up with a curious frown.

"I am truly sorry about your father. If it's any consolation, he will spend eternity as a very happy soul with your mother and sister."

Ty's jaw clenched and tears shimmered in his eyes. He offered Hades a small nod. "It is. Thank you."

Hades tipped his chin, then took a step back. "Safe travels, friends." He struck his staff to the ground. Wind swirled as the portal opened. He stepped back and watched as the four humans, who both aggravated and impressed him, were swept away.

When the wind calmed and the portal closed, Hades stepped over to the unconscious goddess who had collapsed to the floor with the absence of Keira's illusion, which kept her upright.

With one hand, he bent down and grabbed a handful of Hecate's dress at the waist and lifted her. Her body bowed, her hands and feet trailing on the ground as he carried her.

An evil smile covered his face as he headed for the entrance to his dungeon.

Time to have some fun.

Afterword

Thank you for reading *The Chosen*! I hope you enjoyed it. Please consider leaving a rating or review. It would be greatly appreciated!